A Human Condition

A

HUMAN

CONDITION

Lyn Miller

Matador
9 Priory Business Park,
Wistow Road, Kibworth Beauchamp,
Leicestershire. LE8 0RX
Tel: 0116 279 2299
Email: books@troubador.co.uk
Web: www.troubador.co.uk/matador
Twitter: @matadorbooks

ISBN 978 1789016 604

Back cover photo by Michael at Click Photoshop, Morningside, Edinburgh EH10 5HX.

Illustrated by Dave Hill
British Library Cataloguing in Publication Data.
A catalogue record for this book is available from the British Library.

Printed and bound in Great Britain by 4edge Limited
Typeset in 11pt Minion Pro by Troubador Publishing Ltd, Leicester, UK

Matador is an imprint of Troubador Publishing Ltd

This story is largely about family, so I want to dedicate it to my family.

To my parents, Bob and Morag McLarty, and my brother Russell.

Dad loves to entertain by recounting stories of his childhood and young adulthood. I've heard him say that perhaps he should have put his anecdotes down in writing. Mum can spin an elaborate tale from any small everyday occurrence, and is famous for her accompanying expressive gesticulation. Russell embraced the tradition of oral storytelling and has travelled to festivals in the UK, Eire and the USA. And so I've come to realise that by writing books I'm continuing in the family tradition of telling a yarn.

Also to my children, Andrew and Shona, who've always been enthusiastic and encouraging about my writing and to my husband, Dave, my constant support.

Marion

The ringing phone sounded very loud in the middle of the night. Marion was catapulted awake from a deep sleep, sitting bolt upright in bed before she was fully conscious. Years of being on call at nights had produced this Pavlovian reflex to the sound. She shuffled into her slippers and grabbed her dressing gown from a hook on the back of the bedroom door, shrugging it on as she stumbled into the hall. The ring was louder here and wasn't stopping. She felt slightly sick and dizzy, having been woken from her deepest sleep. Turning on the light in the doorway of her study caused her to squint against the brightness as she entered the room. A glance at the wall clock told her that it was two thirty-six. She tossed a mental coin, Rose or Mum, and lifted the receiver.

"Is that Marion?" a voice asked.

"Yes." Her voice produced a dry croak.

"It's Rita Hutchison here, I'm sorry to wake you. I've got your mum here with me, I found her wandering in my garden. She's not making much sense and I don't want to just put her back next door in case she doesn't settle."

"No, no, I understand. Can you keep her with you till I get over?"

"Yes, of course, I'm just about to make her a cup of tea."

"OK, I should be there in half an hour, maybe less at this time of night."

She put the phone down and headed back through to her bedroom. Maybe she should get over her stubbornness about having a phone situated next to her bed. She had banished it gleefully several years ago with the advent of the out-of-hours co-op which meant that she no longer had to be on call from home at nights. She pulled on fresh underwear and grabbed jeans and a favourite red jumper from her wardrobe. Rummaging in her bottom drawer she found a pair of socks and then forced a brush through her thick, unruly hair, clipping it with a large clasp at the nape of her neck to keep it back from her face. What would she need? She retrieved her handbag from the bottom of her bedside cabinet and checked that her mum's house keys were in the side pocket. Maybe she should take her work case. Might as well have the equipment to carry out a basic examination, it might save on having to call out her mum's GP. She went through to her study, picked up the case and then set off downstairs to don her shoes and a thick tweed jacket. She stuck her right hand into the jacket pocket and jangled two sets of keys for her car and her front door which she'd left there when she came home earlier, then stepped out into the cold night air.

She'd always enjoyed driving through the city in the middle of the night. There were hardly any other cars on the streets, and traffic lights, if red, responded at her approach changing to green immediately, facilitating her journey. Her route, via Ferry Road then all along Seafield to Portobello, would be congested and have multiple hold-ups by day. She hummed along to a Sarah McLachlan CD and arrived in front of her mum's bungalow in Joppa by ten past three. All was quiet when she got out of the car; the sharp slamming of the door seemed too loud. She could see a light shining dimly through the curtained side window of Rita's house. In contrast her mum's house was fully illuminated, with all lights blazing and all the curtains fully opened. Rita must have heard the car. She appeared at her front door.

"Come in and have a cuppa," she invited.

"Thanks. Has she settled down a bit?" Marion asked, as she trailed after Rita into the kitchen. Her mum was sitting at Rita's kitchen table nursing a mug between her hands. She was wearing an odd selection of clothes: a black and white knee-length hound's tooth tweed skirt with what looked like a frilly nightie hanging down underneath almost to her ankles. The top part could have been mistaken for a blouse but the bluebird and butterfly fabric betrayed its origins from the lingerie department. She had a red, white and blue silk scarf tied jauntily at her neck and a green velvet beret perched on top of her tightly permed, 'black from a bottle' hair. Her legs under the nightie were bare and the skin was white, dry and flaky. On her feet was a pair of warm sheepskin slippers that Marion didn't recognise.

"Hi Mum," she greeted her, slipping off her jacket and leaning in to kiss her mother's cheek.

"Oh no, dear, you shouldn't wear red with your hair," her mum replied.

Marion was tempted to laugh. Her mum had always been a well-turned-out woman, interested in fashion. As the manageress of a small boutique in Portobello, she loved to give customers guidance on their purchases. Despite her own strange ensemble of clothes tonight, she still had the instinct to advise. She'd always been firm that redheads couldn't wear red clothes. However, Marion's hair was copper rather than carrot and through time she'd developed her own ideas about which colours suited her best.

"How are you, Mum? Did something waken you up tonight?"

"I'm perfectly fine and enjoying a cup of tea," was the reply.

"The slippers are mine," Rita informed, as she placed a mug of tea on the table for Marion. "Sit down. Do you want a biscuit? Or some toast?"

"A biscuit would be nice, thanks. So was she wandering outside in her bare feet?"

"Yes. I heard noises that woke me up, like rummaging around my wheelie bins. I thought it was maybe a fox but then I got up and looked out of the window and saw Betty. When I went out and asked her what was wrong she kept mumbling about seeing someone off, and not wanting Peter to see the man. It didn't make much sense."

"Did she seem frightened?"

"No, not really, but she was whispering as if it was all a secret or a conspiracy."

"Mum, did you think you heard someone outside?" Marion asked.

"I'm not sure... I don't always remember." Betty sounded hesitant, and then added, "But I didn't want him to be disturbing Peter." Marion's dad, Peter, had died five years ago but sometimes her mum forgot this.

"Mum, if you'd thought someone was outside you should have phoned me or called the police. It wasn't sensible to go out by yourself to deal with it."

"Oh, he'd never have hurt me, dear," her mum assured her.

Marion sighed. It didn't sound as if there had been a real intruder, but it was hard to gauge what had been going on. Although Betty's mind was compromised her hearing was still sharp. Could there have been a potential thief who knew that a vulnerable old lady was in the house alone? But such a person might also intuit that the house wouldn't be likely to contain any electronic gadgets or much else that would be of value.

"All the lights are on in the house. It looks as if she'd been up for a while," she told Rita. "Anyway, we should go and let you get

4

back to sleep. Thank you so much for helping out, I'll take Mum home now. I'm sorry you've had a disturbed night."

"You can give me the slippers back tomorrow, or I suppose it's going to be later today. What will you do? Do you have work?"

"No, luckily I don't work on Wednesdays. I'll get something sorted out. Thanks again."

"Bye dear." Rita patted Betty on the shoulder as Marion shepherded her out.

Next door Marion found that both doors were locked and had to use her key to gain access. Her mum had locked herself out. She decided to try and regain a night-time routine, so began to turn off some of the lights. She guided her mum towards the bathroom and suggested she might like to go to the toilet before bed. Meanwhile she closed the bedroom curtains and remade her mum's rumpled-up bed. The bedclothes seemed dry but there was a distinct whiff of stale urine in the room. When she returned from the toilet she helped her mum to take off her extraneous clothes, leaving only the nightie, then tucked her into bed. She noticed that her mum's face was flushed and thought she felt a bit clammy and hot.

"I think you might have a temperature, Mum," she said. "We'll check it in the morning. Night night."

She kissed her mum and left the room quietly, leaving the door ajar so that the light from the hall could shine in a little. She hoped that the childlike routine would be soothing and lull Betty back to sleep. It seemed to work as she didn't hear any sounds from the bedroom while she made up the bed in the spare room. This had been her own room many years ago. Before trying to settle in for what remained of the night she went back and peeped in to check. Her mum was sleeping soundly, lying on her back, snoring gently. She wondered if maybe a urinary tract infection could be making Betty more confused than usual. She'd make a proper assessment in the morning.

Marion emerged from the shower and had only just completed dressing when the doorbell shrilled next morning. The young woman on the doorstep was wearing a short-sleeved lilac uniform top above navy trousers. She looked surprised to see Marion.

"Hello, I'm Rachel, one of Betty's carers. Is everything alright?"

"I'm Marion, Betty's daughter. Come in. We had a bit of excitement in the night, but at the moment I think she's still asleep." Marion filled Rachel in on the details of the nocturnal disturbance as they went through to the kitchen. Rachel filled the kettle and switched it on.

"I'm here to make sure she has some breakfast and takes her pills. She's usually up, washed and dressed already by the time I arrive," Rachel explained. "I'll have a look in the report book for yesterday to see if she was out of sorts at all. Mmmm, it looks as if she'd had a bit of an accident in the afternoon. When Carolyn came in at teatime she was upset and she'd wet herself. That's unusual. Carolyn had to help her to wash and change."

"I think she's maybe got a urine infection."

"Let me pop through and see if she's awake." Marion could hear an exchange of conversation from her mum's bedroom then Rachel reappeared.

"She's just woken up. I sent her to the loo and suggested she just comes through in her dressing gown for breakfast."

"Oh, before she wees can we try to get a sample? What could we use?"

"Betty, hang on a minute," Rachel called. Marion went to the cupboard where mixing bowls and containers were kept and selected a Tupperware bowl that she thought would sit inside the toilet without capsizing. She managed to arrive with it in the bathroom just before her mum sat on the toilet. Betty wasn't too sure about weeing into the bowl.

"Whatever do you want me to do that for?" she asked, irritably.

"It's so we can check out your urine in case you've got an infection," Marion explained.

"Infected? I'm perfectly clean."

"I know, Mum, but this can sometimes happen to people. Can you try, just for me?"

"Oh, alright." Eventually she capitulated and Marion was able to collect the sample. She helped her mum to wash her hands and then to put on her dressing gown. She sent her through to Rachel in the kitchen, still muttering about being perfectly clean. Marion collected her work bag from the hall where she'd left it last night and selected a tube of urine test strips from it. When she dipped the stick into the urine the indicators for white blood cells and nitrates changed colour almost immediately. She decanted a small volume of the urine into a sample bottle, flushed the rest away, then rinsed out the bowl and washed her hands. The sample looked dark and cloudy.

"Looks like a definite infection," she reported to Rachel on her return to the kitchen. "I'll contact Mum's GP surgery and get the sample to them; hopefully they'll give me a prescription for her today."

"Oh well, that's good. It kind of explains why she's gone off a bit. Are you not hungry today, Betty?" Marion's mum was stirring porridge slowly around in her bowl, slopping the milk over the sides, but none had gone in her mouth so far. Her posture was droopy and slumped, her head bent and nodding.

"It's too hot," she complained, continuing to stir.

"Try and drink some of your tea then, and look, here's some toast and jam. That won't be hot," Rachel coaxed. "I'm not sure she'll be able to manage on her own the way she is today," she commented to Marion.

"Yes, I agree. I'll try to get someone to come and stay for a few days. My auntie could maybe come. I've got to work tomorrow, but after that I could take over."

"You a nurse then?"

"No, I'm a GP, but I think it's best if I don't treat my own relatives if possible."

"I think we'll maybe just have to put her back to bed. Look, she's nodding off. Come on, Betty, let's get your tablets down and then I'll tuck you back into bed." Betty cooperated meekly with Rachel's plan.

"You might want to think of getting one of those key safes installed," Rachel suggested to Marion as she tidied up the remains of Betty's breakfast in the kitchen. "It would make it easier for us to get in if Betty's not well or if she's still in bed. She wouldn't have to get up to answer the door."

"Yes, I'll think about it. But maybe I'm going to have to change things more radically than that. I have to face it that Mum's getting more vulnerable living here, and it's not that handy for me to drop everything and come rushing over when things go wrong. And it'll only get worse with time."

"Yes, it's hard to know what's best. I'll probably see you later, then. Have to go now but I'll be back at lunchtime."

Marion made herself some breakfast once Rachel had gone. As she ate she considered what she needed to do this morning and began to write a list. 'Contact the GP, phone Auntie Peggy, email Douglas.' Maybe she'd need to try getting a reserve for curling this afternoon in case Auntie Peggy couldn't get here in time to let her play. It would be hard at such short notice. Perhaps Rita would help out if it was only for a short gap. She'd phone Auntie Peggy first, see what she could manage. Peggy was Betty's younger sister by two years. She lived in Kirkcaldy and joked that if she had a boat she would visit Betty more often. As the crow flies her house was only about twelve miles away but the drive to the Forth Bridge and then around the city bypass and into Joppa usually took well over an hour. When Marion explained the situation Peggy agreed that she could come and stay until Friday morning.

"I've a few things I'd need to organise before setting out. I could probably be there about three."

"That's great, Auntie Peggy. I've got a curling match at two thirty, so I might ask Rita to fill in for an hour or so, but I'll let you know."

"OK, dear. I'll speak to you later."

Next she spoke to the duty doctor at the Portobello practice. On hearing the details she agreed to leave a prescription for collection that morning and asked Marion to bring the urine sample she'd taken so that they could send it to the lab for testing.

As she spoke on the phone Marion was gazing around her mum's kitchen and it occurred to her how shabby everything looked. She didn't usually stop for long enough in the house to really notice. She was always in a rush, organising things for her mum, or collecting her to take her to an appointment, or taking her on an outing for a change of scene. The linoleum was so faded that it was hard to distinguish its pattern or original colours. It was cracked at the edges and in some parts curled up. The fronts of the kitchen units had splatters that looked like dribbled tea and the worktops were cluttered with an assortment of cups, bowls, utensils and numerous piles of papers which looked like several months' worth of advertising junk mail. The inside of the kitchen window was grimy and greasy and the curtains worn and frayed. Spiders' webs hung in the upper corners of the walls and there were black dots, denoting ex-flies splattering the paintwork under each. How had it got quite so tired and grubby? Betty had a cleaning lady who came for a couple of hours every week. Marion thought of her as a friendly soul; she knew that she spent some of her time drinking tea and socialising with Betty. She'd always seen this as an advantage, giving her mum a bit of company. But it meant that in the remaining time her cleaning could probably only skim the surface. Hoovering, dusting, putting on a wash, cleaning the kitchen surfaces and the toilet was probably the most that was achieved. The truth was that no one had really cared for the house since her dad was fit and well. Betty had never been a natural housewife, and during his last illness and then Betty's slow descent into confusion there had been no motivation to decorate or replace worn-out fittings. Marion herself had been too busy with her own life, working and, with Angus at the other end of the country, being left as a single parent to Rose. She sighed. Well, now Rose was grown up and away at university, had flown the nest. Marion had more free time, so she'd have to put more of her energy into sorting things out for her mum.

Nyaga

"There now, Maisie, you're nice and clean. Let's get you dried and into some warm clothes. What would you like to wear today?"

Nyaga began to dry the tiny, wizened woman seated in the bath hoist chair. She towelled the fragile limbs gently, noticing some livid purplish patches on Maisie's shins.

"Oh dear, you've got some new bruises. What can we do? Maybe we should wrap you up in cotton wool to keep you safe from more bumps. Let's go through to your room now and we'll dry your hair. You still haven't told me what you want to wear."

Maisie looked up shyly and her voice was a whisper. Nyaga, who was tall, had to bend down to catch what she'd said.

"Your blue jumper? A good choice, it's cold today and we want to keep you cosy."

Since coming to live in Scotland from Botswana, Nyaga was invariably cold, except while at work. The nursing home building was kept superheated for the benefit of the elderly residents, but the atmosphere was stuffy. Nyaga had an idea that this lack of air might be the cause of her frequent headaches. Her instinct was to open windows to allow a flow of fresh air, but the residents complained of the draughts and she soon had to close them again. She finished dressing Maisie then accompanied her to the dining room for breakfast. Maisie walked very slowly with tiny steps, hunched over her Zimmer frame. It took nearly five minutes to make the journey but Nyaga was patient and encouraging. She liked to foster the residents' independence as much as possible. It would be quicker to put Maisie into a wheelchair and whirl her along, but saving time wasn't always the priority.

With Maisie safely delivered to the care staff, Nyaga made her way to the office to plan her morning's activities. Today was Thursday, so Dr Wallace, the GP, would be making a routine visit. Nyaga sat at her desk and checked the diary where she'd noted down which of the residents she'd like the doctor to see today. She would reassess everyone on her morning drug round and fine-tune the list. She should also strip the dressings down on Iris's leg to see if it looked any better. When she'd last cleaned it, she'd suspected that there could be an infection brewing.

"Hi Nyaga. Thanks for helping with washing and dressing this morning." Linda, the nursing home manager, bustled into the room and immediately began to rummage through the papers on the desk opposite Nyaga's. As a qualified nurse Nyaga didn't usually carry out simple personal care.

"That's OK. I'm just going to do the drug round now."

"I hope Sonia will be back tomorrow, or we'll be toiling." Linda found the folder she was looking for and turned to the duty roster for the week. "I might have to try and get someone from the agency to fill in."

"What's wrong with Sonia?"

"She said she'd been vomiting overnight when she phoned this morning."

"Hnn, better count her out for tomorrow then. We wouldn't want her to come back too soon and infect the residents. I can come in if you're stuck."

"Thanks, Nyaga, that's a kind offer, but you're entitled to your days off."

"OK, but the offer stands."

Nyaga set off down the corridor to administer the residents' morning drugs, taking her diary with her. She began in the rooms of those who liked to have their breakfast in bed or alone in their rooms. She'd catch the dining room crowd later.

At eleven thirty the doorbell rang and Nyaga went to open it expecting it would be the doctor. She could see her familiar profile through the frosted glass. She liked Dr Wallace. She noticed that she treated the elderly residents with dignity and empathy, always talking to them and listening to them, not just dealing with the staff.

"Good morning," she greeted the doctor.

"Hello Nyaga. What do you have on your list for me today?"

"Not too many problems you'll be glad to hear."

"Good. Now, before I forget I want to recheck Jimmy's bloods today, and I expect to have the flu vaccine available next week so I'm going to aim to come earlier, say around ten thirty, and hopefully we can get everyone done."

"That's fine, I'll put it in my diary. Do you want to leave your coat in the office and we'll set out?"

Dr Wallace shed her coat and greeted the manager then she set off along the corridor with Nyaga. The women were of a similar height but Nyaga looked slender next to the fuller figure of the doctor.

Their first stop was in Iris's room. Iris was a small, round woman almost as broad as she was tall. She was reclining on a chair with a built-in footrest. Her abdomen bulged up in front of her and her enormously swollen legs and feet were on display. The skin on the right leg was red and shiny. Both lower legs were dotted with small pits and watery blisters which leaked clear fluid. She smiled up at her visitors.

"Good morning, Iris. How are you getting on? Nurse Nyaga tells me you've been troubled by your leg."

"Yes, Doctor, it's in a terrible state."

"Is it painful?"

"Not really, I mustn't complain."

"I think it hurts you when I have to change the dressing, though," Nyaga suggested.

"Yes."

"You don't need to put up with it if it's sore, Iris. I can give you some painkillers to help. And apart from your leg? Any other problems?"

"I'm a bit out of puff."

"OK, I'll have a look at your leg, check your blood pressure and have a listen to your chest. Is that OK?"

"Yes, Doctor."

After examining Iris, Dr Wallace explained that she had uncontrolled heart failure which was causing her to retain fluid, evident in her swollen legs, and also affecting her breathing. Unfortunately, because of her diabetes she was more prone to skin infections, which could be the reason for the developing cellulitis on her right leg.

"I'll prescribe some diuretics to help take away the fluid, and antibiotics for your leg. I'll need to visit again in a few days to check that you're responding to the treatment. I'll also leave a supply of stronger painkillers in case you need them. Anything you want to ask me?"

"Will it be alright to go out with my son at the weekend? I've been invited to his house for lunch."

"Yes, of course you can go. I hope you enjoy the outing and I'll come back to see you on Monday."

After leaving Iris, the doctor and nurse visited four other residents together and then returned to the office to allow Dr

Wallace to write in the medical notes and also leave prescriptions for those who needed medication. Once she'd let the doctor out of the building, Nyaga went to the kitchen to get a bowl of soup for lunch. She took it, along with a slice of bread and an apple, back to her desk in the office to eat. The manager was tapping efficiently on her computer keyboard and looked up as Nyaga entered the room.

"Nyaga, good news. I've been able to engage two agency staff for tomorrow. So there's no need for you to give up your day off."

Nyaga had mixed feelings. She was weary, always feeling listless and tired, so a longer lie in bed and an easy day might help. But she hated having nothing to do, no one to visit and, to avoid spending money, nowhere to go.

The next morning Nyaga woke up to the sound of running footsteps echoing and gradually receding down the communal stairway in her block of flats. It would be Kyle, the boy from across the landing, heading off to school. She hadn't set her alarm clock but calculated that it must be about quarter to nine. She burrowed back under her downie and tried to doze again, reluctant to get up. Her flat always felt chilly and it was drab and depressing. She knew that she could make it more homely if she spent some time and effort on it but she was loath to put money towards décor. She sent a large proportion of her salary back to her mother in Botswana to help with Lesedi's keep, and the rest she was trying to save to be able to afford a better flat and have Lesedi come to live with her.

After quarter of an hour of tossing and turning she gave up on the idea of any more sleep and pulled on a pair of socks and slippers, then she buttoned a cardigan and fastened a thick dressing gown over her flannelette pyjamas. She went into the kitchen and filled the kettle. Reaching into an overhead cupboard she found the pack of Rooibos tea, put a sachet in a mug and poured over the boiling water. The familiar scent from African bushes immediately reminded her of home. She added milk and honey and put a slice of bread in the toaster. As she put the milk back into the fridge she paused to look at the picture she'd attached to its door with magnets. It was the latest from Lesedi, drawn with crayons and depicting a large sun in a blue sky under which a figure with hair in bunches, presumably Lesedi, was playing with a red ball. Nyaga stroked the drawing gently with her fingertips, filled with longing to hold her child. The toast popped and she turned automatically to collect it, then perched at the breakfast bar spreading butter and jam. She let her gaze roam round the uniformly beige room, the kitchen area; flooring, cupboards, worktops and walls were all various shades of fawn. On the other side of the breakfast bar the carpet, curtains and two-seater couch in the lounge followed the same colour scheme. The square of sky seen from the second floor window was grey. The red kettle, silver toaster, her blue mug and plate and Lesedi's picture were the only objects providing relief from the monotony.

She visited Lesedi in her imagination. They'd be one hour ahead in Botswana. What would Lesedi be doing at ten o'clock on a Friday morning in November? It would be spring, she might be playing in the yard or visiting the market with her granny to shop for weekend provisions. Nyaga drained her mug and took the dirty dishes to the sink. She'd go out. It wasn't good to sit and wallow, it didn't help. She decided to go into town and visit the internet café to check her email account. Maybe there would be news from home.

After showering and dressing warmly Nyaga locked her door carefully, descended the two flights of stairs to the ground floor and braved the icy blast as she left her building. As she set off down the street to the bus stop she was thankful that at least it was dry today. She didn't have long to wait for a bus, the number twenty-five service ran every ten minutes and took her directly to Haymarket where there was an internet café that she frequented. She also made a habit of browsing in the many charity shops on Dalry Road. On arriving in Scotland she'd quickly realised that her clothes weren't warm enough. Although she was earning much more money than she had at home, she was horrified by the prices in the shops on Princes Street. Luckily she met a woman at church who'd suggested that she might find some bargains if she looked for secondhand clothes. Unfortunately because of her height the number of suitable garments was few, but she had found some useful bargains.

In the café she ordered a latte and found a free monitor to sit at. She tapped in her details and opened her email account. She hadn't managed to log on for over a week and a dozen new entries popped up in her inbox. Recognising the familiar names – her mum, her brother and two of her friends – she began to feel better. She opened the letters and read avidly, grateful for the connection. Affection, concern and love seemed to flow towards her from the words on the screen. Her brother had a new job as a kitchen porter in one of the upmarket hotels in Gaborone. He hoped it might lead to promotion, perhaps to some training in catering. Lorato, one of her nursing friends, had bought a new car. Her friend Zeida had had a miscarriage. Nyaga sipped her coffee and considered before sending a supportive reply. Her mum reported that Lesedi had grown again and needed a lot of new clothes. Yesterday she had taken Lesedi to the local primary school and enrolled her there. She would start school at the end of January when the next session began, and was very excited about it.

Nyaga suffered a pang of jealousy as she realised that she wouldn't be the one to take Lesedi to the classroom on her first day of school. She had always relied heavily on her mother for childcare. At home she'd worked for long hours at the hospital. This led her to the mistaken idea that being away in another country wouldn't be so bad. She hadn't acknowledged how each short time snatched with her daughter had nourished her. Most days there had been at least a quick hug on her way to work, or a chance to stroke Lesedi's hair and watch her sleeping peacefully when she returned home. Now Nyaga knew that she'd been naïve when she made the decision to work abroad. The salary on offer had sounded like a fortune, but she hadn't taken into account the more expensive rent, and extra bills for heating (even though she kept the thermostat turned down low and was always cold). She was able to eat some meals at work, but even so food seemed costly. It all added up. So, she wasn't sure that she was much better off than at home, where the cost of living was less and her mother grew vegetables for the household in the yard. She regretted her choice, but felt she had to continue on here to give it a chance. Maybe there was also an element of pride, not wanting to give in and go back too soon, to hear people saying that she'd failed. She'd already had to develop a thick skin as a single mother with no obvious partner in sight. Her own family knew her circumstances and gave her their full support, but she'd been aware of some cutting gossip. This move to Scotland had seemed at the time to be a way to prove herself capable of providing well for her child. But now, lonely and cut off from her culture, she was beginning to wonder if she could endure the cost.

Marion

When Marion opened her mother's front door on Friday morning she heard familiar choral music emerging from the living room. She'd promised to arrive by ten o'clock as Auntie Peggy had a regular Friday afternoon bridge club in Kirkcaldy that she didn't want to miss. Marion listened and recognised Mozart's 'Ave Verum Corpus'. She put her head round the lounge door and saw her mum sitting in an armchair with a book of music open on her lap. She wasn't following the score today. Still wearing her night clothes and dressing gown, her eyes were closed. But Marion could tell that she was listening as her lips moved slightly along with the soprano line and her right foot was keeping the beat. Betty used to be a keen choral singer. She'd been a member of the Edinburgh Royal Choral Union, the Edinburgh Festival Chorus and her local church choir. It amazed Marion that, although she often couldn't tell you if she'd eaten any breakfast and had forgotten that her husband was dead, Betty could still sing complicated music. Her voice had lost its depth and had become quavery but she could still find the right pitch and keep to the tune. Marion was grateful for this continuing interest in music as it filled Betty's days with some purpose and could sometimes act to soothe her if she became agitated. She decided to leave her undisturbed and went to look for Peggy in the kitchen.

There had been a transformation since Wednesday. Although the fittings were still worn and shabby, now everything was spotlessly clean and all of the surfaces had been cleared of debris.

"Wow, Auntie Peggy, you must have been cleaning non-stop!" Marion exclaimed.

Her aunt eyed her over the top of *The Scotsman*.

"Well, I tackled the kitchen because I couldn't bear it, but I'm afraid the rest of the house is still like a midden. Come and sit down, there's tea in the pot."

"I peeped in at Mum. She seemed to be peaceful, listening to her music. How's she been?"

"A bit more lively today I'd say. She slept a lot yesterday and she had quite a few accidents. I've had her wearing those pads, but she doesn't like them."

"No, they won't be her idea of how lingerie should be." The women smiled wryly at each other. They had both been subjected to Betty's 'helpful' comments and criticisms about their apparel in the past.

"How long will you stay with her?" Peggy asked.

"I can stay until Monday. But I've been thinking about the situation and I've come to the conclusion that it's time to make a change. To be honest I hadn't looked closely at the state of the house until Wednesday and it shocked me a bit."

"What do you have in mind?"

"Well, I've been toying with the idea of having Mum come to stay with me."

Peggy's mouth fell open.

"No, don't say anything right now. I know it could be a strain and I'd need some help, especially on my work days. But I have a house to myself now, so plenty of space, and if I sold this house it would release money for nursing help. I realise that eventually we'll probably have to resort to some kind of institutional care, but I think it would be worth keeping Mum in a normal homely environment while she can still recognise us and appreciate where she is."

"And how do you think she'd take to it?"

"I'm not sure. I'd thought of pitching it as coming for a holiday to begin with and see how it goes."

"And what about your own holidays?"

"Well, I'd probably have to start thinking about respite care when I go away anyway, even if Mum was still here. It's getting to be a bit risky having her on her own and I don't think I could relax and enjoy a holiday unless I felt that things were more secure."

"When are you next away?"

"I was planning on some skiing, maybe in February. But I don't have anything booked yet."

"What about Douglas? Couldn't he come over to let you away?"

"I don't think we can rely on him." Marion was angry with her brother's response to the email that she'd sent him about their mum, but she didn't want to go into that with her aunt. "Anyway, I haven't fully decided yet. But in a lot of ways it would be easier to have Mum nearer to me."

"Yes. I can see that. I'll think on it too, but I'd better collect my things and get along the road."

Marion poured a mug of tea for her mum and took it through to the lounge while Peggy went about her packing. The music had stopped.

"Hi Mum. What's that you were listening to?" She put the tea onto the small table next to Betty and sat down on the sofa with the remains of her own drink.

Betty's eyes snapped open.

"It was Mozart. I wasn't sleeping."

"I know. I could see your lips following the singing. You must know that one off by heart."

"We sing it for the anthem in church. I haven't seen you at the service for a while."

"No, I live in Corstorphine now. Would you like to go on Sunday? I'm staying until then. I could take you."

That might be a disadvantage of moving Betty. She did still sometimes go to church if a volunteer from the congregation was organised to pick her up and bring her home. An unfamiliar church might confuse her.

"What day is it today?"

"Friday."

"Well, maybe. But I can't quite remember, what are we supposed to be singing this week?" Betty looked troubled.

"Don't worry. I'm sure you'll manage fine whatever it is. We'll see how you're feeling on the day." Marion tried to reassure Betty and didn't remind her that she wasn't a choir member anymore. She'd decided some time ago that correcting her with up-to-date facts wasn't really a kindness. She thought she might contact Betty's minister to see how often she'd been attending church recently. She didn't think it was more than once a month and at that rate she could always bring her back over to Joppa on a Sunday. Peggy appeared in the doorway wearing a blue anorak and carrying a tartan holdall.

"That's me off then. Bye Betty, you take care. I'll speak to you on the phone, Marion. Don't rush into anything you'll regret."

"Bye Auntie Peggy. Thank you so much for helping out." Marion got up and hugged her aunt then followed her to the front door. She waved as the blue Fiesta drove off.

"Peggy should get a smarter jacket for around town," Betty commented as Marion returned to the lounge. "She looks as if she's going off hill walking."

Marion smiled.

"Well, let's get you into your clothes, and then we can decide what to do with our day."

It turned out that even the minimal amount of activity involved in showering and dressing tired Betty out. She obviously wasn't fully recovered from her infection, as usually she was physically fit, happy to walk along Portobello promenade or around the Botanic Gardens. Today she fell asleep on top of her bed and Marion decided to carry on with the cleaning work that her aunt had initiated. Since she'd been using the bathroom she began there, first taking down the curtains and loading them into the washing machine. As she washed down the tiles and scrubbed the grouting with a toothbrush she was mentally composing scathing replies to her brother. She'd purposefully refrained from a knee-jerk retort to his email, and had deliberately left her laptop and mobile router at home. There was no internet at Betty's, so she had no access until Monday. By then she should have simmered down and be able to send a measured reply. She was well aware that she had a fiery disposition that matched her hair colour and had largely learned how to manage her temper. One of her rules was never to respond immediately to mail that made her angry. She remembered her psychologist telling her that in any debate or argument the person who showed the least emotion was the 'winner'. Marion's experiences as a teenager of furious outbursts, usually immediately followed by tears and then the need for embarrassing apologies, had made this advice seem particularly relevant. But what could she say to Douglas? Having carefully explained about their mum's declining cognitive capacity, the state of the house and the current illness making things worse she'd expected a little sympathy and maybe even an offer to come and visit. But, of course, there was always that 'get-out' explanation that the holiday allowance in Canada was less generous than it was here. When had he last been over? It must be over a year ago now, yes, it was August of last year. Now she could remember. She'd been mad with him because he'd spent most of his time attending events at the Edinburgh Festival rather than with Mum. And he hadn't even thought to get a ticket for Mum when he'd gone to a concert that involved choral music!

Anyway, there was no support from his direction. His reply was critical of her for 'letting things get to this state'. According to Douglas their mum should have been neatly packaged off to a 'seniors' facility' some time ago. Given that things were now getting risky he'd advise institutional care as soon as possible. If she wanted to take on a bigger role and have their mum at home with her, then that was her prerogative and it would be her responsibility. However, he didn't then want her to come over 'holier than thou' and expect him to be grateful to her for the task she was adopting. She was not to make him feel guilty. He thought that 'these things' were best done professionally.

When had he changed so much? She was sure he used to be a sweet, loving little boy who was affectionate towards his parents. Of course he went to work in Canada straight from university. That was twenty-five years ago now, so he'd lived there longer than he had in Scotland. She supposed that contact between them since then had been fairly superficial. They'd always both been busy with their jobs and families. When her father was alive he had been a conduit for news to and from Canada. There had been sporadic holidays across the Atlantic in both directions. Marion had never completely warmed to Mandy, Douglas's wife, who was a PE teacher. She was always on the go, ultra-thin and super-fit. Marion could admit that she probably hadn't tried very hard to bond with Mandy, the woman made her feel like a buxom giant. On her trips to Canada, Marion had toured independently with a short family visit tagged on at the beginning or end of the holiday. Douglas had usually had a similar routine but when in Edinburgh he had always stayed in a hotel, never here at Joppa. And she realised now that he'd never slept in her house either. OK, so they're not close, she'd just never felt it so distinctly before. The tone of his letter was like a manager approaching a tricky business project with a truculent client rather than a brother discussing his failing mother's care with his sister. He did come over when their dad was dying and then stayed on for the funeral. But he left almost immediately afterwards. She thinks that Douglas phones Betty about once a month, but obviously her mum can't be relied on to verify that. It certainly doesn't seem likely that their mum's illness is going to be the agent that brings the siblings together.

With this thought Marion took her bucket of murky water through to the kitchen sink and emptied it there. Then, feeling hungry, she opened the fridge to see what she might make for lunch. She saw a covered bowl and discovered homemade lentil soup. She smiled. Forget about absent brothers, thank goodness for Auntie Peggy.

Rose

"Bye Mum. Love you, speak to you again soon."

Rose waved at her laptop screen then signed out of Skype and sighed. She loved her mum but conversations with her often seemed to be such hard work. Mum invariably gave the impression of being really busy and super-organised. Even when she was spending time with Rose, or speaking to her long-distance, somehow it felt like a planned activity. Marion had timetabled this allotted space to give Rose her full attention. Rose didn't think her mum would ever be able to just 'go with the flow'.

Then again these thoughts made her feel guilty, her mum had needed to be organised in order to work and look after a small girl. She'd always done her best to attend all of Rose's drama performances and sports matches if at all possible and that can't have been easy. Also, although well hidden, recently Rose has been able to sense that her mum has an underlying fragility. She thinks that it's probably still related to her dad. Now that she's older Rose realises that it's a bit strange that there's never been even a hint of another serious relationship with a man. And now Mum has a chance to be more relaxed, but she's talking about having Gran come to live with her. That wouldn't be easy, Gran is getting pretty batty. Rose doesn't want Marion to take on more than she can cope with and then get stressed and ill. Why couldn't her mum just sometimes give in and do what was simplest like everyone else did? No wonder Uncle Douglas had reacted in such a defensive manner, not that her mum would have knowingly tried to make him feel guilty, he just would. It seemed to Rose that contact with her mum could easily leave other people feeling inadequate.

Rose looked at her watch. God, she'd have to rush, she was due at work. Luckily she'd changed into her work clothes before she'd spoken with her mum, so she only had to slip her shoes on and grab her jacket. She rushed out of the front door and into the gravelled driveway. Her part-time job was at the Alma Tavern and Theatre which was just around the corner.

She loved staying in Clifton with her friends. It was a much trendier area than where she had lived last year in halls. They were renting part of an old four-storey semi-detached house that had been renovated and split into flats. It came from an era of large rooms, tall windows and lofty ceilings. She was beginning to realise that it would be more of a challenge to keep warm in the colder weather, but she thought the extra space made it worthwhile. Working at the tavern and theatre also suited Rose very well. She'd gained experience behind a bar, and of front-of-house theatre management over the past two summers at the Edinburgh Fringe. So, one day she'd asked on a chance when passing the Alma if they needed staff. They'd taken her contact details and she'd imagined that would be the end of it. She was pleasantly surprised to receive a phone call two days later asking her to come and speak to the manager. Most weeks she worked on two or three evenings and sometimes, if the bar was quiet, she was able to watch part of the performance once she'd collected all of the tickets, sold programmes and got the audience safely seated. It didn't really seem like work at all. She loved the atmosphere of the theatre and was paid to be there.

After her shift, Rose walked home and went into the kitchen to make a hot chocolate drink before bed.

"Good night at the theatre?" Claire, one of her flatmates, was at the sink tackling a pile of dirty dishes.

"Yeah, I managed to see a bit of the play. It's a Noel Coward and well done."

"Just think, you might be starring there yourself if you get that part in *The Crucible*. When's the audition?"

"It's next Friday."

"And Mark's going for a major character too?"

"Yeah, he's trying for John Proctor. I'm sure he'll get it. He's by far the best actor."

"Not that you'd be biased."

"Ha ha."

Rose took a slurp of hot chocolate and blushed at Claire's teasing. She and Mark had been a couple since the beginning of the semester when they'd met up again at Drama Society. However, Claire knew that Rose had been smitten from afar for most of the previous year, having listened to her friend agonising over the possible significance of any glance or comment from Mark that came her way.

"I'll help you with your lines if you want. Or is Mark doing that?"

"He has his own to do, so thanks, I might take you up on that if you've got time."

Rose was trying out for the part of Abigail Williams. It was a big leap up from last year when she'd won a small speaking part in the production of *Macbeth*. But she felt so much more confident this year; maybe that was the effect of going out with Mark.

"Got plans for the weekend?" she asked Claire.

"I think I'll go back home tomorrow. There's a twenty-first party for one of my friends and I'd quite like to go. It's a chance to stay in touch with everyone. What about you?"

"My dad's coming up to take me out for lunch on Sunday. I'll try to get a bit ahead on that essay for Arthurian Lit tomorrow, as well as learning my part, and I think Mark wants to go to the cinema."

"Where will you go for lunch?"

"I'm not sure. Sometimes Dad likes to drive out to a country pub, but if he wants to stay in town I might suggest one of the places down by the Harbourside. If it's a nice day you can sit outside."

"Yeah, there's a few good places to choose from there. Is Mark invited?"

"Oh, I've not told the parents about him yet. I think it's a bit soon. And I don't know if my stepmum will be joining us or not."

"D'you like her?"

"Yeah, she's OK, quite relaxed."

Rose thought about her dad and Sally. She'd spent half of her holidays with them since she was four. They'd never had children together and, as a short-term visitor, Rose hadn't acquired friends of her own age to play with. Consequently she'd often tagged along with whatever Sally was doing. She was a sports enthusiast and had introduced Rose to swimming, tennis and yoga. They'd also spent a lot of time pottering around in the large garden that Sally had created. The summer weather in the south of England was more reliably warm than it was in Edinburgh and when Rose came to stay, her dad or Sally (and sometimes both) would have arranged to take time off from work to look after her. She realised now that maybe that was why she thought of Sally as being relaxed. She'd never had to juggle work, household chores and the school run for weeks on end like Mum had.

Claire stacked the last few clean dishes and pulled the plug out from the sink to release the scummy water.

"Well, that's my contribution to the chores for a while. I think I'll head to bed now."

"G'dnight, I'll be going too in a minute."

After Claire left there was a chime from Rose's phone alerting her to a text.

'Have sweet dreams about me. C u tomorrow at 6 your place. M xx.' Rose smiled and began to type a reply.

———⁂———

Angus and Sally arrived at Rose's flat at midday on Sunday. It was an unseasonably warm day for mid-November, and dry, so they were happy to go along with the idea of eating in the old dockland area. They all agreed that it was still too early for lunch.

"Why don't we go for a walk to work up an appetite?" Sally suggested.

"OK. We could go via Brandon Hill. I'd like to go up the tower, I've heard that it's open again after the renovations."

"Sounds good. Grab a coat then and we'll head off," her dad chivvied her.

Despite the pleasant temperature it was a grey day, but colour glowed from the gold and russet autumn foliage. Some leaves were still clinging to the trees but many now carpeted the ground. Rose shuffled her feet deliberately through the heaps of fallen leaves, enjoying the swishing sound she produced. There was a lot of busy squirrel activity and she was amused by children, who'd come prepared with nuts, trying to coax the creatures to come closer and eat from their hands. Her dad wasn't so taken by them.

"I hope none of those kids get bitten. They're liable to develop a nasty infection. Come on, let's climb the tower."

They set off up a narrow spiral stairway, Sally setting a brisk pace. The stone steps were high and many were worn down in the centre. Rose began to feel burning in her hamstring muscles before they reached the first viewing platform. The second stairway was even narrower with no space to pass anyone. Luckily it was quiet and they reached the top uninterrupted. Rose and her dad vied to point out the landmarks and university buildings that they were familiar with. Angus and Sally came into Bristol from time to time, as their home in Bath was only about an hour's drive away. Sally's trips were usually for shopping and Angus came to attend meetings and study days held in different hospitals, or at the university medical school.

Back at ground level they headed downhill through the park and steep streets towards the newly developed Millennium Square area next to the floating harbour. They passed houses with brightly coloured walls, a trend in this area. As they approached the row of restaurants along the dockside Sally exclaimed, "Look, a Gromit on a boat!"

The others turned to see what had claimed her attention and saw a blue and white painted statue of the famous dog at the bow of a cruiser tied up by their side. A few years ago a collection of the figures had been made, decorated by different artists and auctioned off for charity.

"I saw another one on a balcony of a house up on Clifton Down just the other week," her dad said.

"And there's one in the Wills Building," Rose added. "I think they're great. In Edinburgh we have cows. I like them too, but Gromit's more of a character."

By the time they began to study the menus on display outside the restaurants Rose was aware of her stomach growling. In addition to sparking an appetite the walk and climb had raised her colour giving her pink cheeks. They decided on Pitcher and Piano, electing to sit at an outside table sheltered under the overhang of the floor above. They all ordered the Sunday roast; Rose opted for pork and the others went for the beef. Rose buttered a piece of bread and took a bite. She accepted a glass of red wine from her dad.

"Well, you're looking better now, Rose. I thought you were a bit pale this morning," Sally commented.

"Yes, you don't think that you're overdoing things with a job and this part in the play as well as your studies, do you?" her dad asked.

"I can always cut down on the job if I feel I'm getting behind at all, and so far the part isn't a given. The audition's coming up this Friday."

Rose tried not to get angry or sound defensive in reaction to her dad's comment. But last year she'd had excellent marks; really he had no grounds to doubt her. She probably looked tired because she hadn't got much sleep last night. After the film she'd gone back to Mark's room but sleeping hadn't really been on their agenda. She couldn't very well tell her dad that a night of love-making was why she was tired though, and she really didn't want to think about sex with Mark while having Sunday lunch. It was too distracting.

"I'm sure you'll do brilliantly and get the part," Sally said supportively.

"When is the actual production?" her dad wanted to know.

"February, so we've got three months to rehearse."

"Well, good luck on Friday, I know it means a lot to you. I think I'll just pop to the gents before our food arrives." Angus got up and threaded his way between tables and then indoors to the toilets.

"Are you sure you're feeling OK?" Sally asked Rose. "Really you did look awful when we arrived, that greenish look you can get and all white-lipped. It reminded me of how you looked when you got those terrible period pains that used to make you faint a few years ago."

"Yes, really I'm fine, just had a late night." Rose sometimes wished that she didn't have medical parents who scrutinised you and made comments about bodily functions in public.

Their food arrived just as Angus came back to the table and they all tucked in hungrily.

"Mmm, this is delicious. Great choice of eatery, Rose." Sally smiled at Rose.

"Mine's good too," she replied while loading up another forkful. But suddenly Sally's earlier comment came into her head, and the apple sauce that had seemed so delicious a second ago turned sour in her mouth.

My period, she thought. *When was my last period?*

She tried counting back several times but always came to the same conclusion: that her last period had been about six weeks ago at the beginning of October. Her relationship with Mark had sprung up quickly and unexpectedly when she arrived back in Bristol after the summer break. She hadn't got around to organising the pill yet; she'd been thinking of going to the family planning clinic several times but had never quite made it. But she and Mark had been very careful, always using condoms. Could one of them have burst and she hadn't noticed? She was usually fairly regular, maybe a day or two of variation.

"Are you full up all of a sudden, Rose? You seem to be flagging." Her dad interrupted the frantic flow of thoughts.

"I probably ate too much bread to begin with. But I'll manage a bit more."

Rose tried to sound cheery while struggling against nausea. Well, she wanted to be an actress, so practise now. Play the part of a carefree student daughter enjoying a lovely free meal out and don't give away the fact that you're terrified that you might be pregnant.

Marion

Marion clicked her mouse to open the records for the last patient on her morning surgery appointment list. Glancing at the time she sighed. She was running twenty-five minutes late. That made her feel edgy, plus she really could do with a toilet break and a cup of coffee. Well, not much longer now and she liked Mr Dickson. She looked through a few screens to remind herself of his recent visits and medication, and then walked along the corridor to collect him from the waiting room.

"Come along in and sit down," she invited him. "I'm sorry to have kept you waiting."

"That's alright, Doctor. I don't have much need to rush about these days." Mr Dickson had a slight but erect build. His thinning silver hair was cut short which made his ears seem prominent. He dressed formally and his jacket, pullover, shirt and tie were always beautifully colour co-ordinated in muted tweedy shades.

"What can I do for you today?"

"Well, I need some more of my medication, but I've been feeling a bit sick and dizzy for the past few weeks so I thought I should come to get it checked out."

Marion began to ask for more details about his complaint, seeking information that would give clues to the underlying cause. She knew that Mrs Dickson was still in hospital following a severe stroke and asked about her.

"Oh, she's just the same really. She can't talk to me but I think she understands everything I tell her. She can squeeze my hand with her good side but her other leg and arm are no use at all. She'll not get back home, they've put her down for long-term care."

"Will that still be at Liberton?"

"Yes, I think so. I'm happy with the care there. The staff are all very good to her."

"But it's not so easy for you to get there, is it?" Marion remembered that Mr Dickson had been forced to stop driving when his eyesight deteriorated because of macular degeneration.

"Well, whichever way I go it's two buses and a bit of a walk, but I've got plenty of free time so it doesn't worry me. Sometimes my son gives me a lift at the weekend, but during the week he's busy at work."

"Are you going every day?"

"Oh yes. She'd miss me if I didn't go."

Marion could remember visiting the couple in their home after Mrs Dickson's first, smaller stroke to find them playing a board game together. That day Mrs Dickson had reminisced about the times when she and her husband had been keen ballroom dancers. Because of her illness they had now stopped attending public gatherings. However, they still liked to put a CD on and waltz gently around their living room. They'd always seemed to be a devoted pair. Marion asked Mr Dickson about shopping and cooking, trying to assess the quality of his diet. Then she weighed him and carried out a basic examination: pulse, blood pressure, eyes, ears, head movements and abdomen. She didn't find anything out of the ordinary and arranged for him to visit the phlebotomist for blood tests and then come back for a review in two weeks' time when the results would be available.

Once he'd left she typed up notes from their meeting. Her opinion was that he was lonely and grieving for his wife. Plus, he was probably wearing himself out with daily hospital visiting. It was a lot for a man in his late eighties to cope with. Males of that generation weren't always the best of cooks, but from what he'd said he seemed to be eating OK. Maybe she should suggest a lunch club if everything in his bloods came back as normal. She closed the screen down and left her room, heading for the toilet and then the staff room for coffee.

"Hi Marion, there you are," Kathy, one of her partners, greeted her. She was standing by the kettle waiting for it to boil.

"Am I last up again?" Marion asked while scanning the room to see who else was seated round the coffee table.

"Yes, but I only beat you by a whisker."

"Many visits?"

"I think there's one or two each at most."

"That's good since we have that meeting at lunchtime, it can be a struggle to get back in time," Marion commented. She poured hot water onto coffee granules, stirred the mixture, selected a biscuit from the tin and went to sit down, carrying her mug in one hand and a digestive biscuit in the other.

Marion worked with four other doctors in a partnership. The two men worked full-time, Susan the oldest of the doctors was there for four days a week, and Marion and Kathy both worked for three days each week. Their hours were arranged to complement each other and to cover the demand for appointments. Tuesday lunchtime was a good time to hold a meeting as everyone was in the practice and generally it wasn't the busiest day of the week.

After coffee Marion collected the notes for the two visits that she'd agreed to do and set off in her car. The first call was to a middle-aged man with severe back pain and sciatica. He could hardly manage to get from his bed to the toilet, so certainly wouldn't have made it to the health centre for an appointment. Marion examined him and prescribed strong painkillers and a muscle relaxant. She thought that he should be substantially improved in seven days, but might not be fit to go back to his work as a plumber, so asked him to come and see her next Tuesday. Her second visit was more complicated, a man with sharp abdominal pain. Her assessment led her to suspect renal colic and after giving him an injection for pain relief she called the hospital and also arranged an ambulance. As she perched on the end of his bed to write a letter with medical information for the receiving doctors, she realised that she would now be late for the lunchtime meeting.

"Do we have to do all of this stuff?" Susan, the oldest of Marion's partners, was asking sounding rather exasperated.

"If we don't do it our income will drop, plus we might lose our training status. We have to be seen to adhere to high standards for quality and clinical governance to be reapproved by the postgraduate department," Kenneth explained and he waved a hefty bundle of papers in Marion's direction which she accepted as she sat down to join the group.

"That's all very well, but I just don't see when we're going to find the time to do all of this. Our days are long and jammed full as it is." Kathy, who had a young family, found it hard to juggle work and home life, often feeling that both areas were compromised.

"Well, if we each take an area it won't be too bad," Hari tried to soothe. "We just need to do the basics, I'm sure there'll be no extra points for excellence."

Marion had been keeping quiet, listening to their comments and studying the requirements while chewing on an egg sandwich. She was sympathetic towards Kathy, as she'd had the same stresses herself when Rose was small. Now she wasn't so worried if work spilled over into her free time. She often chose to come into the practice at the weekend to work on administrative tasks then, rather than staying on until eight o'clock at night when she was tired. There was no doubt that there seemed to have been an explosion in the amount of paperwork to be done. Everyone was putting in very long hours. It was a worrying trend and younger doctors still in training were alert to increased pressure and poor morale in general practice and opting for other specialties.

The documents were from the Health Board asking them to analyse referrals from the practice to secondary care for certain stated conditions, commenting on the outcome and adherence to local guidelines. Now Marion gave a suggestion.

"There are six sections, so one each and one extra. Could we get Judy to look at the referrals and give us the records for each section? That would save a lot of time." Judy was the practice manager.

"Good idea, Marion. Then we might find that some sections have fewer patients, so someone could maybe take on two smaller parts." Hari took the proposal further.

"OK, we'll ask Judy to trawl the records and then we'll assign the sections when we have a better idea of the size of the task," Kenneth summed up.

"Often these things aren't too bad once you get down to them. It might even be quite interesting." Hari had a naturally enthusiastic outlook.

Marion heard a barely suppressed snorting noise from Susan's direction.

"OK, the only other thing I wanted to do was to discuss the next few weeks of teaching for Sarah. As you know I'm off on holiday from Friday, so I've timetabled you all for tutorials and supervision while I'm away." Kenneth was responsible for the GP trainee but the whole team took their part in supporting her. He passed out a timetable to everyone.

"You can see I've suggested topics for the tutorials, but if something else more relevant comes up, like a problem case, then obviously go with that."

"Is mine a joke?" Marion laughed because Kenneth had given her the subject of time-keeping. This morning had been no different from usual. She was always chasing the clock.

"No. I know that it's something you struggle with, Marion, therefore I'm sure you'll have a lot of useful insight and good ideas to impart. It's helpful for the trainees to know that we find things difficult too. It improves their confidence."

"If you were Hari, you'd say that maybe Marion will learn something too," Susan put in.

Marion thought it a rather waspish remark and observed that Hari looked hurt. Kathy had seen it too and changed the subject.

"Where are you off to on holiday, Kenneth?"

Kenneth began to describe his proposed touring route through South Africa and a more pleasant atmosphere was regained.

⁓

Marion had an arrangement to meet her friend Jenny for tapas at Café Andaluz in George Street and she decided to go there straight from work. It was six thirty by the time she'd finished evening surgery, so she tackled some of her accumulation of 'paperwork', which nowadays was all electronic, for the next thirty minutes. She was lucky to slot into a space in the central parking area just in front of the restaurant as another car left it. The restaurant was popular and always busy. A babble of chatter and laughter hit her along with food aromas when she came in through the door. She'd expected Jenny to have beaten her, and she was already seated, surveying the menu, when the waitress guided Marion to their table.

"Hi, I hope you've not been waiting long," Marion said as the friends embraced.

"No, not long. I've ordered us some wine and started to look at the food. I'm not sure how many dishes we'll need. I thought maybe six. How hungry are you?"

"Starving, I only had a sandwich for lunch."

"OK, well let's pick three things each and get some bread too. That ought to do it."

The women chatted while tucking into *gambas pil pil* and *calamares*, mopping up the sauces with their bread.

They'd first met at a postnatal support group after Rose was born. Jenny had just given birth to her second baby, Callum, and both women were suffering from postnatal depression, hence their referral to the support group. For Marion the illness had been overwhelming and severe. She still felt that her depression had been a major contributor in the break-up of her marriage. Jenny had recovered more quickly and had even gone on to have another baby, something Marion didn't think she could ever have contemplated for herself. She and Jenny had remained firm friends. When their families were young they met up with toddlers in tow and often helped each other with childcare. Marion and Rose had spent holidays with the White family; they'd been on a canal-boat tour near Oxford and had rented a gîte in Brittany. Now the friends spoke most weeks on the phone and met about once a month for dinner. They had decided to arrange a holiday together, just for themselves, and this was their current topic of conversation.

"Are you sure that Martin is OK with you going off without him for a week?" Marion was checking.

"Yes, because it gives him a chance to go on a golf trip to Portugal with his mates without feeling guilty. So don't worry about it."

"OK, then February should be fine. I'll have to check when Rose's play is on, though, I can't miss that. Plus it relies on getting respite arranged for Mum, but that would be the same for any week."

"Have you definitely decided to have her to live with you?"

"Yes. I'd like to give it a try. But we'd need the holiday respite anyway. I don't think it'd be worth going away if I was worrying about her all the time. I've arranged an appointment with a social worker to get the process started."

"Good, when's that going to be?"

"It's the week after next, but we've got about ten weeks from then until we're planning to go away, so I think we should just go ahead and book once I've spoken to Rose."

"Will she still do the play if she doesn't get the part she's going for?"

"I imagine she'll be offered a smaller part if she doesn't get Abigail. She's so mad on drama I'm sure she'd still want to be involved."

"Alright, so does France sound good?"

"Yeah, you've been skiing there before and know the resorts, so I'm happy to go with whatever you recommend."

Marion was really excited about going on holiday with Jenny. Recently it had been harder to organise holidays. Rose wanted to travel with her own friends and Marion wasn't keen on going alone for longer than an extended weekend. Last year she'd gone to Tenerife for a week with Kim, another divorcee from the curling club. It had been a disaster. They'd always got on well at curling and Kim seemed to be chatty and good fun. However, on the first night in Los Cristianos, Kim had hooked up with a man that they met in the bar over drinks, and that had been the last that Marion had seen of her until they left. She just seemed to move in with the bloke. Marion tried to make the most of her time there, but felt lonely having expected to have a companion to explore with. On the journey home, Kim seemed to think that Marion's objection to being abandoned was down to jealousy that she hadn't managed to catch a man for herself.

They were rather cool with each other now when they met at the ice rink and Marion was leery of agreeing to accompany anyone else on a trip unless she knew her companion very well. Anyway, this should be great; she loved Jenny's company and knew that Jenny would never go off and abandon her.

Nyaga

Friday was Nyaga's seventh day at work without a break and it was becoming increasingly difficult to hide her weariness. She always tried to stay cheerful and positive when dealing with the residents, but she must have let her mask slip in interactions with the other staff. Sonia had commented this morning that Nyaga looked tired and now the manager had held her back after their lunchtime report.

"Nyaga, I'm worried about your health. I have no complaints about your work or efficiency but you seem to have lost the enthusiasm that you originally brought to the job. And I've noticed that cough of yours isn't clearing up."

"I'm just a bit tired, looking forward to a weekend off. The cough is nothing, only a tickle." Nyaga was keen to deflect concern.

"Well, it sounds like more than a tickle to me. I'd like you to make an appointment with your GP to get it checked out. I'll obviously allow you time off to attend, just let me know when you've arranged it." She wasn't going to allow Nyaga to wriggle out of going.

"OK. I will."

Nyaga left the office and went to the staff toilet, locking herself in. She closed the lid down over the toilet seat and sat down, propping her elbows on her knees and leaning her face into her outspread palms.

She'd actually been telling the truth about her anticipation of a Saturday off. It didn't happen often, and it meant that she could attend church. When her pastor at church in Gaborone had heard that she was moving to Edinburgh to live he told her about the African and Caribbean Christian Fellowship, urging her to seek them out. It had taken Nyaga a few weeks to find time to attend the group, but she'd immediately felt welcome and accepted there. She didn't consider herself to be particularly religious. At home her work had made church-going a sporadic activity and she wasn't one for prayers or bible-reading in her own time. However, the atmosphere at West Richmond Street on those Saturday afternoons reminded her strongly of home. So now she made it a priority to attend if she could.

Although she'd been trying not to admit it, her cough and general fatigue had been causing her concern. Nyaga knew that she'd been deliberately playing her symptoms down and trying to ignore any possible significance. Experience from life in Botswana made these kinds of symptoms frightening, they could be potentially life-threatening. Maybe it all added up to something less, but if she gave rein to her imagination she quickly began to fear the worst. The toll of HIV in her country was immense and she didn't want to face a possible diagnosis.

She wasn't a nun or a saint; she'd had a few boyfriends. Sometimes they'd used condoms but she couldn't truthfully say that she'd been protected for one hundred per cent of sexual encounters. And then there was Joseph, Lesedi's father. He'd been very responsible, knowing all about infection risks and safe sex, so the pregnancy was a complete surprise. Not that Joseph knew anything about it. He was a visiting medical student, seconded to Gaborone from Cape Town for six months. She'd loved him, but knew that their relationship was for that short time only. By the time that her pregnancy became apparent he'd already gone back home to South Africa. She could have made enquiries and it probably wouldn't have been difficult to contact him. But it wasn't what she'd wanted. He hadn't asked for a child, but she was ready to be a mother. She didn't want to burden him or gain support which was given grudgingly. She could envisage initial interest and involvement which gradually tailed off as the rest of his life took over. She preferred her happy memories of him, and her daughter to be hers exclusively. Only now she was thousands of miles away from Lesedi and might have contracted a fatal disease.

Well, the decision had been taken for her; she was expected to see a doctor so she couldn't hold off any longer. She'd only been into the medical practice once, to register, so didn't really know any of the GPs. But, wait a minute, didn't Dr Wallace come from that surgery? Nyaga decided to ask for an appointment with her. She emerged from the toilet feeling calmer and went to the office to make the phone call before she lost her nerve.

⊶⊷

By Sunday Nyaga's energy levels felt at least partially restored. She'd been able to sleep for longer on both weekend mornings and had managed to keep active through the days, filling the time enough to keep her worries and loneliness at bay. Yesterday she'd dropped off a bundle of dirty washing at the laundrette she used in Gorgie then walked along to Haymarket where she spent an hour at the internet café. As always, email contact with home lifted her spirits.

Then she caught a number thirty-one bus which took her along Princes Street and up the Bridges. She got off at Surgeons' Hall which was just around the corner from church. She was early

45

for the service but recognised people that she'd spoken to there before and was absorbed into their group. After the meeting, Amelia, who was also a nurse, originally from Cameroon, invited Nyaga to join in with a crowd who were going on to have a meal together. They went to Nando's, which was just a short walk away along at the other end of Chambers Street. Nyaga hadn't realised that this restaurant chain, so familiar from home, had branches in Scotland. It was another positive thing in her day. If she suffered from some guilt about spending so much money on one meal it was offset by her enjoyment of the food and the company. She also got an idea for a free Sunday activity. On their way along Chambers Street, Amelia pointed out the National Museum which was a huge building occupying most of the south side of the street. She told Nyaga that it was open every day of the week and that there was no entry charge. So that's where Nyaga was on Sunday afternoon. She meandered slowly through the galleries, engrossed by the variety of different exhibits. Currently she was learning all about the construction and operation of Scotland's lighthouses. She found the stories fascinating, perhaps because she came from a landlocked country with no coastline. The exhibition made her want to travel to the seaside, to see the sea and maybe even visit a lighthouse. There were probably lots of other things about Scotland that she'd find interesting. Maybe she hadn't given the place much of a chance. Sam, another of the group from last night, had suggested that she find her local public library. Apparently she could borrow books and use the internet free of charge once she became a member. There was bound to be a branch near to her flat or her work. She'd find out next week. Glancing at her watch she realised that she needed to hurry if she was going to make it back to the laundrette on time to collect her clean washing; it closed at five o'clock. Well, never mind, she could come back to the museum on her next day off.

Marion

"Look at that boy, paddling in the sea on a cold day like this! I'd get a row from my mother if she saw me doing that. Should we be getting back for our tea now? She'll be looking out for us."

"No, it's OK, we've still got a bit of time," Marion reassured Betty.

She was spending Sunday with her mum. They'd gone to church together in the morning, and then had driven to Leith to have lunch at The Shore restaurant. The weather was dry after lunch so Marion suggested a walk along Portobello promenade before returning to the house. Betty was on good form today. She'd joined in lustily with the hymn-singing in church and luckily seemed to have some insight that she wasn't to sing when the choir gave their anthem. She managed to restrain herself to quiet humming; it was obviously a piece that she was familiar with. At lunchtime she tucked away a large helping of fish and chips followed by crème brûlée and was now striding out along the shore commenting on the other people around them.

"Look at that woman. Did she forget to put her skirt on?"

Betty had always had a habit of remarking on the appearance and dress sense of people around her, often in a complimentary way. However, with the progression of her dementia all discretion had gone and now her observations were voiced at full volume. She'd always hated leggings and thought that they should be especially avoided by anyone over eighteen years of age or more than a dress-size ten. The woman who'd just walked past them broke both of Betty's rules. Marion had given up being embarrassed by her mum's opinions long ago. In fact, now she found that she often agreed with her and was secretly amused by Betty's loud utterances.

"That's a cute wee dog." Betty stopped to pet a passing shih-tzu. "My mother won't let us have a dog, even when Peggy and I promise we'll look after it."

"Well, they are a lot of work," Marion soothed.

She was surprised by her mum's sudden enthusiasm, as their family had never had a dog either. She could remember that she and Douglas had raised similar pleas, to be told that her parents didn't like dogs. She also found it strange that in Betty's world the mother figure seemed to be strict and authoritarian, usually giving Betty a telling-off or having to be appeased in some way. Her maternal grandmother had died when Marion was seven years old but she recalled her as being a warm and cuddly woman, often producing sweets for Marion from her handbag. Either her character had mellowed in her older age or Betty's memories were skewed. There was one occasion last year when Betty's behaviour had been different, suggesting that there were some tender feelings for her mother. Betty had taken a heavy fall in her garden, sustaining a large cut on the back of her head. Marion had to take her to the A&E department as she needed stitches to the wound. Throughout the procedure Betty had clutched Marion's hand tightly and cried for her mum.

Back at the house, Marion settled Betty into her reclining chair in the lounge and put some gentle music on the stereo. As she'd hoped, after the combination of a glass of wine at lunchtime and fresh air and exercise, Betty quickly fell asleep. Now that the kitchen and bathroom had been cleaned Marion planned to systematically tackle the rest of the house. She would leave the rooms that her mum used most until she was sure that moving to stay with her in Corstorphine was going to work out. But if she had some of the house cleared out it would mean that she could move more quickly to put it on the market. Spring was usually a good time to try selling a property.

With this in mind she gathered cleaning supplies and the roll of bin bags that she'd brought with her today and entered the dining room. She couldn't remember the last time that anyone had eaten in here. It was probably before her dad died. Now meals were eaten at the kitchen table or from a tray in the lounge. There was a coating of dust on all the surfaces and it smelled stuffy and unaired. She opened a window and sprayed some furniture polish as she dusted. Then she vacuumed, reaching up with the hose attachment to suck up cobwebs from the cornice. Next, she began to empty the sideboard. She discovered her mum's Royal Doulton wedding china, seldom used and so still in good condition. This might be of interest to somebody. She'd noticed a trend for using old china tea sets in some of the restaurants and cafés in town. There was also a large selection of crystal glassware. She put the good things onto the table. Next time she visited she'd bring boxes and newspaper to pack them up for delivery to a charity shop. Anything that was chipped or outdated went into a rubbish bag. She sorted through the drawers – tablecloths, placemats and cutlery. Holding up a bag full of mismatched, partly burned candles she began to feel overwhelmed. The task she'd set herself was going to take ages; this was the first room and possibly the easiest. She took a deep breath and tried to be positive. She would just have to pace herself, do a little at a time, and if it got too much she could engage one of those house clearance firms to finish off. She decided to take a break and make a cup of tea. Her mum would probably be awake again soon.

—∞∞—

"Nyaga Sejewe," Marion called into the waiting room. A tall, elegant black woman with close-cut hair rose to follow her along the corridor. She looked familiar but Marion knew from scanning her notes that she was a newly registered patient, so she hadn't consulted with her before.

"Come in and have a seat." She gestured towards the chair and closed the door.

"Good evening Dr Wallace."

As soon as the patient spoke Marion was able to place her.

"Hello Nyaga. I know you from Dellview of course, but I haven't seen you here before. What can I do for you?"

Nyaga began to describe her symptoms, beginning with the tiredness and headaches and then mentioning the cough. Marion first questioned Nyaga about the cough, her diet and her sleeping pattern, listening carefully to the replies.

"How long have you been living in Scotland now?" she asked.

"Nearly three months."

"And how are you settling in?"

There was a pause which Marion allowed to grow, knowing that often silence would draw more detail from a patient than twenty questions would.

"Not so well," Nyaga eventually admitted, with a grimace. "My work is OK, but I miss my family and friends."

"Who do you have back at home?"

"My daughter, my mother and my brother."

"It must be hard being so far away from your daughter. How old is she?"

Nyaga told Marion all the latest about Lesedi, including the enrolment at school.

"Do you think you might be depressed?" Marion suggested.

"I am lonely, and I'm low some of the time but I don't think I'm depressed. I actually had quite a good weekend and enjoyed a night out with people from my church."

"So, what do you worry about most?"

"Not being well enough to work."

"And?"

"HIV."

"Yes, I wondered if that would be a concern." Marion went on to ask more specific questions about possible contact with the virus.

"Now I need to examine you." She asked Nyaga to go behind the curtain and remove her top and then followed her through to carry out an examination. Once Nyaga was dressed and sitting down again Marion gave her opinion.

"I think you have a chest infection; there are a lot of wheezes and crackles when I'm listening to your chest, so I'd advise a course of antibiotics. This infection could be making you feel tired and run-down. However, there is also a possibility of an underlying illness. It could be physical, like HIV, or it might be psychological. We need to do some blood tests to find out more. Unfortunately it's too late in the day to send blood off now, so I'd like you to make an appointment with the phlebotomist later this week. Then I need to see you back again to discuss the results and to see how you feel after the antibiotics are finished. Is that OK? Do you have any questions you'd like to ask me?"

"How long will it take for the results to be back?"

"They should be back in a week, so book a time to see me for a week after the blood test. You're not allergic to penicillin, are you?" Marion typed and her printer spewed out a piece of paper which she checked and signed before handing it to Nyaga.

"Then here's your prescription. Take one capsule three times a day, and they'll last for a week."

"OK, thank you. I'll see you then, Doctor."

"Yes, I'll see you next week, although we'll probably meet up at Dellview before then. And, Nyaga, I think you'll feel an improvement after the antibiotics. And I think it's better that you get this test done rather than just worrying about it. Hopefully the HIV test will be negative, but if it should be positive at least we'll be able to start treatment very quickly. A lot more can be done now."

"Yes, you're right. I know that."

Nyaga stood up, gathered her belongings together and left the room. Marion sat for a moment in thought before typing up the record of their consultation. She'd liked Nyaga immediately since her arrival at Dellview. She had a lovely, caring manner with the residents and seemed to genuinely enjoy their company. She also seemed to be an efficient and knowledgeable nurse. Marion had never previously considered her social background and was saddened to learn that she was so lonely. She hoped that the HIV test would come back negative, but the virus was widespread in Botswana and there was no doubt that Nyaga had taken some risks. She began to type a summary of their meeting and to set up instructions for the blood work that she wanted to be done.

Rose

Rose had been frantically busy for the last two weeks and consequently she'd managed to bury her worries about the late period and possible pregnancy.

On the days leading up to her audition she'd immersed herself in the play. She read it through several times to learn the plot thoroughly and familiarise herself with all of the characters. She tried to imagine how Abigail would interact with each of them. Then she began to learn the lines that were required for the audition. She needed to have an American accent and she found it difficult to keep it consistent. She recorded herself and listened to the playback with a critical ear. To get fully into her part she dressed in an old full-length nightie with a high buttoned neckline and long sleeves. She used a throw from her bed as a shawl and practised walking and moving in the way that she thought appropriate for a girl in the seventeenth century.

She was nervous when she arrived at the hall on Friday. She knew that Mark would already have been heard, and that he intended to stay on in the audience to watch her. Luckily when her turn came her anxiety seemed to evaporate and she was able to lose herself completely in the role. Afterwards she met up with Mark outside the hall. She rushed up to him and flung her arms around his waist, burying her face into his scarf, clinging on tightly.

"You were great," he said immediately, returning her hug. "I can't imagine that any of the others have a chance, you were definitely the strongest candidate."

"Thanks. I'm exhausted now, my legs feel all shaky. How do you think you did?"

"It went OK. I think I have a chance."

"I definitely need a hit of sugar to revive me."

"OK let's go. We're near Caffe Clifton, they do cakes."

They linked arms and set off to dissect their performances comprehensively over coffee and Danish pastries. The results would be posted tomorrow.

Rose didn't want to log onto her email on Saturday morning. It felt like waiting for exam results; she wanted to know but she didn't want to look. Just after midday her phone chimed. It was a text from Mark.

'Congratulations u got it. Me 2. M xx.'

Yes! She jumped up and danced a jig accompanied by air punches. She was so excited, but there was no one to share it with. The flat was empty. Claire and Joanna had gone out shopping and Trish was staying over at her boyfriend's flat. She quickly replied to Mark's text.

'Brilliant + well done c u after work 2 party R xx.'

Then she fired off texts to Marion and Angus and powered up her computer. She logged onto Facebook to update her status and chat with any friends who were available.

That night she had a shift at the theatre. For the whole time at work she was in a dream, envisaging how it was going to feel in February when she was in the cast, on the stage. She was still fizzing with excitement when she arrived at Phil's flat where everyone was congregating prior to going out in a group to a club. She'd been to his house before as it was close to the hall where the drama society rehearsed, so he often offered coffee or drinks afterwards. There was a crush of bodies in the hall as she was one of the last to arrive. She received lots of hugs, kisses and congratulations from all sides as she squeezed by, heading for the kitchen where the alcohol would be stashed. She poured herself a large glass of white wine and then looked around, trying to locate Mark. Usually his straight blonde hair was easy to spot above other heads since he was taller than average.

"Rose, well done. We all thought you deserved the part. You're going to be amazing." She was greeted effusively by Angie, who was Phil's girlfriend.

Angie grasped Rose's forearm but swayed and staggered slightly, causing some of Rose's wine to spill.

"Whoops, these heels are a bit high. Let me find a towel." She presented Rose with a grubby dishcloth.

"Thanks. I hear you got Mary Warren," Rose said while swabbing down her skirt; luckily it was white wine.

"Yeah and Becky got Elizabeth Proctor." Angie's speech was slightly slurred; she was obviously fairly drunk. She must have started drinking a while ago.

"Cool." Rose was distracted, wanting to find Mark. "Have you seen Mark?"

"I think he's in the front room with Phil and Becky. Let's go and find them. I think we'll be heading out soon."

Rose and Angie edged their way back through the jam in the hall and from the doorway of the front room she could see Mark. Becky, who was to be his stage wife, was pressed close up to his side and she appeared to be whispering something into his ear. He caught Rose's eye, straightened up and swept back his long forelock, combing it with spread fingers. It was a characteristic gesture.

"Rose, you're here at last," he greeted her.

"I found her in the kitchen." Angie made the discovery sound like a major achievement. Meanwhile Rose received more hugs and kisses from the occupants of the front room.

"Now you're here we can go and party," Phil announced.

Gradually the group began to disperse with the intention of meeting up again at The Bunker, which was a favourite student spot for dancing and was open until late. Rose linked arms with Mark as they set off.

Sunday was a lost day. Rose didn't surface until late in the afternoon and felt decidedly hung-over. Her mouth was dry and her head seemed to be thumping in time with her pulse rate. She rummaged in her bedside drawer looking for paracetamol and then propped herself up on pillows in bed sipping ginger beer to wash the tablets down. She had two assignments due this week, one on Wednesday and the other on Friday. She'd done some preparatory reading but knew that she was going to have to concentrate and put in long hours to meet the deadlines. She decided to start tomorrow, then burrowed back underneath her downie. The next five days were spent reading and typing, beginning at eight o'clock in the morning and continuing for as long as she could manage before sleep overtook her, usually at around 2am. There were brief breaks for food and drink but apart from a foray to Tesco to restock the fridge Rose didn't leave the flat. She pressed the 'send' button at four fifty-five on Friday evening with five minutes to spare. Then she stood and stretched.

Phew. That was a marathon. Now I need a bath, she thought. She went to run the water, adding a few drops of lavender oil which she'd heard had relaxing and reviving properties. She almost drowsed off as she soaked and therefore decided that she wasn't going to be able to drag herself out, or to be sociable that night. She opted for toast and jam, hot chocolate and catching up with a few episodes of *Made in Chelsea* instead.

She woke on Saturday morning feeling alert and refreshed, glad that the essays were completed. She got up intending to have a quick breakfast and then head to the farmers' market on Whiteladies Road to buy some good food. She'd been surviving on toast and baked beans and now had a craving for crisp apples, crunchy celery and tangy cheese. As she was brushing her teeth her stomach suddenly heaved and she retched into the basin. Nothing much came up as she hadn't eaten yet today but she tried to be sick several more times. Perching on the side of the bath she wiped her face with a warm, damp cloth to wash away the sweat that had gathered. Then she rinsed her mouth with Listerine. She was never usually sick, in fact she was famous for having a stomach of steel. This was evidence, she couldn't ignore it any longer. She had to face up to the likelihood that she was pregnant.

After breakfast Rose went shopping as planned and when she was out she also visited a pharmacy to buy a pregnancy testing kit. On returning home she opened the box and read the instructions. The leaflet advised you to do the test first thing in the morning, but she was impatient to know straightaway. There were two sticks; if there was any doubt she could do the other one tomorrow morning as a check. She went into the toilet and held the stick under her as she peed. Then she sat with her eyes closed until she thought the three minutes were up. She wasn't surprised to see the strong pink line. What should she do now? She decided to go and see Mark.

Mark lived in one of the modern flats, purpose-built for students, just off Park Street. Rose set off down Pembroke Road heading towards Queen's Road. As she walked she rehearsed what she might say to break her news to Mark. When she reached his building, there was a gaggle of students emerging. They held the door open for her and she went in past them and called the lift, pressing the button for the third floor. She had just raised her hand to knock on Mark's front door when it opened from the inside and Chris, one of Mark's flatmates, emerged dressed in jeans, a leather jacket and a beanie hat.

"Hi Rose. Come to see the man?"

"Yeah, is he in?"

"Think so, but I haven't seen him. I'm just up and running late as usual. Meeting some of the lads to watch the footie."

"Hope you win," Rosie called to his retreating back and he gave her a wave in acknowledgement.

Rose looked into the kitchen, which was a mess, and the lounge, which wasn't much better. No sign of Mark. She went along to his room, tapped on the door and opened it. The room was gloomy with the window blind still down.

"Hi Mark. I've got something…"

She froze mesmerised by the tangle of naked limbs that she could make out on the bed. There was silence for what seemed like aeons but must only have been a few seconds. Then the couple must have become aware of her presence. Mark's head emerged from the blur of bodies and one of Becky's nipples slipped out from his mouth. Rose suddenly found the ability to move again. She backed out of the room, closed the door and then ran down the hall and out of the flat slamming the front door behind her.

As she retraced her steps her brain was jangling with conflicting and sometimes bizarre thoughts. How long had this been going on? Obviously Chris can't have had any idea that Becky was there or he'd surely have headed Rose off. What was she going to do now? Somehow it didn't look as if she could rely on Mark for advice or support about the pregnancy. She didn't like to admit it to herself but she'd known that Mark wasn't the staying kind. He had a reputation for flitting around lots of women. Why had she thought that she was any different from the crowd? She'd never noticed before that Becky had such large breasts. Of course, they weren't usually on full display. How was she going to manage to carry on with the play? She'd have to keep seeing both of them. Why wasn't she crying? Shouldn't she be heartbroken? Actually, her main emotions were anger, embarrassment and fear.

When she arrived home Claire and Joanna were watching

the DVD of *Les Mis* for about the thousandth time. They took one look at her face and hit the pause button.

"What's wrong?" Claire asked.

Rose spilled out her unfortunate experience, only omitting the reason behind her sudden urge to visit Mark. Both girls rallied immediately to support Rose.

"Oh my God, how awful for you." Claire sprang up from the sofa and enveloped Rose in a huge hug.

"Well, you're definitely too good for him, Rose," Joanna declared.

"You know I tried to like him for your sake but he's a right poser," Claire gave her opinion.

"Yes, too full of himself. Always preening and flicking his hair back. Thinks he's God's gift to the females of the species," Joanna agreed.

"But how am I going to face them? I'm going to see them all the time at rehearsals." Their sympathy had released her emotions and Rose was sobbing now.

"Well, I'd just be polite but ignore them otherwise. Keep your dignity," Joanna advised.

"Didn't you tell me when we were doing the lines for your audition that Abigail had a past with Mark's character?" Claire asked.

"Yes, she and John Proctor had an affair when she was their maid but then his wife found out and fired her."

"Well, can't you try to use what's happened with you and Mark and Becky to help build your character?" Claire suggested.

"Yes, maybe." Rose could see that Claire had a point. "I'll need to think about that."

"And don't forget he'll probably drop Becky soon anyway," Joanna said.

"Or two-time her," Claire added.

Rose was grateful to her friends for their encouragement but of course she hadn't confided in them, or anyone else, her other major worry. Well, she'd managed to suppress her fears before and at the moment that seemed to be the easiest option. She joined the other two girls, snuggling up close together on the settee. They passed the bowl of popcorn along to her for sharing and unpaused the DVD. She let Eddie Redmayne's rendition of 'Empty Chairs at Empty Tables' fill her mind and immersed herself in the film.

Marion

"Sweep! Hard!" the skip shouted from the house. Marion and her teammate jogged along, scrubbing furiously with their brooms at the ice ahead of the curling stone. It kept its speed and line and hit the opposing stone with a satisfying crack. The red stone was propelled out and their stone now sat near to the centre.

"Well swept." The skip praised them as they slid back down the ice to be ready for the next delivery.

This evening's event was a Bonspiel with a St Andrew's Day theme. The teams had been made up by mixing curlers from a selection of clubs. Marion didn't really know the others in her team, although she recognised the skip from previous competitions. Her opposite number in the red team had a daughter who'd been in Rose's year at school, so she'd met her a few times in the past at school events. Everyone had been asked to wear something tartan. Curling wasn't really a game suited to kilts but some of the men sported tartan trews. Marion had pinned a tartan scarf across her shoulder like a sash and had a matching tammy which threatened to fall off when she had to put any effort into sweeping. Currently the blue team were two stones ahead and there was only one more end to play, so it was a close competition.

The next red stone narrowly missed hitting the recently placed blue.

"We'll put up a guard," the skip muttered as he slid past up to the hack. His stone was well judged in weight and only had to be swept lightly into its place. It looked as if they'd still be in the lead going into the last end.

Ten minutes later the teams shook hands. It was a win by three stones for the blues.

"Can I buy you a drink?" Marion asked the number two from the reds. It was traditional that the winners stood the first round of drinks.

"I'll have a lager, please." They stowed away their brushes, changed their shoes and headed up to the bar. In line with the Scottish theme there was to be a meal of haggis. Marion bought the lager and a cider for herself and went to sit at a table beside the people she'd been playing with. "I'm sorry, I know that we met at school functions, but I've forgotten your name. I'm Marion," she said as she placed the drinks on the table.

"Yes, you're Rose's mum. It's Pamela, my daughter is Janey."

"Of course. It's hard to believe that it's been eighteen months since they left school. What's Janey up to these days?"

"She's up in Aberdeen studying law. She seems to be enjoying it. Didn't Rose decide to go to an English university?"

"Yes, she's at Bristol. It's close to her dad in Bath."

"How's she getting on?"

"Well, OK I think." Marion explained that the previous weekend Rose had been euphoric about getting the part she wanted in the drama production. But that when she phoned this weekend she'd been tearful because her boyfriend had been cheating on her.

"It's quite difficult when they're so far away to judge how they're coping with things like that," Pamela commiserated.

"I know, but I suppose it's all part of growing up. She'll be home for Christmas in about three weeks, so hopefully she'll manage until then."

"She might be ready for some mothering and home comforts. Oh, good, here's the haggis, I'm starving. It must be after all that sweeping. It was a good match though, close."

"Yes, it could have gone either way quite easily. Did you see any of the European championships?"

The talk moved onto international curling and drew in other folk from around the table. Marion enjoyed the company and the chat. It took her mind away from worrying. She'd actually been quite concerned about Rose after their Skype conversation yesterday. She'd looked pale and red-eyed and had sounded very flat, so Marion had asked her if she was OK. When she'd explained about finding out that her boyfriend had been two-timing her Marion felt sorry for her. But she hadn't even been aware that Rose had a current boyfriend, she'd never mentioned him before, so surely their relationship can't have been terribly serious yet. However, the poor girl had looked quite pathetic. Pamela was right, it was hard to gauge what was going on from a weekly phone call and occasional text messages.

"Would you like another drink, Marion?"

"No thanks, I'm fine with water." Marion smiled at her companion as her attention was drawn back to the group. The food was simple but hearty and they were provided with coffee, shortbread and a 'Rusty Nail' to finish off.

"I'm not sure we should be driving after this. It must be quite alcoholic," one curler worried. Everyone had become extremely cautious since the new stricter drink-driving rules had been passed.

"Och, it's only a small measure," one player reassured.

"We'll just have to sit on for a bit and chat for longer until we metabolise it," another suggested.

The mixture of whisky and Drambuie burned as it went down; Marion liked the fiery warmth. She leant back in her chair to listen as the Bonspiel organiser stood to announce the overall scores and clapped as the prizes were presented.

Wednesday, Marion's next day free from work, was the day arranged for the social worker to visit Betty. Marion set off towards Joppa after breakfast, stopping in at a supermarket en route to buy some biscuits. If left to her own devices Betty couldn't be relied upon to remember to eat, but sometimes she could also forget that she'd had a meal and be prepared to eat another one straightaway. Later in life she had developed a sweet tooth and, uncannily, she seemed to know if there were biscuits in the cupboard. Regardless of meals she could demolish an entire packet in no time at all, leaving none available for visitors. So, now Marion only restocked the biscuit supply when someone was expected to visit.

When she arrived at the house she let herself in and called out to her mum. There was no reply. She looked into the lounge and Betty's bedroom but no sign of her. Maybe she was in the toilet. As she moved down the hall she became aware of a cold draught of air and looking into the kitchen found that the back door was ajar. She stepped out into the back garden where she spotted Betty crouching, hunched over by a flower bed. As she drew nearer she could see that her mum was still wearing her nightie and was digging into the soil with a spoon. The front of her nightie was grubby with earth.

"Mum, what are you doing? It's too cold to be out here in your nightie." She also noticed that Betty's feet were bare. It was a dry morning but only around three degrees centigrade; Marion hoped that Betty hadn't been here for long.

"I need to dig a hole. It's a poor wee..." Betty wasn't finding the word she needed. She gestured, and there was the body of a house sparrow lying on the path beside her.

"OK, Mum, but I think you should come into the house and get dressed first. Why don't we wrap the bird up and we can bury it later?" She produced a tissue from her jacket pocket and used it to scoop up the stiff bird corpse. "We'll put it on the window ledge for now."

"I don't want the cat to get it," Betty said clambering stiffly upright. Marion took her hand to lead her indoors; it was very cold.

Betty loved to see birds in her garden and had always attracted them by providing seeds, fat-balls and coconut. Keeping these supplies topped up was now another of Marion's tasks. She undertook this happily as the birdwatching gave her mum so much pleasure. Conversely, Betty thoroughly disliked the cat from two doors down the street which was a hunter by nature and the probable cause of the sparrow's death. She was quick to chase it off if she discovered it in the vicinity.

"I think you should have a bath to warm up. Then I'll make you a cup of tea."

Marion led Betty through to the bathroom, inserted the bath plug and turned on the taps. She wondered what had happened to the carers this morning. She'd installed a key safe as they'd requested, so they had no difficulty with access now. There probably wasn't much point in asking her mum if anyone had been. She'd look in their notebook once Betty was in the bath.

"There was something... what was it I wanted to do? Sometimes I forget, you know," Betty told her.

"I think maybe you were going to feed the birds. We can do it later once you're dressed," Marion soothed. She helped her mum into the warm bath and left her soaping herself. The carers' file was in the kitchen and there was no entry for today.

Later Marion was recounting the events of the morning to the social worker.

"If I hadn't happened to come this morning, Mum could have been out there for hours. You can see why I feel she needs more supervision," Marion concluded.

"I agree, but generally the carers have attended four times daily. I think it's unusual for them to have missed a shift. However, we must stress to them that you should be informed if they're unable to cover one of their slots."

"Often there wouldn't be much I could do. I live at the other side of the city and I work. I can't rely on Mum's neighbours to step in. It's one of the reasons I'm thinking of having Mum come to stay with me."

"That could have some advantages. But moving could also make Betty more disorientated, I'm sure you're aware of that."

"Yes, I thought we'd try things out over the Christmas holiday period first. My daughter will be around to help and I was assuming we would still be able to have carers for the days when I work. If Mum didn't settle we could move her back here. I wouldn't decide to sell her house unless I thought the move was permanent."

"Hello Mrs...?" Betty appeared in the doorway. "Are you here to see my mother?" She appeared to be shy in the presence of the visitor, perhaps because she was unsure whether this was a person that she should already know and recognise.

The social worker, whose age Marion had estimated as around thirty, rose to greet Betty, shaking her hand and introducing herself.

"Hello Betty. I'm Mrs Morrison, I'm here to visit you. I've been chatting to Marion here about your carers."

"Come and sit down, Mum, and have a cup of tea."

The social worker had arrived just as Betty was dry after her bath. Marion had left her to dress and she and Mrs Morrison were ensconced in the lounge with mugs of tea by the time Betty appeared. She had chosen to wear a peacock-blue cocktail dress with sequined detail around the neckline. Her black mohair cardigan and fluffy pink slippers spoiled the elegant effect somewhat.

"Your carers?… What's that?" Betty sounded puzzled. Then she spotted the plate of biscuits.

"Yes, I'd like a biscuit, please," she said, eyeing up the selection as she sat down.

"Mrs Morrison has come to talk to you about going away for a short holiday." Marion tried to introduce the subject of respite care.

"And my mother and father would be there?" Betty wanted reassurance.

"No, but there would be other nice people to look after you," Mrs Morrison clarified.

"No, I don't want to go back to Guide camp ever again." Betty was firm. "It rained all the time and the tent dripped on me. There were beetles and creepy crawlies."

"It wouldn't be tents, more like a hotel. And there would be lots of people there to keep you company." Marion gave more details.

"Well, I'm not sure. I'd need to ask my mother. Would Peggy be coming?"

"Not to stay the whole time, but she could visit you. Peggy's her sister," Marion explained for Mrs Morrison.

"Well, I agree that respite would be appropriate for Betty. Do you have any firm dates that need cover?"

"Can I have another biscuit, please? I'm hungry," Betty declared.

"Yes, you must be after missing breakfast," Marion commented as she offered the biscuit plate up for Betty to choose from. "It'll be February sometime. My friend is making the arrangements but I'll let you know as soon as it's confirmed."

"That should be plenty of time. I'll give you this list of possible locations. If you can look through and let me know your preference I can try to arrange placement there. However, we can't always guarantee a specific unit, so if you can pick out two or three that you'd be happy with that would be helpful. After the first visit we'd always try to keep to the same place." She handed a sheaf of papers to Marion. "Now, I'll need you to help me to fill in this application form." She rummaged around in her handbag to find a pen and then began to write in Betty's details as Marion supplied them. Betty lost interest in the conversation and drifted off to sleep. Eventually the paperwork was completed and Mrs Morrison was ready to leave.

"Now, are there any questions that you have before I go?" she asked.

"Can I just ask you about planning for the future? I realise that eventually Mum might need residential care full-time. I suppose I'd hoped that she might get used to a home on respite visits and then it wouldn't be such a big step if she had to stay long term."

"Absolutely, you're quite right. We always try to continue to return clients to familiar surroundings so that it's less confusing, because of course that leads to less disruption for everyone."

"That's good."

"Try not to worry. Your mum might be perfectly content in a care home. It's often thought of as the last resort but lots of my clients have bloomed after a move to a secure environment."

"Yes. Thank you for coming and I'll get in touch once I know my dates and have gone through the list. Is email best?"

"Yes. I'm often out and about, so phoning can be a bit hit and miss. I'll process what we've discussed today and look forward to hearing from you."

"OK, bye." Marion sighed as she closed the front door. There was no doubt that having to face up to Betty's deterioration and thinking about what the future held for her was disheartening.

Nyaga

A small boy was crouched down on his haunches, running a yellow truck around the floor and accompanying his movements with a vrooming lorry sound. His route brought him within a few inches of Nyaga's feet but he didn't look up, intent in his play. Most of the eyes in the waiting room followed his progress, although one man in the corner was hidden behind a newspaper which rustled whenever he turned a page. Nyaga felt very uncomfortable, her heart racing and her nerves jangling. She tried to reassure herself with the fact that she was definitely feeling better after the course of antibiotics. Her cough had improved and the breathlessness was almost gone. But…

The toy lorry banged into her foot.

"Lewis, come here. Say sorry to the lady," a young woman called to the boy.

"It's OK." Nyaga smiled at her as the boy retreated slowly, now making a beep-beep-beeping noise for reversing the truck.

"Nyaga Sejewe."

Nyaga's stomach lurched when she heard her name, she felt sick. She got to her feet and followed Marion along the corridor. Had there been a smile as her name was called? Well, that could just be a social thing; she tried to read the doctor's body language for clues.

"Come along in and sit down, Nyaga." The door closed behind them and Nyaga thought that the sound of her heartbeat must be filling the whole room and not just her head. She licked her lips.

"Good morning Dr Wallace."

"Nyaga, I'll tell you immediately as I know that you're worrying. The HIV test is negative."

Nyaga's ears were ringing and she felt dizzy. Tears sprang into her eyes.

"Are you OK? Would you like a glass of water?"

Marion handed Nyaga a tissue then crossed the room to the sink and ran cold water into a paper cup which she set on the desk in front of Nyaga. She was quiet, allowing Nyaga to cry and release some of the tension that had been building up inside her for weeks.

"Are you ready to hear more?" Marion asked after a minute had passed.

Nyaga nodded, not yet able to look Marion in the eye.

"Well, as I said the HIV test is negative, but you are anaemic. The blood picture shows a macrocytosis, which just means bigger red cells than normal. This can be caused by a vitamin deficiency, but from what you told me last time you eat lots of fruit and vegetables, so I don't think you'll be short of folic acid. I suspect that you have pernicious anaemia. You'll be familiar with that?"

Nyaga looked up, crushing the wet tissue in her hand.

"It's the one that needs injections. But isn't it something that old ladies get?"

"Well, you know, I thought that too. But I looked it up on the internet and while in a white population it generally presents at around sixty years of age, apparently there is a high occurrence rate in young black women."

"Oh."

"So I think that's the most likely diagnosis, but we need to send off some more blood for vitamin B12 levels and intrinsic factor antibodies to confirm it. If I'm right then it's easily treated with injections as you said. How are you feeling after the antibiotics?"

"I'm a bit better, coughing less and not so breathless."

"That's good. Let me just listen in to your chest again, then I'll take some blood."

After the examination and blood test Nyaga began to dress, preparing to leave.

"Your chest sounds a lot better, it seems that the antibiotics have done their job. I think you should make another appointment to see me in about ten days' time. If the bloods show I'm right I can begin the injections then. You'll need a loading course twice a week for a month, then onto a three-monthly regime. Our practice nurse can arrange all of that. Any questions for me?"

"No. I'm just so relieved. I don't think everything has sunk in yet."

"Are you off work today?"

"Yes."

"That's good, it'll give you some time to absorb everything I've told you. I'll miss you at Dellview, though. I'll be visiting there after surgery."

"Oh, I left a list of things for you. Bernice, the relief nurse, will look after you."

"I'm sure she will. Enjoy the rest of your day off. Do you have any plans?"

"I'm not sure. I'd thought of going to the library, but now I feel I might need to be out of doors. I feel quite agitated, probably I need to let off some steam."

"Yes, it's a lovely day. A walk along the Water of Leith or the canal might be the thing. I'll see you soon."

The women shook hands and Nyaga left the consulting room still feeling somewhat dazed.

⸺ ∞ ⸺

Outside the sky was blue and there was sunshine today, although it was quite bitingly cold and Nyaga's breath made clouds in front of her face as she exhaled. She knew vaguely that the name given to her place of employment had something to do with a river and she'd also seen brown signposts to the Water of Leith riverside walkway, but she'd never been curious enough to go and explore. Now, still feeling a bit wobbly, *like a newborn kid*, she thought, she decided that the doctor's suggestion might be a good one. She needed to stretch her legs and feel their strength return. So she walked along the road towards one of the route markers for the walkway. It led her downhill and then to a steep set of descending steps. She could hear water running and smell damp vegetation. Trees and bushes covered the steep valley sides. Apart from a few conifers the trees were bare, their branches creating a crazed pattern against the pale blue sky. Decaying leaves squelched underfoot after overnight rain. These were mainly grey or brown where people had trampled over them on the path but there were still some carpets of rusty red and gold leaves underneath the trees off to the side. Green could still be seen where thick ivy enveloped tree trunks and bright velvety moss softened walls and boulders. Nyaga also spotted holly bushes sporting vivid red berries. At the bottom of the steps she found a sign pointing to Colinton and Craiglockhart dells in one direction and Currie in the other. She turned in the direction of the dells and made her way along a well-worn path. She was amazed that the environment was so peaceful; the only sounds were the river rushing past just below her, a few notes of birdsong and a dog barking in the distance. It was hard to believe that she'd only just left the city streets behind; she felt that she could be deep in the countryside.

She let her mind float as she walked along, still not quite able to trust the good news that she'd received. Deep inside she'd really believed that the result of the AIDS test was going to be positive. Her eyes began to leak again as she gave a prayer of thanks to God for what seemed to be a deliverance. She found a tissue in her pocket and dabbed at her face. Things had to change. This good news should be a pivotal event. Once she had her health back she must grasp hold of her life again, make some serious decisions and stop just drifting along. First of all after her walk she'd go to the library, as she'd originally planned, and use the computer to read up about her anaemia.

She came to a stone bridge and wondered if she should cross the river or carry on along this bank, worried that she might get lost on the other side. She saw a woman approaching accompanied by a small black dog and decided to ask her about the paths. It turned out that there were two more bridges downstream, so she could choose how far she wanted to walk and come back along the opposite bank. Nyaga thanked the woman and carried on towards the next bridge. She began to pay more attention to her surroundings, noticing a pair of ducks on the water and a small bird hopping on the path ahead. She recognised it from the picture on the office calendar for December and was able to identify it as a robin redbreast. It was surprising how much the discovery of this familiar bird pleased her. It was almost as good as meeting a friend. She took a few steadying deep breaths and appreciated for the first time that cold air could be invigorating and even agreeable.

—⚬⚬⚬—

The next day Nyaga was back at work and thankfully seemed to have her emotions back under control. Yet there must have been something different about her. She found people commenting to her.

"You've got your lovely smile back today, Nurse Nyaga," Iris said, as Nyaga handed her the small cup which held her morning medication.

"That's a happy tune," Linda, the nursing home manager, observed when they were in the office together. Nyaga hadn't even been aware that she was humming quietly to herself as she wrote up a drug order form for the pharmacy.

Later she was sorting through a box of tinsel in the residents' lounge. She and Sonia had been asked to organise the Christmas decorations. Sonia was trying to untangle a skein of fairy lights.

"You're like a cat that's stolen the cream today," Sonia remarked. "If I didn't know you better I'd think you had a new man."

"What? You think that's so unlikely?" Nyaga tried to sound insulted.

"From what you give away, which isn't much, I think you live like a hermit."

"Well, not quite, but maybe you're not far wrong. Do you think we should throw this out? It doesn't look very good." She held up a balding tinsel wreath which had once had several silver-sprayed pine cones attached, but now only one remained and there were obvious gaps where the others were missing.

"Yeah, I'd bin it. Can you help with these lights? If you hold this end at the top of the tree I'll try to drape them round."

"I've noticed a few trees lit up in house windows at night, they look pretty."

"Do you have Christmas trees at home?" Sonia asked. "Of course it must be quite different because Christmas is in the summer. That must be weird."

"Some people have artificial Christmas trees like this one, but not my family. We have lots of decorations that we've made over the years by threading small beads, and also garlands made

74

from paper and material. We put them up around the house and we string lights out in our yard over the trees and bushes."

"And is it hot?"

"Right now probably around thirty-five degrees in the day."

"Wow, that's boiling."

"It's more pleasant at night, nice to sit out in the yard with the lights twinkling."

"You must miss it," Sonia intuited as she finished placing the lights and plugged them in. She smiled when the tree lit up. "Success! Now for the baubles."

"Yes, I do miss it but it isn't forever. I'll be home by next Christmas."

Nyaga wasn't sure when she'd made this decision. The words had just popped out unprepared, but the pronouncement seemed to be valid. She continued hanging the tree ornaments humming softly. Meanwhile Sonia described the Christmas Eve traditions, or *Wigilia* as she called it, that she would celebrate with her family at home in Krakow.

Marion

Marion had started some research based on the list of care homes given to her by Mrs Morrison. She'd decided to look at places which were located either close to her house or to her work. If Betty was going to end up in care full-time then it would be best if it was convenient for visiting. She was familiar with the establishments that fell within her practice area having visited patients there. Some she wouldn't consider for her mum. One building always seemed dark and dingy, and another had a prevailing smell of stale urine. Dellview was a possibility and another that Hari took responsibility for. She decided to ask his opinion on Monday. She'd looked on the internet at the homes that were in Corstorphine but it was hard to judge them just from their websites. She knew one of the local GPs, Jane, who'd been in her year at university and had phoned to ask her for advice. They'd agreed to meet for coffee and so Marion was waiting, scanning the headlines of the weekend *Scotsman* and sipping a cappuccino.

"Marion. Sorry I'm a bit late. I had to deliver the youngest to rugby." Marion folded her paper and smiled at her harassed-looking friend.

"I've been perfectly happy reading my paper. Sit down and relax."

"I was quite relieved to have an excuse to just drop Jack off and run. It's much too cold for hanging around a playing field this morning." Jane shrugged out of her coat and settled opposite Marion. A waitress came to take her order.

"How're things with you?" Marion asked.

"Oh, hectic as usual and it'll only get worse in the run-up to Christmas."

"Is it only Jack at home now?"

"Yes, the other two are at uni. They've got exams just now but should be home in a couple of weeks. You'll be expecting Rose back soon."

"She should be finished down in Bristol in about ten days' time. I'm going to move my mum across to stay with me for Christmas too."

"But you're looking at care homes for her?"

"Well, only for respite initially, but it may have to be permanent at some point. She has Alzheimer's."

"Mmm, that's hard to cope with. Is it getting risky to leave her on her own now?"

"Well, yes, we've had a few incidents recently that concern me. I certainly couldn't go away on holiday happily with the current arrangements."

"OK, well let's have a look at your list and I'll try to shed some light on the local places."

Jane's input was very helpful and by the end of their meeting there were two homes in the area that seemed to be worth considering.

"I'd phone them and ask to visit, see for yourself what the atmosphere's like," Jane recommended.

"I will. I'd like to get everything firmed up soon, my holiday's in February."

"Well, good luck. Let me know if there's anything else that I can do. I'd better go though, a muddy youth to be collected."

"Thanks, I hope his team won." Marion waved as Jane strode past the café window towards her car.

<hr />

I think I might have found it, Marion thought to herself as she walked away from Hilltop Care Home on Sunday afternoon. It had been Jane's top recommendation and was only four streets away from Marion's house, so she'd phoned to arrange a visit. The building was a redevelopment of an old mansion house rather than a purpose-built home. So while there were fewer facilities like en-suite toilets for each resident, Marion felt that the place had character. It seemed like somewhere that you could live and put down roots rather than a temporary stop or a hotel. She quite liked visiting Dellview; it was neat, warm and clean. But she'd always thought that the rooms were all on the small side, a bit pokey and stuffy. Also the uniformity of the rooms and corridors tended to make it feel impersonal. Hilltop's rooms were large and irregular, not one the same, and there were no long hallways. Wouldn't that make it less likely that a confused elderly person would get disorientated and lost? When she was admitted into the front hall she noticed fresh flowers on a side table, soft light classical music playing and a delicious aroma of cooking wafting through from the kitchens. She'd then started to actively look for the flaw that would spoil her first impressions: a casual attitude, doped-up-looking residents or hidden grime somewhere. She'd found the nurse on duty to be friendly and informative, some of the residents were sitting in the conservatory in a small group knitting with a carer and the furnishings throughout were pleasant, light coloured and fresh. She broached the problem of her mum's confusion.

"We're a small unit with only twelve residents, so we've found that it's easier to give each one the attention they need," the nurse, Christine, replied.

"And you take people for respite?"

"Yes, we keep one room free for respite and have a small group that come to us on a rota. I'm not sure if we have space for another allocation just now, but our manager will be in tomorrow and I can ask her to contact you with more information. Once your mum's on our rota then there should be no problem as long as you give plenty of notification about potential dates."

Marion supplied her contact details and as she walked home she felt much more positive about how things might work out.

———— ∞∞∞ ————

Monday morning at the practice was busy as usual and Marion's stomach was growling as she climbed the stairs to the staff lounge for lunch. She carried a box containing the sandwiches she'd made at home last night and an apple. She filled the kettle and dropped a teabag into a mug. Once she'd made her tea she went over to sit beside Hari.

"Hi Marion, busy morning?" he asked while scooping up a forkful of pasta salad from a Tupperware container.

"Yes, as usual. I'm glad to catch you, though. I wanted to ask you about The Towers nursing home. I'm going to need respite care for my mum when I go on holiday soon and it's one of the possible places on the list. I know you're in there quite a lot and wondered what you think of it?"

"I'm sorry, Marion, obviously that must mean that your mum's condition's deteriorating. If you'd asked me the same question three months ago I'd have been happy to recommend The Towers but they've had a change in management and the care has really gone downhill under the new regime. A lot of the original staff have left or are thinking of moving on and the calibre of the new people just isn't the same. I've had a few concerns and if things don't pick up I'm considering notifying the Care Commission."

"Oh, well, I'll rule that one out then. I saw a nice place near my house yesterday. I'd be happy with Mum going there, but they haven't got back to me about availability yet."

"I hope it'll work out. Can I ask you something in confidence since we seem to be alone?"

"Of course." Marion wondered what on earth Hari was going to come out with.

"Well, I'm a bit worried about Susan. I know I get on her nerves but I wonder if she's stressed or getting burnt out. I saw a patient last week that Susan had been dealing with and I think she'd missed something pretty obvious. And then today I had a lady who complained about Susan's attitude, said she'd been very 'offhand' towards her. And she didn't seem like the chronic complaining type."

"Oh dear. I certainly don't think Susan's very happy. She's upset by all the changes that come up. I don't mean medical advances, it's the increase in admin and all the new targets that drive her mad. I suspect she's probably counting down to when she can retire. But it would be awful if she made a big mistake or had a complaint at this stage in her career."

"Do you think she might be depressed?"

"I hadn't considered it before, but she often seems hassled and a bit bad tempered. Maybe one of us should speak to her."

"I think we should probably wait until Kenneth gets back next week, but just keep an eye on things meantime. Oh, hello Sarah, come and join us." Hari greeted the registrar as she came into the room.

"I think you should talk to Kenneth since you have the facts," Marion advised Hari, and then as Sarah approached she greeted her too. "Hello Sarah, we've got a tutorial after lunch, haven't we? How was your weekend?"

The conversation moved on to discuss films currently running at the cinema as Sarah spooned up a bowl of lentil soup that she'd heated in the microwave. After lunch Sarah and Marion took a cup of tea each back down to Sarah's consulting room. They had ninety minutes set aside for their tutorial.

"I know we're going to talk about time-keeping but is there anything else you want to ask me about? Problem patients, funny results or anything like that?"

Sarah retrieved a notebook from her desk drawer and proceeded to talk over a few cases where she had questions about how to proceed. Then they moved on to tackle the main subject.

"You realise that Kenneth gave me this topic because I personally still find it a challenge?" Marion began. "So although we might outline some general tips and strategies today, I think you have to accept that some days you'll run late. You can't predict what's coming through the door and if you get a couple of complex problems, someone who needs admitting to hospital and three people that burst into tears in the same surgery then it's bad luck and you just have to do your best."

Sarah laughed.

"I do worry, though. Because at the moment I've got longer to see everyone than the GPs and I still run behind," she admitted.

"Well, some of that's because you're still learning consultation techniques and you need the extra time to practise different ways of doing things. Eventually you'll find out what works for you and what feels comfortable and you'll get into a rhythm that comes more naturally. It's like a lot of other skills – learning to drive, playing a musical instrument; at first there seems to be a lot to concentrate on and then eventually a lot of it becomes automatic. Once you get to that stage of consulting you get quicker because your brain is clear to work on the medical problem without having to worry about all of the other things."

"That sounds reassuring."

They talked about patients with multiple problems and ones who arrived with written lists of complaints.

"First of all acknowledge to yourself that often you won't be able to deal with a patient completely in one visit. Once you've done that you can actually begin to use time as a tool. Arrange to see the patient again, do some tests, wait and see what happens, try things and see how they work out," Marion suggested.

"Yes, I think that the patients kind of expect me to get everything sorted out straightaway."

"You have to negotiate with the patient and agree priorities. You might think some things are medically more important, but if you don't deal with a subject that's the patient's main concern early on then they won't be happy with you," Marion advised. "Why don't we practise that? I'll be a patient with a list and you're the doctor."

They acted out a role play and then swapped roles over so that Sarah could experience being the patient. Marion played two contrasting examples, one where she proceeded to share concerns as she'd advised Sarah to do, and another where she doggedly followed a doctor-based agenda without involving her 'patient'.

"It did feel very different," Sarah commented. "I much preferred the first doctor."

"Yes. We all like to think that we're being listened to and that the doctor is on our side. OK, hopefully you've got a few things to think about?"

"Oh yes, definitely. Thank you very much."

"Well, we can always come back to this again if you want, but I think we both have surgeries starting in fifteen minutes and I know I need a loo stop first." Marion collected her cardigan from the back of her chair and smiled at Sarah as she left the room. Walking past the reception desk on her way to the toilet she was hailed.

"Dr Wallace, there was a message for you from a care home." The receptionist handed her a piece of paper.

"Thanks Moira."

Marion glanced at the note as she continued along the corridor. The message was from Aileen McNiven, the manager of Hilltop Care Home. There was a potential space for respite, so she should contact Mrs Morrison, the social worker, as soon as possible to get the arrangements underway.

Rose

R ose glanced up from her magazine. A huddle of sheep was congregated in one corner of a field, avoiding a large area of lying water. The train sped past a river two fields farther along; it was brown and murky, swollen and fast-flowing. There had been a lot of news coverage about flooding over recent days and the passing Cumbrian countryside certainly looked waterlogged.

She checked the time on her phone; just under three hours until she arrived in Edinburgh. She was ready for a break away from Bristol. The past two weeks had been difficult. Thankfully most of her assessment this semester was on coursework, so she'd only had one exam. She'd had plenty of time to prepare for it and managed to concentrate, working steadily. After completing the paper yesterday, she felt confident that she should get a reasonable mark. She wasn't too worried about uni. The grades that she'd attained for the essays handed in three weeks ago were good, keeping her on track for a 2:1.

She hadn't spoken to Mark apart from essential interaction 'on stage' at drama rehearsals. He'd sent her several texts later on that awful Saturday, and again on Sunday. Eventually she'd replied with a text telling him that she didn't want to receive any further communication from him. She'd evolved a routine for coping with rehearsals. She timed her arrival to be one or two minutes into the session. Muttering apologies she'd sit as far away from Mark as possible and keep her head down in the script when she wasn't actively involved. When the group broke up she retreated swiftly from the hall, grabbing her belongings and tugging her coat on in the corridor. Even with this strategy Mark had run after her the first week and, catching her up, had entreated, "Hey Rose, no hard feelings eh? You know we never promised to be exclusive."

She'd turned and glared at him before rushing out of the building letting the door slam behind her. She wasn't only angry about his cheating on her but also that he'd spoiled the best part of her life. Drama Soc and rehearsals used to be the highlight of her week, and getting the part of Abigail was all that she'd aspired to. Now she dreaded rehearsals, feeling like an outcast. She was working very hard on her part, determined to show everyone that she could still be a good actress. But it was all for the wrong reason, her heart wasn't really in it. It was down to pride. He'd ruined it all.

Yes, it would be good to be back home in Edinburgh and normally she'd be looking forward to relaxing into a bit of pampering from Mum. But of course there was the pregnancy to face up to and she wasn't sure how she was going to do that. She wasn't stupid and knew that her tactic of ignoring things couldn't last forever. Her mum was a doctor after all and probably the person who knew her best; she was bound to notice something was different. The morning sickness was still there intermittently and Rose was beginning to find that some of her jeans wouldn't button up. Also, her breasts were quite tender and seemed to be growing larger, but she didn't think that anyone else would notice a change in her figure yet. Thankfully, because it was winter, she could stick to wearing sweatshirts and baggy jumpers. But presumably she should be arranging to see a midwife – getting scans and check-ups, looking after herself and the baby. There! She'd admitted to herself that there was going to be a baby, not just some never-ending, vague pregnant state. She would need to suddenly be responsible, someone's mother. Her mind skittered around the edge of that mountainous concept, then veered off. She didn't want to go there yet and purposefully focused her attention back to the article in her magazine about home-made Christmas decorations. Mum had said they'd go shopping for a tree together tomorrow and then decorate the house. Maybe she could try making some of these candle holders.

The train pulled into Edinburgh Waverley at just after eight o'clock. The redesign of the station meant that cars couldn't drive through anymore, so Rose had arranged to meet her mum at the exit on Market Street where, hopefully, there would be a parking space. Rose hauled on her backpack and pulled her suitcase behind her, making for the lift up from the platform. She emerged onto the dark, damp street and spotted her mum immediately. She was wearing a cream-coloured jacket and the orange-tinted street lighting caught her chestnut-coloured hair, making it glow brightly around her head. She saw Rose and waved.

"Hello, so good to see you. How was your trip?" she asked as she hugged Rose tight.

"Hi Mum, it was fine. Everything ran to time."

"The car's just along here." Marion pointed and then they linked arms and walked along together. Marion stowed Rose's suitcase and bag in the boot and they set off for home.

"Oh, look, the big wheel's up and the Christmas tree," Rose commented.

"Yes, you get a good view of it all from here," Marion agreed. They were stopped at the traffic lights waiting to turn onto The Mound and could see all along Princes Street. "Are the lights nice in Bristol?"

"I suppose they're OK, but it's not so dramatic as here. So we're going to get our tree tomorrow?"

"Yes. I waited for you coming home. And if you don't mind I'd like you to help with moving Gran on Sunday."

"Yeah, fine. But how do you think she's going to be at ours?"

"Well, I've been telling her it's just a visit for Christmas. So, then I thought we'd see how well she settles in and if she's OK just extend the visit indefinitely."

"And do you think she understands about Christmas?"

"Yes, I think so and if we have all the decorations up before she arrives it'll act as a reminder."

"And what about when you're at work?"

"The social worker is rearranging the system of carers so that people will come to our house instead of Joppa. And then you'll be around to begin with which will be an extra help."

"I'm not too good at getting up early in the holidays, though."

"That's OK, you shouldn't need to. A carer should get Gran up, make her breakfast and supervise her tablets. And did I tell you I've got a nursing home set up for my skiing holiday and coming down for *The Crucible*? How's that going by the way?"

"Well, it's OK, but a bit awkward because I'm trying to avoid Mark. It's spoiled the fun of it all really but I'll do my best with the part."

"I'm sure you'll be great. I'm sorry things didn't work out with Mark."

"Yeah."

"Well, here we are. I hope you're hungry. I left a lasagne in the oven."

Marion pulled into her driveway and parked the car. Then mother and daughter lugged Rose's case and bag up to the house. A welcoming aroma of food met them as Marion opened the door.

Rose slept well back in her familiar bedroom. She was a bit anxious when she got up in case she was going to be sick. She pulled on her dressing gown and stepped into slippers. On venturing downstairs to the kitchen she found a note from her mum placed in the middle of the table. 'Gone to Corstorphine for papers and milk,' she read in her mum's scrawl. It was just as well that Marion was out, as Rose had to race for the kitchen sink to vomit after eating her first few mouthfuls of toast. She rinsed her mouth out and sipped hot tea from a mug. Then she tried again with the toast, just nibbling a tiny corner at a time. This time it stayed down and by the time Marion returned Rose had finished breakfast and was showered, dressed and ready to go.

"Can I just grab a coffee before we set out? I thought we'd try the garden centre out past Hopetoun House," Marion suggested. "They usually have a good selection of trees and we can probably pick up some decorations from their shop. I think our tinsel is all a bit tatty and tired."

"OK by me."

"Maybe I could find a plant or something in their shop for Jenny," Marion mused.

"I haven't even started my Christmas shopping yet. But I won't be seeing Dad and Sally for a while, so I suppose it's just you and Gran I need to buy for and maybe the girls from school will be doing a Secret Santa."

Rose and Marion accomplished their tree shopping companionably, then after lunch Marion went up into the attic for the boxes of decorations. They spent a happy afternoon adorning the tree while listening to Christmas music, Rose singing along. Then they placed other ornaments around the room. The angel chimes went on the mantelpiece and the reindeer bells hung from the light fitting. Rose liked to bash the bells gently, setting them jingling, every time she passed by. From time to time Rose's phone pinged with an incoming text and she'd type dextrously in reply. She was getting in touch with some of her friends from home.

"Mum, I'm meeting up with Fiona in town for a pizza. She's back from Aberdeen," she announced after several more pings.

"It'll be nice for the two of you to catch up."

Marion plugged in the vacuum cleaner. There was a scattering of pine needles and tinsel threads to be tidied up after their labours.

"Yeah, we'll probably join up with some of the others for a drink after. I won't be late back, though, and I'm still OK to come with you to Gran's tomorrow."

"Will we aim to get there late morning? Then we can take her out for lunch and we won't be too late in getting back here. Give her time to settle in before bedtime."

"OK, sounds good." Rose headed upstairs to change and put her make-up on in preparation for going out.

⁂

"A Coke, thanks," Rose replied to Adam who was buying the next round in at the pub.

"Not like you to be on the soft stuff," Laura observed.

"I kind of overdid it at the end of term, sickened myself," Rose fibbed.

This was the second time she'd had to make an excuse for not drinking alcohol tonight. She'd bought the last drink for herself so no one noticed. At the restaurant with Fiona she'd pleaded lack of funds and having to buy presents and ordered tap water. In fact she hadn't had any alcohol since the party four weeks ago. She'd been working hard, then made a point of avoiding end-of-term drinks. On the bus journey into the city centre she'd toyed with the idea of confiding in Fiona about the pregnancy. However, once they met up she realised that, although they were still friends, eighteen months and five hundred miles of separation meant that they'd both changed. They were no longer bosom buddies who would share intimate secrets. She was beginning to ask herself if her silence about the baby wasn't only fear but also partly a defence. If she waited long enough no one could advise or coerce her into considering an abortion. Maybe that's what Mark would have recommended. She was sure her flatmates would have raised the subject. To Rose it had never seemed to be an option.

"Hey Rose, where are you? Wake up, head-in-the-clouds." Adam had returned with the drinks and was thrusting a Coke towards her.

"Thanks, end-of-term fatigue. I really need a holiday," she joked.

"We all do," Adam agreed.

Marion

"OK, Auntie Peggy, I really appreciate that and we'll look forward to our visit with you on Boxing Day. Bye now."

Marion put the phone down.

"How's Auntie Peggy?" Rose asked.

"She's fine. She's going to pop over on Tuesday sometime to check how Mum's settling in. So you'll see her if you're around. I think she's a bit sceptical about Mum being here longer term."

"Well, you'll never know if you don't give it a try. Has it been difficult with all the to-ing and fro-ing recently?"

"Yes, I've told you about some of the things that've happened. I don't like Mum being on her own so much, especially not overnight."

"I think she'll like the way you've done the spare room up for her, it's really cosy."

"Thanks. And it'll look more personal once we bring more of her things here."

"So are you nearly ready to go?"

"Yes. I just need to get my handbag."

Marion ran upstairs and as she passed the spare room she stopped to look in. She'd brought home some soft furnishings from her mum's house in an attempt to make the room seem familiar. The curtains were a pair that she'd found on a high shelf in a bedroom cupboard and altered to fit. She remembered that they'd once hung in the dining room at Joppa in earlier days when Betty used to change her décor for summer and winter. The thick rose-coloured velvet had been chosen to keep out winter draughts and suited the new location in the bedroom. She'd managed to find a bedspread and quilt in Betty's linen chest which toned in. She'd hung a treasured painting, which had been bought on her parents' honeymoon in Girvan, opposite the bed. It was a seascape featuring Ailsa Craig and also came from the dining room at Joppa. She'd placed a cushion with a cover embroidered by Betty's mother and antimacassars to match on the armchair. She was pleased with the effect but, yes, it would definitely look more homely once Betty's hairbrush, jewellery box and lotions were on the dressing table and her radio on the bedside cabinet. Marion hadn't wanted to remove any everyday items before her mum moved in. If Betty missed something from her house she might think that it had been stolen. There had been a misunderstanding last month when Betty had 'lost' a brooch and accused one of the carers of stealing it. Marion had discovered the brooch pinned to a jacket hanging in Betty's wardrobe. When Marion apologised on behalf of her mum the carer had been surprisingly understanding; apparently that kind of charge from confused elderly clients was common. Marion pulled the door closed and went into her own room to fetch her bag.

When they arrived at Joppa, Betty was snoozing in her armchair.

"Hello Mum. We thought we'd take you out for lunch. Hope you're hungry." Marion kissed Betty on the cheek.

"Hi Gran." Rose leaned in to kiss her too.

"Now, who's this you've brought today? My mother doesn't like strangers in the house," Betty declared.

"It's Rose, your granddaughter. She's been away at university and now it's the Christmas holidays," Marion reminded her.

"Rose?... There's an Ivy at my school. Do you know her?"

"No, Gran. I don't think I've met Ivy." Rose was used to not being recognised now that there were long gaps when she didn't see Betty.

"Let's find your jacket and some shoes for going out," Marion suggested. Betty heaved herself up out of the armchair and began to lead the way through to her bedroom to choose outdoor garments.

"Maybe you should go to the toilet too before we set off."

"Thank you. I'm not a baby, you know," Betty said huffily. She could sometimes be annoyed by too much instruction.

⁕

That night in bed Marion found it hard to fall asleep. She was alert to every tiny creak and faint click as the house cooled down, noises that she would normally ignore. Now she imagined that it was Betty padding about. Maybe she had woken up and was wandering about disorientated. What if she wanted to go to the toilet and couldn't find it? What if she took a wrong turn and fell down the stairs? Marion had plugged in a glowing night light in Betty's room and left the landing light on too, but it might be sensible to invest in a stair gate.

Overall she'd been pleased at how well her mum had settled in this evening.

They'd driven down the coast to Dirleton and had enjoyed a pleasant lunch at the Open Arms Hotel. This establishment had always been a family favourite; the food and service were good and after eating, children and adults alike used to enjoy exploring the ruined castle across the road. There was also an extensive garden to wander through. However, the weather was too cold for outdoor pursuits so today after lunch they had driven straight back to Joppa where she and Rose had packed up toiletries, clothes and other essentials for Betty's 'holiday'. Betty dozed happily after putting away a large meal; there was certainly nothing wrong with her appetite.

Once they arrived in Corstorphine, Betty seemed to find her surroundings familiar, she certainly wasn't distressed at all. She'd commented on the Christmas tree and decorations and had to be gently restrained from eating the chocolate tree baubles.

"They're for after Christmas, Gran," Rose had admonished.

"I suspect we'll find that they gradually disappear," Marion said. "You know your gran has developed a sweet tooth."

Betty had been pleased with her bedroom.

"Is it all for me?" she'd asked. "Where will Peggy sleep?"

They'd helped her to unpack and showed her where the bathroom was, right next door. Then Marion had turned on the television in the lounge for *Songs of Praise* as her mum liked to sing along with the hymns. They'd also all watched a repeat of *Dad's Army* and then, after a drink of hot chocolate accompanied by a slice of banana loaf, Marion had helped Betty to get ready for bed. Since then it had been quiet; presumably Betty was sleeping peacefully. Marion hoped that the new carers would appear in the morning as planned, because she had to leave the house before eight o'clock for work. Well, at least Rose was here as a backup. She could muddle through with her gran if necessary.

Eventually Marion must have drifted off to sleep. She woke up suddenly. Opening her eyes she found a figure looming over her. She started, catching her breath and clutching the downie to her neck. Then she realised that it was her mum peering at her.

"Is this Robert's house? Where's Peter?" Betty whispered.

"No, Mum, it's OK. You're visiting with me, remember?" Marion glanced at the bedside clock; it showed four fifteen.

"Did something waken you up, Mum?"

"Where's Peter?"

Marion hated it when her mum asked for people who were dead. She didn't like lying but it didn't seem kind to upset Betty by telling her that her mother and her husband Peter, the people that she asked after most, were dead. She wasn't sure who Robert was, maybe another relative? She wasn't at her most mentally agile when woken at this hour.

"He's visiting Douglas," she said. This was a deceit that she often resorted to and it usually satisfied Betty. Luckily she'd forget both having asked the question and Marion's reply very soon.

"It's still the middle of the night, Mum. Will I take you back to bed?"

"I'm a bit thirsty."

"OK. Let's tuck you up and I'll fetch you a drink. What would you like?"

"A cup of tea would be nice."

Marion winced internally. By the time she made a hot drink and then got Betty settled down again there probably wouldn't be much more chance to sleep tonight.

On Monday morning Marion was on the rota to be duty doctor. This meant that, instead of taking a surgery and then a share of visits, she dealt with patients who telephoned asking to speak to a doctor or for an urgent appointment. Many of the interactions could be resolved over the phone, either by Marion giving advice or offering to write a prescription or a medical certificate allowing absence from work. She arranged for some patients to come for a consultation later in the week, or to be put onto the visit list. And she saw some people personally that morning. There was less structure to her routine than usual so she was able to call home at ten o'clock. Rose reassured her that a carer had been to the house. Apparently today Betty had already got herself up and had dressed independently. The carer had made some breakfast and supervised her medication. Rose wondered if it was OK to take her gran for a walk around the block for some exercise as long as they were back by the time the next carer was due at lunchtime. Marion thought that was a good idea and thanked Rose. She felt a lot happier after their conversation and settled down to her list of callbacks.

Later that morning Marion was returning to her room, after delivering a pile of signed prescriptions and certificates to the reception desk, when she met Nyaga coming in the opposite direction along the corridor.

"Hello Nyaga. Have you been having one of your injections?"

"Hello Dr Wallace. Yes, I've just seen your nurse, and I think I'm feeling stronger already after just one week of the treatment."

"That's good to hear. And what are your plans for Christmas?"

"Oh, I'm working. That way someone with a family can enjoy their day off and I get lots of company."

Marion remembered how bleak and lonely Nyaga's description of her life had sounded and thought how much she must be missing her little girl, especially at this time of the year. Suddenly she decided.

"When does your shift finish? Would you like to join me and my family for Christmas dinner?"

"Oh." Nyaga looked taken aback. "I wouldn't want to put you out."

"Really you wouldn't be. There's just me, my mum and my daughter and we can eat at any time of day, early or late. Please say you'll come." Somehow it now seemed to be tremendously important that Nyaga should accept the invitation.

"Well, I finish at four o'clock and I've arranged for one of the other staff members who owns a car to give me a lift home as there won't be many buses running that day. Maybe they could drop me at your house instead."

"Or if not my daughter Rose could drive over to collect you. I'll probably be busy in the kitchen. So you'll come?"

"Yes. I'd like that very much."

"Why not come along to my room just now and I'll give you a note of my address and phone number. If you need us to collect you give me a ring, otherwise we'll expect you around four thirty."

"Thank you. I'll look forward to it."

Nyaga

Nyaga woke on Christmas Day with a sense of pleasant anticipation. It was a long time since she'd had such a feeling; she snuggled in under her downie and hugged it to her. Because there were very few buses running on the holiday, Dellview had organised for a taxi to collect her from home. So the beginning of her day could be more leisurely than usual. She'd already packed a bag with clothes to change into after work and she'd wrapped an African cloth that her mum had sent her to take as a gift for Marion.

Standing under the shower she allowed herself to think about her other excitement. As it was Christmas, Linda had given her permission to use the nursing home telephone to call home. She was to pay back the charges once the itemised bill came in. It was months since she'd spoken to her mum and Lesedi. She'd survived on emails and occasional parcels. To hear their voices would be a treat.

She towelled herself dry and donned her uniform. Then she went through to the kitchen to make some breakfast. She'd kept one of the two cloths that her mum had sent. It was draped over the settee and seemed to radiate its colours into the beigeness, dispelling some of the gloom. She ate fruit and yoghurt, then toast with honey and drank strong tea. Even her appetite seemed to have improved now that she was having the B12 injections. She wasn't sure how much of her recovery was purely physical; there was no doubt that the release from worry also played a large part in her new sense of wellbeing.

The taxi arrived as planned and swept her off to work. The streets were almost deserted and she arrived within ten minutes. After breakfast and the medicine round were finished the staff encouraged residents who were dressed and mobile to collect in the lounge. A recording of carols from the choir of King's College, Cambridge was playing quietly in the background and the cooks had prepared warm mince pies and a choice of mulled wine or non-alcoholic fruit punch. Then Santa appeared, the husband of one of the kitchen staff who'd been 'volunteered' for the role. He played his part well, with cheerful greetings and jolly banter for the residents. Everyone received a gift and then Santa went to visit the frailer nursing home inhabitants in their rooms. Some people were expecting to be collected by family members, who would take them to join in with celebrations at their homes. One or two residents had invited guests to the special Christmas lunch at Dellview. All of these changes from the normal daily routine raised an atmosphere of excitement in the building and time seemed to fly past.

Nyaga spent a large part of the morning tending to Jessie who was very weak and unwell, coughing, breathless and running a high fever. Dr Wallace had called yesterday and prescribed antibiotic syrup and Nyaga was trying to make her patient comfortable, encouraging her to take sips of iced water through a straw, and bathing her forehead and arms with a cool cloth. She murmured and hummed to her, keeping her company. She felt sorry for the old lady; it wasn't nice to be ill and alone on any day, but somehow it felt worse today. When she had to leave to attend to other duties she arranged for one of the auxiliary staff to sit with Jessie in her place. She called into the office to check in the records, wondering if there were relatives nearby who might come. A son and his family lived in Australia and there was a cousin in Inverness, so no one local. She'd see how things went today but she might phone the cousin tomorrow if there was no improvement.

Christmas lunch was more elaborate than the usual Dellview fare and there were crackers and party hats provided. Afterwards most of the residents went for a nap or settled down to watch television. The Queen's speech was eagerly awaited by some. This quieter interlude gave the staff a break and a chance to have something to eat. Nyaga restricted herself to a turkey sandwich and a mince pie to leave plenty of space for dinner. The office was piled high with tins of biscuits and boxes of chocolates given to the staff by residents and their relatives.

"I don't think we'll need to buy any biscuits before Easter," Linda had commented when she'd attempted to clear some space on her desk yesterday.

The relief nurse arrived for her shift at three thirty and Nyaga brought her up to date with essential information, mainly about how Jessie was faring. Then at quarter to four Nyaga sat down at Linda's desk, with her diary open to the page where her home telephone number was noted down preceded by the international dialling code. After some beeps and crackles on the line she heard ringing.

"*Dumela*." It was her mum's voice.

"Hello, it's Nyaga," she managed to reply in Twsana. Her voice had come out as a squeak; it was the first time that she'd heard or spoken her native language for months.

"Nyaga. Oh, how wonderful to hear from you."

Once they had established that both individuals were well and that Nyaga was calling from her work her mother called for

Lesedi to come and speak. Lesedi chattily told Nyaga about her day, about going to church in the morning where there was a baby Jesus in the manger and then there was a big party in their yard with lots of good things to eat.

"… and ice cream," she listed twice. "Here's Granny." Her description came to an abrupt end.

Nyaga spoke for a little longer with her mother, telling her about the invitation to dinner. Her mum was pleased to hear that she was making friends.

"But don't stay away from us for too long," she requested.

When Nyaga hung up she found that although she was smiling, tears were also tracking down her face. She'd need to wash her face and apply some makeup in addition to getting changed. She hurried through to the staff toilet as she didn't want to keep Ruth, her driver, waiting.

Nyaga had seen Corstorphine Hill to the north across the city skyline, but had never travelled in that direction. She was surprised by the steep approach up towards Marion's street.

"Your friend lives almost next door to the zoo," Ruth commented.

"Oh. I didn't know that."

Nyaga wasn't quite sure what a zoo comprised. She knew that it was some kind of a park for animals but she couldn't imagine that there was enough space for a game reserve here in the city. The car was drawing up at Marion's house number. She opened the door and collected her belongings.

"Thank you for the lift, I hope it wasn't too far out of your way."

"Not at all. Have a nice time." Ruth smiled and waved cheerily as she drove off.

Nyaga went through a wrought iron gate and climbed up six steps on the path approaching the front door. A heavy wooden outer door was standing open. Light spilled out and she entered a small tiled porch. She rang the doorbell and could see a figure inside the house advancing towards the partially glazed inner door. A teenage girl opened the door. She had long, straight dark hair, caught back from her face in a partial ponytail, and was dressed in black jeans with a loose, coral-coloured, silky shirt on top.

"Hi, you must be Nyaga. Come in. Mum's in the kitchen but she'll be out to see you in a moment. I'm Rose, Merry Christmas."

Rose took Nyaga's coat then guided her into a room on their left and encouraged her to take a seat. Nyaga perched on the edge of an armchair. Yellow and gold were the predominant colours in the room with some features picked out in jewel tones. The cushions were gold, ruby, emerald and sapphire and the curtains and hearthrug picked up the same tones. There was a real Christmas tree by the window; Nyaga could smell its fresh pine scent. Lit candles flickered on the mantelpiece and were reflected in a large mirror hanging on the chimney breast. Nyaga noticed a piano with a pile of music books perched on top. She realised that this was the first time that she'd been inside an Edinburgh home apart from her own dreary flat.

"Nyaga, hello and Merry Christmas." Marion came into the room. "Now, can I get you something to drink?"

Nyaga accepted a glass of wine and recounted a little of her day's activities.

"It must have been great to speak to your family," Marion commented.

"How old is your daughter?" Rose asked. Rose and Marion were both very interested in Nyaga's family and asked questions about where they lived. She offered her gift and they appreciated its rich colours and African design.

"Where's Gran?" Rose eventually asked when Marion mentioned that their meal would soon be ready to serve.

"I think she must be asleep in her room. Could you go and fetch her?" Marion asked. She then explained to Nyaga that her mum had dementia and had only just come to stay.

"So she can be a bit confused."

"Oh, I'm used to that," Nyaga laughed. "But not easy for you to cope with."

"Well, so far it's been better than I expected," Marion admitted.

Just then Betty entered the room. Today her clothes were well co-ordinated: a tweed skirt in heathery shades of pink and mauve and a cream blouse with the same colours edging the collar.

"Hello, we have a visitor. Oh my, you could be a fashion model. Look at how tall and elegant you are." Betty gaped up at Nyaga when she stood to shake hands.

"Let's all go through to the dining room while we're on our feet," Marion encouraged them. Betty seemed to be mesmerised by Nyaga and took her hand as they moved to the dining room.

"Are those big hoops not heavy for your ears?" she asked. Nyaga had put the earrings in after her shift. They reached almost to her shoulders.

"No, they're not gold, just imitation so I won't hurt my ears," she reassured Betty.

They sat down and pulled crackers. Nyaga enjoyed the meal. Nothing was elaborate but the ingredients were all fresh and very tasty. Conversation seemed to flow easily and touched on fashion trends, Rose's play in Bristol and different Christmas traditions. Nyaga asked about the zoo along the road and mentioned her wish to go and see the sea. Rose seemed keen to help out and offered to drive Nyaga along the coast to St Abb's Head on her next day off if the car was available.

"There's a lighthouse there. And we could go to the beach at Tyninghame on the way back. You'd need to wrap up, though, as it'll be cold."

"Yes, I've only just discovered that sometimes a walk in the cold can be enjoyable," Nyaga admitted. "At first I hated it and was miserable. I didn't have warm enough clothes when I arrived."

After dinner, when they returned to the lounge, Rose sat at the piano.

"I thought Gran might like to sing some carols," she suggested. "I've been practising." She opened a book with a mixture of carols and Christmas songs and proceeded to play while the others sang along. Betty and Rose carried the tunes and Nyaga added some harmonies. They finished with a rendition of 'White Christmas'.

"When we had snow one time... I built a snowman with my sister and then my father lent us one of his... those puffy things to put in its mouth."

"Was it a pipe, Gran?" Rose clarified.

"Yes, and we put chuckies for the buttons."

"What are chuckies?" Rose wanted to know.

"It's a Scots word for pebbles or wee stones," Marion explained. She was grateful for moments like these when Betty could still interact socially. "I think we had a few snowy Christmases when I was young, but now with global warming we get a lot less snow than we used to," she commented.

"Except there was all that snow in 2010 and it lay for weeks. We even had a snowman-building competition at school," Rose remembered.

"I built a snowman with my sister Peggy and we gave it buttons and made its nose with a carrot." Betty's conversation could be repetitive.

"Have you ever seen snow, Nyaga?" Marion asked.

"Not close up. I think there was some on the tops of the hills last week."

"We might get more in January, that's when the temperature usually drops," Marion predicted.

When she noticed from the clock on the mantelpiece that it was eleven o'clock Nyaga felt that it was time to leave.

"Thank you so much, I've had a lovely time," she said to Marion as she buttoned up her coat.

"You're welcome," Marion replied.

"Will you come back again?" Betty asked.

"Yes, I will if you'd like me to."

"And we've got our seaside trip coming up," Rose reminded her. She was also donning outdoor clothing, getting ready to drive Nyaga home.

"Don't let my family boss you about too much," Marion warned.

"That's OK. I'm very happy to go along with their plans," Nyaga said, laughing.

She waved to Marion and Betty as the car pulled away.

Marion

"Mum, I need to talk to you."

"Mmmm?" Marion looked up from her book. She was enjoying a lazy day after cooking on Christmas Day and then driving to Kirkcaldy yesterday to spend the day with Auntie Peggy. Rose was planted in front of her chair, feet apart, one arm dangling loose and the other bent up with the fist bunched in front of her mouth. Something about her stance alerted Marion and she began to pay attention.

"OK," she said closing her book and putting it down. "Why don't you sit down? Are you worried about something? Is it uni?"

Rose sat in the neighbouring armchair.

"I'm pregnant," Rose blurted out.

It felt to Marion that she'd received a physical blow; she froze. This wasn't what she'd imagined at all. She tried to steady herself by taking a few deep breaths. She was shocked and very aware of the need to tread gently.

"You're sure?"

"Yes. I'm about three months."

"And are you OK?"

"A bit sick, but I think so otherwise. I waited till now to tell you because I didn't want to spoil Christmas."

Marion felt as if her thoughts had been stirred in treacle. It was so hard to extract one and to know what to say next.

"Does your dad know?"

"No. I haven't told anyone else. I was going to tell Mark and that's when I discovered he was cheating on me. So, I couldn't tell him then." Rose began to cry.

Marion couldn't imagine how lonely and frightened Rose must have been, dealing with all of this on her own.

"I wish you'd told me earlier, it must have been scary," she said. Rose's tears seemed to unlock a basic, maternal reaction and Marion was able to move again. She crossed over to sit on the arm of Rose's chair and hugged her daughter close. Digging into the pocket of her jeans she found a clean tissue and offered it to Rose.

"I didn't want to tell you on the phone and I was so busy with the play and uni that I didn't feel I could afford to come up for a weekend. I couldn't have told Dad before you."

"So, what are you thinking?" Marion knew that if Rose's estimated date was correct they would need to move fast if she was considering a termination. But she didn't know if Rose knew this.

"Well, I worked out that the baby will be due around the beginning of July. So I don't see why I can't finish up second year and then come home to have it here."

"So you definitely want to go ahead?" Marion had to be sure that Rose was given the opportunity to think about the other option, no matter what her own opinion might be. And, if she was being honest with herself, she wasn't too sure about that right now. It was all very well having broad principles, but it seemed different when they had to be applied so close to home.

"Mum, I couldn't kill it. It's my baby."

"I just need to know that you've thought it all through, and that you realise how much it'll change your life if you have a baby. You know I'll support you all I can, but in the end it's going to be your responsibility."

"I have been thinking about it. Not at first. To begin with I just pushed it all to the back of my mind and wouldn't go there. But since I've come home I've faced up to it, and I am sure."

"OK, then we'd better get you an appointment for an antenatal check-up before you go back to Bristol."

Marion had to slam her internal brakes on. She'd almost said that she'd phone and arrange it after the holiday weekend. She and Rose had fallen out before over Marion assuming control. It was hard for her to stop thinking of Rose as a child and just taking over. She was going to have to be even more careful now.

"I can get you the number to phone," she said instead.

"Thanks, Mum, and thanks for being here for me. I feel better now that you know."

"Well, any time you want to talk about things let me know. What about telling your dad? Will you phone him or wait until you're back in Bristol?"

"I think I'd rather tell him in person. They're expecting me to visit on the Sunday before term starts. We're going to have lunch and exchange presents then, so that'd be the obvious time to break the news."

"And Mark?"

"I really don't know, Mum. I'd rather not involve him at all, but once I start to show he's going to work it out, isn't he? I'd considered writing him a letter. I don't want to face him."

"Well, you've got time to think about it before you go back. Want a cup of tea?" she asked getting up.

"Yes please. I think I can hear Gran in the kitchen, she's probably on the lookout for a snack. I can't understand why she isn't really fat because she eats non-stop."

They went through together to find Betty rummaging through one of the kitchen cupboards. Packets and tins were strewn across the worktop.

"I'm a bit hungry. I was looking for a biscuit," she said.

"They're in this other cupboard here, Mum." Marion showed Betty again where the biscuits were kept. "We were just coming through to put the kettle on for a cup of tea."

The next day Marion was still on holiday and as it was a crisp, frosty morning she decided to go for a walk around Corstorphine Hill. The paths could often be very muddy, but today they were frozen into ridges and troughs with embedded icy crystals that cracked underfoot. Marion hadn't slept well and her head felt fuzzy, her thoughts in terrible disorder. She hoped that the sharp breeze would be reviving.

She and Rose had talked again last night after Betty went to bed. So now she understood about Rose's long-standing infatuation with Mark. He was apparently very handsome and exuded charisma, especially for girls. Rose's friends had even warned her that he liked to play the field, but in her obsession she hadn't seen it. She was just so amazed that he'd noticed her. Looking back she could admit that she'd probably thrown herself at him. Rose also now recognised that other girls did the same and that sometimes Mark chose not to resist. Marion couldn't help but see some similarities to her own relationship with Angus. But she didn't want to revisit that old subject. And she certainly wouldn't mention it to Rose. She'd made a rule for herself long ago not to bad-mouth Angus to Rose. She deserved to have the best relationship that she could with her dad without any taint from Marion's bitterness.

Reaching the top of the steep path Marion stopped to catch her breath. She'd emerged into a clearing and because the surrounding trees were bare the sun was able to penetrate. A rim of ice outlined every twig, fallen leaf and blade of grass, and everything sparkled in the sunshine. Marion's exhaled breath billowed out in clouds and her eyes watered. She dabbed at them with a tissue and carried on towards Corstorphine Hill Tower.

Marion knew that she shouldn't be thinking about how Rose's situation would affect her personally. She tried not to mind that some people might see the pregnancy as a bad reflection of her parenting. You'd expect a GP's daughter to know better about family planning. She'd had that opinion herself, why wouldn't others think the same way? Rose admitted that she'd been so swept off her feet that she'd never got round to making an appointment to see about the pill. They'd used condoms, and Rose could only deduce that one had leaked. So, Marion had to conclude that Rose had been taking care, and that the pregnancy was down to bad luck and not recklessness.

By now she'd walked past the stone tower, a monument to Sir Walter Scott, and come out onto some huge slabs of rock. The going here was tricky as the rock surfaces abutted each other at odd angles and the covering of frost made everything very slippery. Marion wished that she'd brought her walking pole for extra balance. She slid a few times but avoided falling over and safely reached an outlook point above a grassy field. Here she stopped to assess the progress of work on the new Forth Bridge which she could see in the distance. The white sail-like structures had definitely grown larger since she'd last observed them, as more of the supporting wires had been put into place. It looked much bigger than the other two bridges and was definitely going to be a dramatic and impressive addition to the landscape once it was completed. She picked out Cammo Tower and the airport control tower rising like chess pieces from the flat plane to the west. They reminded her of a castle and a queen respectively, and of the epic battles that she'd had with her dad playing chess.

As she continued to walk she worried about the changes that were ahead for Rose. She brought to mind some of the teenage girls that she'd looked after recently during their pregnancies, and on into early motherhood. Most of the girls were very good with their babies and managed admirably. Nearly all were single mums, often living with their own parents. Only a few set up home with their partners. Some girls went on to further studies at college once their babies were older, and eventually gained good jobs, enabling them to support their children. At least attitudes to single parenthood were more relaxed nowadays. Girls weren't ostracised and their children were accepted. Education had become more flexible with more opportunities for part-time studying. Childcare was easier to access and she knew that many colleges had their own crèches and nurseries on campus. It didn't make single motherhood a breeze, but maybe it wasn't a total disaster for Rose. She might be able to finish her degree if that was still a priority. No doubt her focus would change. She'd have to grow up quickly. In many ways she still seemed like a child to Marion, however she knew that she wouldn't have considered herself to be a child at the same age, approaching twenty. And she was sure that Rose thought of herself as an adult.

The path wound round the north of the hill and then flanked the eastern side. She had glimpses across to Granton where she could see the old gasometer and the Firth of Forth. Then she was walking above Ravelston and Murrayfield golf courses. The route would take her along the boundary fence of the zoo and then back out onto Kaimes Road and the way home.

What if Rose took after her and suffered from postnatal depression? Marion knew that there could be a genetic link. She hated to think about those dark, despairing months and wouldn't wish the experience on anyone, and certainly not Rose. Well, at least she'd be on the alert, and if Rose showed any symptoms once the baby was born they'd be able to react quickly to get help. As far as she knew Betty had been fine after her pregnancies, so in her own case it hadn't been inherited.

Thinking of Betty, Marion thought that they should go out somewhere together this afternoon to make the most of the sunshine. Where could they go? Maybe the Botanics, but there wouldn't be much in flower at this time of year; Cramond foreshore might be better. She'd give Betty the choice. It was certainly handier having her mum living with her. Previously an afternoon outing would have included an extra hour of driving to and from Joppa. And she did seem to be quite settled. There had been one or two occasions when she'd been upset at not being able to find something, but she'd never asked about her own house or wanted to be taken home. Marion supposed she'd need to take a drive over to Joppa soon to check up on the house. Rita from next door was keeping an eye on things and would let Marion know if there was a problem but she didn't want to impose on her too much. She could bring a few more of Betty's clothes back. She still intended to put the place up for sale in the spring if things with Betty were continuing to go well.

She wondered if her preoccupation with her mum had caused her to neglect Rose. Would she have noticed a change in her daughter if she hadn't been so wrapped up in concerns about Betty? Probably not. Rose was a good actress after all and hadn't wanted Marion to guess anything before she made her announcement. With hindsight, she knew that it was out of character for Rose to constantly wear such baggy clothes. She might have been suspicious of her volunteering to drive so much too, presumably as an excuse to avoid alcohol without any comment. And she'd been very stay-at-home, none of the usual clubbing with her friends until three in the morning. Presumably she'd been avoiding the need to wear skimpy outfits and drink cocktails. If Marion remembered early pregnancy correctly Rose had probably also just felt too tired. Marion had put it down to still being upset about breaking up with Mark and so feeling less sociable, and maybe that did play a part too. Adding it all up now, it was easy enough to solve the clues retrospectively. But she came to the conclusion that, at the time, the signs had been very subtle. She decided that she could excuse herself for not catching on.

Marion arrived back at her front gate and began to climb the path up to the front door. As she passed she noticed a Christmas rose in flower in the border. She stopped, squatting down to gently stroke its white petals. There were also some early green shoots of snowdrop bulbs breaching the soil. She loved to see these early signs of spring appearing at what seemed to be the deadest time of the year.

Rose

Rose lay in a dimly lit room on top of a high, narrow examination couch. Marion was perched on a stool by her side and they held hands. Rose was glad that she'd been able to arrange an antenatal appointment for a Wednesday so that her mum could accompany her.

"OK, Rose, this will be a bit cold."

The ultrasound technician smeared icy jelly across Rose's lower abdomen, causing her to shiver. Then she slid the probe across her skin, spreading the jelly with fluid movements. She adjusted some settings on her monitor.

"Here's a good view," she said and swung the screen round so that Rose and Marion could see the image.

Rose was amazed. Everything looked shadowlike and grainy but she could make out an obvious dark kidney shape and lying along the bottom of it was a tiny grey baby. Its head looked relatively large and she could see its eyes and nose. It had stubby little arms and there was a whiter line visible along its back that the radiographer identified as its spine.

"I just need to take some measurements now." The woman turned the screen back and tapped at her keyboard.

"The noise you'll hear next is the baby's heartbeat."

A rushing, whooshing noise began, sounding a bit like a fast train. Rose looked at her mum and smiled. She noticed that Marion, although smiling, had tears in her eyes and gave her hand a squeeze.

"Did you want a printed photo?"

"Yes please," Rose said.

"OK, that's you done. I'll give you a paper towel to wipe your tummy, and then if you go back along to the waiting room the midwife will call you. Your photo will be at reception as you leave, it'll cost £2."

"That's great, thank you." Rose let go of Marion's hand and stood up from the couch scrubbing her stomach clean with the soft paper towel. She readjusted her clothing and followed Marion out into the corridor.

"Wasn't that amazing?" she beamed at Marion. "Of course you'll have seen lots of scans before."

"No, I haven't really. We can use a sonic aid to listen for the foetal heartbeat at the surgery but we don't have ultrasound."

They sat down together in the waiting room. Rose noticed that she wasn't the only one to be accompanied by another woman. When her name was called Marion stayed behind.

"Off you go, I'll wait here," she said.

Rose was relieved that her mum was acting so tactfully and treating her as an adult. She had a few questions that she wanted to ask the midwife which she'd rather not raise with Marion there. She'd begun to have a nagging anxiety that perhaps Mark could have passed on some kind of sexually transmitted disease. If his sperm had got through a condom maybe bacteria or viruses could have too. And he might be a high risk if he'd had a lot of other partners. Although she felt alright she thought that some of these things could be lurking there without many initial symptoms.

The midwife asked a series of questions and entered Rose's answers onto a form. She explained that the details and measurements from the ultrasound scan confirmed the gestation that Rose's dates had suggested. That meant that her estimated date of delivery was the seventh of July. She measured Rose's height and weight, took a blood pressure reading and then prepared to draw off some blood. Rose used this opportunity to raise her questions. The midwife was reassuring without being dismissive and told her that they did some routine testing which would uncover any potential problems. After the blood test was completed they discussed the practicalities of arranging her next few antenatal checks down in Bristol.

"When do you expect to be back in Edinburgh?"

"Probably by the end of May or beginning of June. I don't have my exam dates yet but I was finished by the middle of May last year."

"OK, I'll give you a return appointment here for the second week in June. By then you should only have a month to go. You can always rearrange if your plans change. Anything else you want to ask?"

"No thanks. I think we've covered everything."

"That's good. I hope you'll keep well through your pregnancy and make sure to look after yourself. Stop off at reception on your way out for your appointment date and your photo."

"I will, thanks. Bye."

Rose was surprised to find that it was almost lunchtime when she and Marion emerged from the building into the car park.

"Wow, I didn't realise we'd been in there for so long. I'm famished," she declared.

"Yes, I managed to read a few chapters of my book," Marion commented. "Let's head home for some lunch. The carers will probably have been in to feed Gran by now but there should be enough soup left for us."

"Are you finding it OK with those people coming in and out of the house for Gran?" Rose asked as Marion drove up to the barrier at the car park exit.

"It is a bit intrusive, but needs must. There's no way we could manage without them on the days I'm at work. And I still want to be able to come and go a bit on my days off and have the odd evening out without worrying."

"You know, I think Gran's been a bit better. Maybe having more company is good for her. She was probably a bit lonely at her own house."

"Yes, she might have been. She'll miss having you around after tomorrow. And so will I."

"I've been feeling nervous about going back and having to tell Dad and my flatmates and other people about the baby. But after seeing the scan it seems exciting too."

"And don't forget you've got the play coming up. It's only about five weeks away, isn't it? That'll keep you very busy. I'm looking forward to coming down for it."

"And then you're going off skiing with Jenny straight after. Is that the plan?"

"Yes. We're meeting up at Gatwick and going on to Geneva from there."

"Sounds good. And Gran's definitely going to Hilltop while you're away?"

"Yep, it's all been confirmed and it seems really nice. I think she'll be OK there."

<hr />

After lunch Marion left for the ice rink and her regular Wednesday afternoon curling match. Betty was snoozing in her room so Rose decided to look through her clothes and begin packing. She'd booked a train to take her down to Bristol on Friday, giving her the weekend to settle in before classes started on Monday. She knew that there was no point in taking some things back with her as they were already too tight. She could get away with wearing some of her jeans held together with elastic bands and safety pins at the waist for a bit longer if she matched them with a baggy top. It was too early to start wearing real maternity clothes but she was going to have to find a few additions to her wardrobe. To that end she had a date with Nyaga. They'd agreed to meet tomorrow at Haymarket and then visit the charity shops on Dalry Road where Nyaga shopped regularly.

Rose had spent the previous Friday with Nyaga on their expedition to the sea and had confided in her about the baby. She'd thought that Nyaga was totally cool about the whole thing. She was a single mum herself and was used to working hard and making do. She'd been the one to suggest charity shops as a possible cheap source of extra clothes.

Their excursion had been a great success. Luckily the weather that day had been dry and relatively calm. Rose had insisted that they needed to drive east beyond North Berwick to really experience the sea.

"Before that it's still the estuary, not the real sea," she'd explained and demonstrated to Nyaga on the map.

"OK, I'm happy to take your advice but it means a longer drive for you." Nyaga had been concerned not to cause too much bother.

"Not a problem, we're good and early and I've brought a picnic. We'll go to St Abb's Head first. It's brilliant there, high up above the sea on the cliffs. Then if we've got time we can stop at a beach on the way back for a contrast."

"You've got it all planned out," Nyaga laughed.

Setting out from Nyaga's flat they arrived at the National Trust car park at St Abb's by ten thirty. They wrapped up well with hats, scarves and gloves and followed a marked way towards the cliffs. As they drew nearer to the coast they could see seabirds wheeling above the cliff edges. The birds were screaming noisily and there was a rhythmic booming which could be felt as well as heard. When they reached the viewpoint over Starney Bay, Nyaga gasped. The view straight out to sea seemed endless. The sky was huge and the various shades of grey in the sky and the water melded together at a distant horizon, hazy and difficult to perceive. Looking down they could see birds perched on narrow ledges and white spray flung up from the waves crashing on the rocks below. Rose was pleased with the drama of the scene and by its obvious effect on Nyaga.

"Wow, it's all so noisy and there's so much strength in that water," Nyaga said. "I thought it would be calm and blue like a picture postcard."

"When it's sunny with a blue sky it probably looks prettier. And if you come in the summer you get a lot more birds," Rose commented.

"Look at all the different colours and stripes in the rocks, those ones over there are red and pink. And what's that smell in the air? Is it fish?" Nyaga was sniffing.

"It's just a seaside smell, probably a combination of fish, the birds and seaweed," Rose reckoned.

They walked on farther along the clifftops and spotted a few ships out on the water but decided not to complete the loop of the marked walk as they wanted to leave time to visit the beach. Back at the car Rose decided that it might be more practical to visit Gullane beach than the Tyninghame sands.

"It'll get dark by about half past three and it's quite a long walk through the woods to get down to the beach at Tyninghame. So since it's the beach you really want to experience I think Gullane will be fine. We can park much closer there and it's still an impressive beach."

"You're the expert." Nyaga fell in with Rose's revised plan.

They set out back along the A1 and it was while they were driving that Rose decided to tell Nyaga about the baby.

"I didn't tell my mum until after Christmas, so she didn't know when you visited us," she'd explained.

Nyaga spoke about her daughter, Lesedi. She told Rose how she'd gone back to work when Lesedi was three months old and her mum had looked after the little girl. They all lived together and, because Nyaga was a nurse, it made sense for the family to benefit from her higher wages. She admitted that sometimes she'd felt jealous of Lesedi's strong attachment to her grandmother, although it was natural when they spent most of their time together.

"My mother does a bit of this and that. She has a few cleaning jobs in clients' houses, but they don't mind if she takes Lesedi along with her. She also brings home washing and ironing and she has a large allotment where she grows lots of vegetables and keeps hens. She sells the eggs and excess produce from a market stall. She is someone who is always busy," Nyaga had concluded.

Rose revealed something that had begun to worry her: that she wouldn't be up to standard as a mum. Marion had always been so organised.

"You'll be your own kind of mum," Nyaga had reassured her. "There's not only one recipe for success. Anyway you've organised this day very well and prepared these delicious sandwiches."

By now they were parked above Gullane Bents and eating their picnic in the car. Rose had made cheese and pickle and egg mayonnaise sandwiches and they drank apple juice from cartons with straws. After lunch they donned warm clothing again and found the track that led between grassy sand dunes to the beach. It was difficult to walk. With each step their feet sank into the soft sand and their calf muscles were soon burning. When they emerged onto the beach Rose led them to the firmer sand at the water's edge where the going was easier. The water here in the estuary was much calmer. Waves rolled in languidly, depositing a lacy froth of bubbles on the hard sand. There was a frill of seaweed marking the high tide margin. Nyaga was interested in everything, prodding the seaweed with her toe, sifting dry sand through her fingers and writing their names with a stick in the wet sand.

Rose had really enjoyed Nyaga's company and was looking forward to meeting her again tomorrow to go shopping. She heard Betty leaving her bedroom and start to make her way downstairs. Maybe she should join her and make a cup of tea. At least she'd made a start on her packing.

"Hi Gran. Want a cup of tea? And how about a game of Snap?"

Rose had discovered that Betty could still remember the rules of the simple card game and seemed to enjoy playing.

"Yes, that would be nice. And do we have any biscuits?"

Marion

The phone rang out in the consulting room. Marion was behind the curtains with a patient, examining her upper abdomen. She tutted.

"Sorry, Mrs Watson, I'd better take this call."

The receptionists were trained not to put calls through to the doctors during a consultation unless it was another medical colleague or something urgent. She lifted the receiver.

"Yes?"

"I'm sorry, Dr Wallace, I know you're with a patient but it's your mum's carer and she sounds a bit panicky."

"OK, Gwen, put her through."

There was a crackle on the line and then the carer's voice.

"Dr Wallace, I don't know what to do. Betty's not here."

"What do you mean not here?" Marion thought that the woman sounded garbled.

"She's not in the house. I've come in to make her tea and there's no sign of her anywhere. I've checked."

Marion sighed. What should she do? She was in the middle

of a surgery. Was this bad enough to abandon her work and rush home?

"Can you see her in the garden?"

"No. There's no sign of her. I was in at lunchtime and she seemed fine. I saw her up to bed for a nap after her lunch. When I looked in her room just now her cardigan and slippers are still by the bed. I don't know what she's wearing and it's cold."

Marion processed this information and envisaged her mum wandering through the streets on this cold, dark January evening wearing only thin clothes and in her stocking soles.

"OK, I'll try to get away as soon as possible and come home. Can you stay in the house until I get there in case she comes back?"

"Yes. I'll phone my supervisor and let her know what's happening."

Marion finished up as quickly as she could with Mrs Watson, apologising and explaining that there was a family emergency. She felt jittery and her hands were shaking as she phoned through to Kenneth to explain the problem.

"I'm really sorry but I have to go. Can you share out the rest of my patients between you? I definitely wouldn't be able to concentrate on anything else right now anyway."

"Of course you should go. I hope your mum's alright. Keep in touch."

Marion drove home imploring the cars in front of her to speed up and fidgeting at every red traffic light.

"Hurry up, hurry up, come on, come on," she muttered.

Arriving at the house she burst in through the door and strode into the kitchen where the carer was sitting at the table looking frightened.

"Nothing?" she asked.

"No."

"Do you think we should call the police?"

"It might be best. She could have been gone for quite a few hours."

"I'll just take a look upstairs first."

Marion ran up to Betty's room. The bed covers were pushed down and, as the carer had described, Betty's slippers were standing neatly by the side of the bed and her pink cardigan was draped over the back of the armchair. Marion looked in the wardrobe. There didn't seem to be any shoes missing and she thought that all of the jackets were hanging in their usual places. She ran downstairs to the coat stand in the hall but again all of the usual garments seemed to be accounted for. She returned to the kitchen. The carer was talking to her supervisor on her mobile phone. She looked up as Marion came in.

"My supervisor thinks you should call the police," she informed Marion.

"Yes, I think we'll have to. She might not be far away but there are a lot of streets to cover. I wouldn't know where to start looking."

She pulled her phone out of her pocket and dialled 101.

"Police Scotland," a woman's voice answered.

Marion took a deep steadying breath then began to speak into her phone.

Three hours later Marion was driving slowly along Hillview Terrace. She'd already checked the roads running between Clermiston Road and Kaimes Road and now she'd moved onto the block of streets to the west, bordered by Drum Brae. She crawled along peering up paths and driveways.

The police had taken Betty's disappearance very seriously, noting details over the phone to relay to officers in cars and sending someone round to the house to collect more information. Marion and the carer had passed on everything they could think of. They reckoned that Betty was wearing a white blouse and a ruby-coloured tweed skirt and probably only her tights below that. The officer had asked if they secured Betty in the house between the carers' visits. Marion wondered if she'd been negligent in this respect but in the month since Betty had been living with her in Corstorphine she'd never seemed unsettled or shown any tendency towards wandering off. She'd racked her brain, but she couldn't think that anything had been different today. Perhaps Betty had been missing Rose's company since her return to Bristol. She had asked after 'that girl' a few times over the past week.

Marion came to the end of the street, turned right then right again to search Hillview Road. This driving about was probably futile but she couldn't just sit in the house waiting. She'd called Auntie Peggy who'd come immediately and was presently keeping watch in the house in case Betty showed up there. It seemed unlikely that her confusion would allow her to find her way back, but they agreed that someone should stay just in case. Marion checked the temperature gauge on her car again – one degree centigrade. She was really worried that Betty would be suffering from hypothermia if they didn't find her soon.

She travelled criss-cross around the grid of streets for a second time before returning to the house. It was now after ten o'clock.

"Marion?" Peggy came to meet her at the front door.

"Nothing." Marion shrugged off her jacket and hung it on the coat stand.

"Nothing from the police either," Peggy said gloomily.

"I'll put the kettle on." Marion went through to the kitchen.

"Have you contacted Douglas?" Peggy asked.

"No, not yet. I hoped to be able to report that she was missing but found. There's nothing he can do from so far away anyway."

"No, but it's his mum too."

"I suppose I think he'll give me a hard time over this, say it was my fault. I'm not sure I can face that just now."

"He might surprise you."

"Hmmph. I'd better phone my senior partner before it gets too late. I don't think I'm going to be able to go to work tomorrow. They'll need to arrange to cover my appointments."

"Well, off you go and do that and I'll make the tea and some toast. I don't expect you've eaten anything and you need to keep your strength up."

She felt a bit better after talking to Kenneth. He was very sympathetic and reassured Marion that they'd manage to cope without her, she wasn't to worry about work. The tea and toast also helped to restore her. She went upstairs to make up the bed in Rose's room for Peggy and encouraged her aunt to go and lie down for a rest, even if she didn't think she'd sleep. However, she didn't follow her own advice and settled herself in an armchair in the lounge to keep vigil.

Marion hadn't expected to sleep at all, but woke with a painful neck caused by her cramped position in the chair, and feeling cold as the central heating had gone off for the night. The clock on the mantelpiece showed that the time was ten to five. Marion dragged herself stiffly through to the utility room to advance the central heating boiler, massaging her neck with her hand. She glanced out of the window to see frost sparkling on the ground. Would that be better or worse than wind and rain if Betty was still outside? She didn't know, just hoped that maybe in a few hours, once people were up and about for the day, that someone would come across Betty. She climbed the stairs to take a shower and put on fresh clothes. She didn't know what to do after that. She wasn't hungry and wouldn't be able to concentrate well enough to read anything. She decided to tackle a pile of ironing, so set up the ironing board in the lounge and turned the radio on quietly to break the silence.

When the phone began to ring at ten past seven she almost tripped over her own feet and the flex from the iron in her eagerness to reach it.

"Yes?"

"Dr Wallace, we think we've found your mother. A member of the public has come across an elderly woman matching her description."

"Is she OK?"

"The ambulance crew are with her now. She's alive but very cold. She was lying in the doorway of the pavilion in Roseburn Park. They'll be moving her to A&E at the Royal Infirmary. I suggest you make your way there."

"Yes, I will, thank you."

Marion rushed up the stairs to be met by Peggy at Rose's bedroom door.

"Was that the phone? Is she alright?"

"They said she's alive but very cold. We're to go to the Royal."

"OK, just let me go to the toilet and tidy up a bit. Where was she?"

"Roseburn Park. It's about two miles away, beside Murrayfield Stadium. She was in the doorway of the pavilion, so she maybe had a bit of shelter. Oh, Peggy."

Marion broke down in sobs and messy tears. She found it hard to bear the thought of her mum spending the night scantily dressed on a cold doorstep. Peggy wrapped her arms around Marion and patted her back.

"Come on, let's get you a hankie and we'll make a cup of tea. I expect we'll have a lot of waiting around at the hospital, so it would be sensible to have a bit of breakfast."

They left the house just before eight o'clock, hoping that the rush hour traffic wouldn't have built up to its full volume yet on the city bypass. The Royal Infirmary was situated diagonally across the city from Marion's house, on the south-east. It had been relocated to a greenfield site since Marion's days as a medical student. The old hospital buildings near the city centre, overlooking the Meadows, were now being redeveloped as offices and luxury apartments. Marion didn't think she'd like to live there; she felt that there might well be ghosts haunting the premises. They were lucky; the traffic travelling east was much lighter than in the opposite direction. They drove past long queues on the other carriageway.

"I'm glad I don't have to make that journey every day," Peggy commented.

"Yes, apparently people leave home at six and seven o'clock to avoid the hold-ups, but they do the same from Fife to get into town over the bridge."

"I wonder if it'll be any better once the new bridge is open."

They pulled into the hospital car park after forty minutes of driving and walked through the emerging daylight, taking care over the icy pavements, to the A&E department. Marion gave their names at the reception desk.

"Oh, the lady from the park. She's not been able to speak to us, so we'll need you to confirm that it's definitely your mum and then give us all of her details, please."

"How is she?" Peggy asked.

"She's in Resus at the moment under assessment. I'll get a nurse to take one of you in. Just have a seat over there for a minute."

The receptionist gestured to a huddle of plastic seats in the waiting area, empty at this time of the morning, but with a scattering of empty crisp packets, soft drinks cans and plastic cups and bottles strewn around their legs. They had only just removed their coats and seated themselves when a woman dressed in pale blue theatre pyjamas approached.

"I'm Staff Nurse Wilson. Can one of you come with me, please?"

"I'll come." Marion stood up and gently clasped and squeezed Peggy's shoulder before following the nurse, who stopped in front of double swing doors.

"The lady's unconscious and hypothermic. From the description that you gave the police and the location quite near to where she was last seen, we assume it's your mum, but we need you to identify her positively for us. Then you can stay for a short time, but the team are working hard to stabilise her condition and get her warmed up. You might find the room and all of the equipment a bit overwhelming. I'll be right beside you," the nurse encouraged Marion while leaning on one of the doors to let her go ahead into the room.

Activity was focused around a central operating table in the white-tiled room. The figure on the table was swaddled in white cotton blankets and looked very small. There was a mask delivering oxygen over the lower face and an arm was exposed where a medic was preparing to insert a drip. Marion had to go closer to be able to distinguish any features. Betty's eyes were closed and a few strands of her dyed-black hair had escaped from the shawl-like blanket around her head.

"Yes, it's my mum," she managed to articulate.

"OK, well we're giving her some moist, warmed oxygen to breathe and keeping her well wrapped up. We'll put some warm saline through that drip once it's up and going and hopefully she'll come to when she heats up. Her feet are a bit of a mess so we'll need to attend to them, but we haven't found any other injuries."

Marion found herself being ushered back into the corridor without having mentioned that she was a doctor so could take things in her stride. And she had to admit to herself that the nurse had been right, she had found the scene and the atmosphere distressing.

"If you just sit back down here one of the doctors will come to take medical details from you about your mum."

Marion sat back down beside Peggy. She tried to smile.

"Not good?" Peggy asked.

"She looked so tiny and frail," Marion replied.

"Don't forget she's always been feisty too." Peggy tried to boost her morale.

After twenty minutes the nurse reappeared.

"We've moved your mum out from Resus into Medical Assessment now. You can come and sit with her if you like."

She led them into a large square room with no windows. Each wall of the square was divided by curtains into cubicles and there was a medical work area in the middle of the space. She twitched a curtain open to reveal Betty lying on a trolley still tightly wrapped in white blankets. The oxygen mask remained over her mouth and nose. There was a tube with clear fluid leading from a drip stand and heading in under her wrappings and another thicker tube lower down running out and under the trolley, presumably a urinary catheter. Her eyes were still closed. Marion and Peggy sat on two seats which had been placed on either side of the trolley.

"Hello Mum, we're here beside you."

"Betty, it's Peggy. I'm here with Marion."

There was no response.

"Her temperature has come up by point two degrees. But I'm afraid that so far she's only been responding to painful stimuli. That doesn't necessarily mean that she can't hear you, and isn't aware that you're there, though." The nurse wrote something onto a clipboard and hung it on the end of the trolley. "The doctor will be through to speak to you in a few minutes." She closed the curtain and left them. Peggy drew her chair closer to Betty on the trolley and stroked her arm through the blankets.

The next two hours were spent dealing with administration, first with a doctor, then with the receptionist and last with the police who wanted to sign off their case. Then Marion went outside to the car park, relieved to be able to take some deep breaths of cool, fresh air. She'd had to go out via the waiting area which was now crowded, and hot and stuffy with strong odours of cigarette smoke, unwashed bodies and a tang of vomit. You weren't supposed to use your mobile phone in the assessment area and there was no privacy in the waiting area, so while she was out she phoned her work to give them an update. It was too early to call Canada, only the wee hours of the morning there. So she put that off again, still hoping that she'd have better news if she waited longer. She felt the nagging of a headache building up above her right eye and scrabbled around in her handbag, searching for some co-codamol tablets. There was a water dispenser just inside the front door of the department, so she filled a plastic cup and washed the medication down. She took a fresh cup in with her for Peggy.

"While you were out the nurse told me they're about to move her up to a ward," Peggy reported. "And she gave a wee groan when they blew that blood pressure machine up. That's good, isn't it? Maybe means she's coming to a bit."

"Yes," Marion agreed.

Nyaga

Nyaga clapped hard, helping to swell the applause as the curtain came down and the house lights brightened the theatre. The palms of her hands were stinging as Amelia turned to her, smiling.

"Well, what do you think?"

"It's amazing," Nyaga replied. "I've never experienced anything like it."

"I'm going to have to squeeze past you to go to the toilet."

"OK."

Nyaga stood and the seat of the chair flipped up behind her. Squashed into the backrest with the seat in front only just coming up to her knees she felt dizzy for a moment. The stage looked a long way down. Once Amelia had gone she pulled her seat down and flopped back into it. The performance was so extravagant – the music and singing, rich and colourful costumes, just the sheer drama of it all. She could remember attending the theatre in Gaborone once with a group from school. They saw a play which had been touring from South Africa, but it was on a bleak, stark set and the theme was very serious, steeped in politics. It was nothing like this show. She enjoyed music and had gone to a few big concerts in the sports stadium at home. Usually the bands came on tour from Zimbabwe or South Africa. She could see Amelia approaching, a wave of people in their row bobbing up to let her past. She was clutching two ice-cream tubs and gave one to Nyaga as she pressed by her then sat down.

"Thank you." Nyaga found the plastic spoon hidden inside the tub's lid and scooped a sliver of vanilla onto her tongue.

"Have you been to many shows like this one?" she asked Amelia.

"I saw a few when I worked in London – *The Lion King*, *Les Mis* and *Wicked*. You've got a lot of theatres showing big productions all the time down there."

"The girl playing Christine has a great voice. It's not a type of music I normally listen to, but I think she's very good."

"What would you listen to at home?"

"Oh, local bands at bars or nightclubs. A mix of pop and African music I suppose."

"We could go out some night to one of the bars that have live music here. There's one up near Nando's that features folk music, 'Sandy Bell's.'"

Nyaga suddenly had a small social life. After dinner with Marion there had been the seaside and shopping trips with Rose. Then Amelia had mentioned that she had a spare ticket to see *Phantom of the Opera* as her other friend had backed out. Now there might be music nights in bars.

"I'd like that," she said.

The lights were gradually dimming and music heralded the opening of the curtain for the second act. The stage was bright; women were wearing sumptuous gowns, wigs and boas and men were in evening dress, everyone hiding behind a mask for the masquerade ball.

The next day at work Nyaga felt tired. But it wasn't the horrible weariness that had plagued her before. This was the result of a late night and then getting up early for her shift. It was a good feeling. She found herself humming one of the tunes from last night's show.

"Glad that someone's happy at their work," Linda commented. "How do you think Mabel's settling in?"

"It's hard to say, her appetite seems to be improving, but she's very quiet. I'm going to introduce her to Dr Wallace this morning, get her checked over."

Jessie had died two days after Christmas. Luckily the Inverness cousin had managed to come before the end, and Nyaga thought that Jessie had been aware of that. So a room was empty and now there was a new occupant, Mabel. She'd just arrived at the beginning of the week after a prolonged stay in hospital. Nyaga found this aspect of working at the nursing home difficult. She didn't like to dwell on the fact that it acted as a holding place before death. In previous jobs a few of her patients might die, but most of them got better and went home. A Dellview resident might leave for a hospital stay and then return, but the only permanent departures were when someone died. She'd also developed close relationships with the residents because they lived here for months or years, not just the span of a short hospital admission. So it made the deaths that occurred more distressing.

"There's the doorbell," Linda commented.

"I'll go. It's probably the doctor." Nyaga left the office to go and open the front door. She recognised Marion's silhouette through the frosted glass.

"Good morning," she called cheerily in greeting, but on seeing Marion close up she was shocked by her appearance. Her usual creamy complexion was greyish turning her freckles from gold to dull brown. Her eyes looked pink and their surrounding skin was puffy with purple semicircles underneath. She gave a watery smile.

"Hello. What have you got for me today?"

Nyaga made a quick decision to keep to their professional roles for now, as there was work to be done. But she hoped that she'd be able to speak with Marion more personally before she left to find out what was wrong, and whether she could help at all.

"Well, first is our new resident Mabel. Then I have a few small problems. You were also going to check Archie's chest and ankles to see if he still needs the higher dose of diuretic."

"OK. Lead the way."

Nyaga took Marion along the corridor to Mabel's room and made the introduction between the doctor and her new patient. Mabel was a small, painfully thin woman with a sharp nose and chin. Her cheekbones were highly prominent and the notch above her sternum was a deep cave. She had fluffy grey hair, which helped to soften her features slightly and reminded Nyaga of a dandelion clock. She offered to leave the two alone together, but stayed at Mabel's request.

"How are you feeling? Is it good to be out of hospital?" Marion asked.

"Yes, I'm glad to be out of hospital and everyone's very nice here, but I'd really wanted to get home. I don't suppose I will now." Mabel's last sentence was almost whispered. She was obviously upset.

"That's hard for you, I know."

Marion allowed a short silence, acknowledging Mabel's unhappiness. Then she encouraged Mabel to tell her about her home, asking her where it was, how long she'd lived there, were her neighbours friendly and lots of other questions which got Mabel chatting. Soon she was confiding in the doctor, telling her about her health problems and disabilities and describing the struggle that she'd had in coping even before her recent hospital admission. Nyaga admired Marion's technique. She was learning a lot about her new resident. No one else had got Mabel to open up and talk so freely to them. That was probably because they were all too busy telling Mabel how well she'd be looked after, and that she'd soon settle in here, instead of actually listening to what she wanted to say. Marion spent half an hour getting to know her new patient then moved more quickly round the other residents that Nyaga had lined up for her. They finished up in the office to allow Marion to write some prescriptions.

"I wondered if you'd like to eat some lunch with me," Nyaga asked. "It would be simple – soup and bread – but I owe you some hospitality."

Marion lifted her gaze from her writing but before she could reply Nyaga added, "Plus I think maybe you have some trouble. I'd like to help if I can."

Marion bit her lip and then rested her face on the palms of her hands. She rubbed in a circular motion with the flat of her hands, massaging around the sockets of her eyes before looking at Nyaga.

"Soup would be very nice, thank you."

"OK, I'll leave you here to finish off the prescriptions and go to set up our lunch. We can sit in the staffroom, it's usually quiet at this time of day."

Nyaga returned five minutes later and Marion followed her to the staffroom. It was simply furnished with softly upholstered chairs grouped in an oval around a low table. There was a tray on the coffee table holding two bowls of steaming orange-coloured soup and a plate with buttered slices of brown bread. They sat down.

"The soup is carrot and coriander. Our chef always has a pot of good homemade soup available, it's my regular lunch," Nyaga commented as they took up their soup bowls and spoons. She went on, "You don't look your best today."

"No, I don't expect I do, I haven't had much sleep for the past three days."

Marion began to describe the events surrounding Betty's disappearance.

"Oh, you must have been so worried. And poor Betty wandering in the cold, it must have been frightening for her. How is she now?"

"Not great. Unfortunately she developed pneumonia after her exposure, so she's still in hospital, on oxygen and IV antibiotics."

"And you don't know why she went out of the house?"

"No, she hasn't been able to tell us. To begin with she was unconscious and now the infection has increased her confusion. She's just rambling really, not saying anything that makes much sense."

"Apart from the dementia is she usually quite a fit lady?"

"Yes, she doesn't really have any physical problems. The only pills she's on regularly are for high blood pressure and her dementia."

"So hopefully she should pull through this chest infection OK."

"Yes. I hope so."

"Should you be at work today? You look very tired."

"I'm alright. I had to run off from work on Monday and I wasn't in on Tuesday. Wednesday and Friday are my usual days off, so I felt I should put in the hours today. My brother's arriving from Canada tomorrow."

"That will be good. Betty will like to see him."

"Yes, she will. We don't always get on too well, but I'm pleased that he's making the effort to come."

Marion scraped the last of the soup out of her bowl then wiped the sides with the end of her bread before popping it into her mouth.

"The soup was very good, thank you. And for listening."

"I like Betty. Maybe I can visit her once she's getting better."

"I'm sure she'd like to see you. Now, I'd better fly back to the surgery to try and catch up with my paperwork before the afternoon consulting."

Nyaga walked with Marion to the front door and stayed watching as she stowed her medical case in the boot. She waved as the car pulled out from the car park into the street. Returning to the staffroom she tidied the bowls and spoons onto the tray and took everything back to the kitchen. She was pleased that she'd managed to give some hospitality and support to Marion. Since the Christmas invitation she considered the doctor to be a friend. She wondered how Rose was coping at university, pregnant and no doubt worrying about her gran. She would go to the café or the library on her day off tomorrow and include Rose in her list of correspondents for email messages. But right now she'd better get on with the after-lunch medicine round.

Marion

The automatic doors swished open as Marion approached. Once inside the terminal she had to dodge people coming towards her pushing highly laden luggage trolleys or trailing suitcases on wheels behind them. She consulted an electronic noticeboard which confirmed that Douglas's flight from Amsterdam had landed ten minutes ago. Turning left she headed for the international arrivals area and found a seat which gave her a clear view of the doorway. He'd have to collect luggage and go through passport control, so Marion reckoned he'd probably be quite a while yet. She settled down to wait. A steady trickle of passengers emerged as she kept watch.

She wondered if Douglas would want to go straight to the hospital, or have a rest at the house first. At least she'd be able to tell him that Betty was making progress. She'd been much more lucid when Marion had called in to visit this morning, seeming to recognise her for the first time and answering simple questions. Apparently she'd eaten some breakfast and the doctors were considering taking down her drip and switching to oral medication if she kept her fluid intake up today. Betty didn't like the drip and it had a huge protective bandage around it now, as she kept attempting to pull it out. She didn't like the nasal prongs for her oxygen delivery either and was now only tolerating them when she was asleep. Marion smiled to herself, thinking that her mum had been a much easier patient when she was unconscious.

Her heart lurched as her brother came through the exit. She'd forgotten how much he resembled their father. She stood and waved to him and he arrived in front of her and gave her a firm hug.

"Hey sis, it's been a while."

Anyone observing the reunion would know that these two were related. Both were tall and generously built. In Marion's case, there were Junoesque curves. Douglas was broad in the chest but still had a flat stomach. Both had the Celtic colouring of red hair, pale skin and freckles – a cause for teasing when they'd been children but now much more fashionable in the wake of the Disney film *Brave*. Marion led her brother through the airport towards the multistorey car park.

"Have they changed the airport round again?" he asked as he tagged after her.

"Probably. There always seems to be building work going on somewhere."

She inserted her ticket into the machine at the pay station and then slotted in a £5 note. Some change clattered out at the bottom and she retrieved their ticket.

"So, what would you like to do?" she asked as they went up in the lift.

She filled him in on Betty's condition earlier in the day and he elected to go to Corstorphine to have a shower and change his clothes before visiting the hospital.

"I know all I've done is to sit on two planes but I still feel all rumpled and stale. It would be good to freshen up."

It was a short drive to Marion's house, only taking fifteen minutes. Once there Marion showed Douglas up to Betty's room.

"I've put you in here just now. Auntie Peggy was using Rose's room and she'll probably be back at some point over the weekend. You might have to move if Mum gets discharged, but I can't see that happening for a few days yet."

"Thanks. You've made this nice for her," Douglas commented on the décor.

"Want a cup of tea?"

"I'll have my shower first if that's OK."

"Fine. I'll put the kettle on in twenty minutes." Marion ran downstairs leaving Douglas to unpack and organise himself. She reflected that so far they were getting on well, no arguments or point scoring in their first encounter.

———

Marion and Douglas rubbed their hands with the antiseptic gel placed by the door of the hospital ward. Betty was in a four-bedded room and they could see her propped up in bed as they approached. Her head had slumped to one side in her sleep. The nasal prongs were in situ but the drip had been removed.

"Hello Mum," Marion called softly while grasping Betty's arm to waken her. "Look who's here to see you."

Betty opened her eyes slowly and took a few seconds to rouse. She looked at Marion groggily, then straightened her head and scrabbled at her nose with her hands, pulling out the nasal prongs. Suddenly she noticed Douglas who was standing at the foot of her bed.

"Peter," she said.

"No, Mum, it's Douglas," he replied, coming towards Betty and leaning in to kiss her and give her a hug.

"Well, I don't think anyone could blame Mum for making that mistake because I thought you looked just like Dad when you arrived this morning," Marion commented.

"I suppose," Douglas admitted. "So, Mum, what have you been up to, worrying us all?"

"I don't know how I got here. I think I'm in hospital."

"Yes, you are," Douglas confirmed.

"How long do I have to stay?"

"Well, we're not sure yet, but I hear you're getting a lot better."

"You sit down and chat for a bit and I'll try to catch one of the nurses." Marion smiled at Douglas as she squeezed past and made her way to the nursing station.

The staff nurse looked up from the form that she was completing as Marion approached her desk.

"Hello, you'll see we've taken down your mum's drip. She ate all of her lunch and she's drinking fine."

"That's good, it must mean she's recovering. She usually does have a good appetite. My brother's here for a few days to visit."

"Is that Robert? She's been asking for him a lot and also Peter."

"No, my brother's called Douglas. Peter was my dad, he died about six years ago now. I don't know any Roberts but I think she's mentioned the name before. It could be someone from the past, a cousin or something. She often thinks she's a wee girl again. I'll ask my aunt, maybe she can tell us."

"Could you bring in some clothes next time you come? We'll want to try to get her up and dressed soon."

"Of course. I'll bring them tomorrow."

Marion left the nursing station and decided to go for a wander. She'd let Douglas have some time to himself with Betty. She strolled along to the hospital mall where there were a few shops and bought some cartons of juice for Betty. When she arrived back on the ward Douglas stood, ready to go. Marion opened one of the cartons and inserted the straw, putting the others on the bedside cabinet.

"Here's some juice, Mum."

She proffered the carton and Betty drank thirstily.

"That's good, drink up, it'll help you to get better. We'll say bye now and be back to see you tomorrow." She bent over and

142

gave Betty a kiss. Douglas waved from the end of the bed and then they left.

"Well, how did you find her?" Marion asked as they walked along the corridor.

"She's definitely more confused than last time I saw her. I don't really think she knew who I was talking about when I mentioned Mandy and the kids. I'm not sure if that's a general decline or because she's ill."

"Probably a bit of both. Do you think she knew you, after her initial mistake?"

"It's hard to tell. I was doing most of the talking."

"It's funny, she keeps asking about someone called Robert and I just can't place who that would be."

They'd reached the car by now and Douglas looked hard at Marion over the roof.

"You really don't know?" he asked. "I always wondered, but I thought probably not."

"What do you mean?"

Marion was in the car now and fastening her seatbelt.

"Robert Gilchrist," he said, settling himself beside her.

Marion repeated the name enquiringly.

"I'm still not getting it."

"The musical director of one of her choirs. They had an affair for years."

"What?" Marion spluttered. She'd been about to start the ignition but now she turned and looked at Douglas.

"I didn't know if you knew but, because of how you reacted after what happened between you and Angus and the way you've always looked up to Mum, I thought you were in the dark."

"But how do you know?"

"I got sent home early from school one day. I think there had been a power cut or something. Anyway, when I came into the house it wasn't hard to work it out."

"When was this?"

"I'd have been fifteen. You were at uni."

"Did Dad know?"

"No. Mum confessed to me but begged me not to tell Dad. Said she didn't want to leave him and that it would all stop with Robert. I don't think it did immediately, and I hated her for cheating on Dad but I didn't want to hurt him."

"So that's why you've never had much time for her."

"Yeah, I found it hard to keep up the deceit. Dad was a decent man and he adored her, he didn't deserve to be treated like that."

"I've been thinking that you're a callous bastard all these years, when you've seemed so cold and offhand about Mum."

"I'm sorry, but I didn't know how to tell you at the time and then it seemed too late."

Marion tried to take a steadying breath; she felt faint, off balance with a buzzing in her ears. Her parents' relationship had always represented one of the core certainties in her life. Her own failed marriage hadn't measured up to their standard. And now that pillar had been destroyed and the ceiling was falling down around her. She couldn't calculate all of the implications.

"Do you think you could drive?" she asked Douglas, undoing her seatbelt and getting out of the car. "I really don't think I could concentrate well enough right now. It's OK, I added you onto my insurance for this week."

They swapped places and Douglas drove them home. Initially their progress was decidedly jerky, as he hadn't driven a car with gearshift controls for some time, but he gradually became accustomed to the clutch. Marion didn't really notice their faltering progress. She was trying to process what Douglas had told her.

For the rest of that evening things from the past would come into Marion's mind and acquire a new significance. There was the whole thing about Douglas's cool treatment of Betty. She remembered now that he'd originally planned to go to Edinburgh University to study engineering, then suddenly that switched and he was desperate to leave home, opting for Glasgow University in the end. Of course teenagers grow up and change their opinions, but this now made a different sense. Then he'd immediately gone abroad to work and seemed so offhand, especially after their dad was gone.

She tried to picture Robert Gilchrist. She remembered an enthusiastic man with floppy fair hair. He was famous for the colourful bow ties that he used to wear for choir performances. She was sure he was married and had three or four children. Didn't he move away? Yes, he was a music teacher and got a head of department job somewhere up north. Mum had been devastated, saying that the choir wasn't up to scratch without him. In fact, hadn't she stopped attending that choir soon after? So it wasn't all about Robert's musical talent. Of course Mum used to go to lots of 'extra rehearsals' because she was a soloist. Was that all a sham?

Marion's thoughts moved to her dad. She was very glad that he'd never known about this. He was such a gentle person, she'd sometimes wondered how he managed to control a class of secondary school children. Except that his interest and enthusiasm for his subject could be infectious and somehow that captured your attention. And he was good at explaining things. Marion had struggled with physics in school but her dad had been able to make it seem much clearer. He was so courteous to Betty, doing chores about the house to help her at a time when men didn't generally get involved in housework. He often presented her with flowers or chocolates for no obvious reason or occasion, and when they were together he always walked on the outside of the pavement.

When she and Angus separated she can remember that Betty spoke out strongly for an attempt at reconciliation. At the time Marion thought that she hadn't wanted Rose to grow up without her father around. Now she wondered, given her own love life, if it was just that Betty could be more forgiving of his infidelity.

By nine o'clock she was exhausted by the thoughts whirling around her head. She felt as if she was on an endless merry-go-round ride. Douglas had retired early, tired after his long flight and time zone shift. Marion poured herself a glass of wine and sipped it in front of the television, hoping that it would help her to sleep. She found an episode of *Poldark* that she'd recorded and tried to lose herself in the fortunes of a different family.

∞∞∞

When her aunt arrived on Saturday morning she had hardly stepped into the house and removed her coat before Marion's interrogation began.

"So, what do you know about Robert Gilchrist, Auntie Peggy?"

Peggy looked affronted.

"Well, good morning to you too. A coffee would be nice, thank you, Marion. And then we can sit down and have a civilised conversation. Hello Douglas, it's good to see you, son."

Douglas came into the kitchen and gave his aunt a hug while Marion took the hint and began to make the coffee.

"I'm fine, thank you and you look very fit yourself. Don't mind Marion too much, she got quite a shock and she's been like a dog worrying at a bone since I told her yesterday," Douglas commented.

"Do you want the coffee here or in the lounge?" Marion asked.

They elected to take their mugs through to the more comfortable seats in the lounge. Once Peggy was settled she began to talk.

"I didn't know anything about the affair while it was going on. But Betty told me about it maybe a year after Robert had moved away. I don't know why she decided to confide in me."

"I just can't get my head round it," Marion admitted.

"I was surprised when she told me, but now maybe I understand better. Betty always loved Peter, but I think he wasn't lively enough for her sometimes. The thing with Robert gave her excitement that she needed. She never had any intention of leaving Peter and I think it was the same for Robert and his wife. Maybe your mum was more content and the marriage with Peter worked better when she had this other man too."

Marion snorted.

"I didn't think you were so modern in your outlook, Auntie Peggy."

"It takes all sorts of people to make a world. And remember your dad was perfectly happy."

"I'm not sure how I'm going to cope with Mum now though," Marion admitted.

"She's not the same woman today. She wouldn't understand any debate on the subject," Peggy warned.

"Oh, I know. I'm not going to mention it to her. It's just that I'm not sure that I'll be able to relate to her in the same way."

Peggy nodded.

"Yes, I can understand that. I've had a long time to mull things over and reach my conclusion."

"Marion, you might struggle for a while but I think you should try to treat Mum in the same way as usual. You're one of the stable, certain things amongst her confusion, a kind of anchor. She might get a lot worse if you changed towards her." Douglas gave his advice.

Marion shook her head and sighed.

"That might be easier said than done," she admitted ruefully.

Rose

Rose had arranged to meet Sally at Café du Jour on Park Street. She arrived first, and ordered peppermint tea and a spiced apple muffin while waiting for Sally to appear. She found it hard to believe that she really couldn't drink coffee any more; she used to consider herself a bit of an addict but now it tasted like burnt rubber. It was mentioned as one of the common pregnancy foibles. She'd read about it in her antenatal blurb. Raindrops were tracking down the outside of the large windows that looked out over Park Street and up towards the Wills Building. To an observer, Rose might appear to be gazing into space, but in fact her mind was very busy running through dialogue from her script. She filled most free moments in this way, currently working on Abigail's court appearance in Act Three. There was less than a week to go until the opening night and she couldn't afford to relax now.

"Hello. How's it going?" Sally arrived, showering drops from her rain jacket onto the floor as she removed it before sitting down.

"I'm fine, thanks."

"Was it today that you had your check-up?"

"Yes, it was first thing this morning and the midwife was happy with me. My bump seems to be the right size for my dates and everything else was OK. Oh, I've ordered, thanks," as the waitress appeared. Sally chose a latte and a slice of carrot cake.

"I've been feeling little flutterings for the past week or so."

"That must be exciting, but strange."

"It's very faint and just when I'm lying still in bed at night before I fall asleep. It feels a bit like my tummy rumbling, but there's no noise."

Sally smiled.

"And how are the rehearsals going?"

"Oh, it's starting to get frantic. We'll be working this evening and all weekend. We get into the theatre on Monday evening for the first time."

"I'm looking forward to the performance, but I know I'll feel nervous for you."

"You're coming on the last night. If I haven't got it right by then I'll be really worried," Rose laughed.

"Don't you get anxious?"

"I do before I go on, but once I start acting my part takes over and I forget about outside things. The only thing is that the Alma Theatre is so small and intimate, I think it might actually be harder to ignore the audience than in a bigger venue."

"Well, I'm sure most people will be friends and relatives of the cast so they'll all be well-wishers too. Mmm, this cake is yummy. Do you want to try a piece?"

"OK, we'll do bit for bit. Here's some of my muffin." Rose cut off a slice and offered it to Sally in exchange for a quarter of the carrot cake.

"How's your gran getting on now?"

"She's much better, thanks. She went into a nursing home when the hospital discharged her. She was due to go there anyway for the next two weeks to cover my mum's holiday and they were able to take her sooner."

"It must have been so worrying for your mum when she went missing."

"Yes. I'm a bit surprised that Mum didn't seem to want Gran back home. But maybe the whole thing was too traumatic. And my Uncle Douglas was around. He's always been more in favour of a care home for Gran."

"Maybe your mum blames herself for your gran wandering off."

"I'm not sure. I'll see her next week and I'll be able to talk to her properly about it then."

"Look what I bought for you. I hope you don't mind." Sally rummaged in her shopping bag and produced a pale-yellow cotton blanket. She unfolded it displaying two rows of embroidered white ducks along the top and bottom borders.

"It's so soft, I just couldn't resist it." She rubbed it gently across her cheek, and then handed it to Rose.

Rose also touched the soft cotton to her face.

"Thank you, it's lovely," she said. "I haven't even looked at any baby things. Maybe once the play's over I will."

"Oh, I know, there's loads of time to think about all of that yet. I just had a few minutes to spare and I was in Lewis's and wandered into the baby department. There are so many cute things. Are you going to find out whether it's a girl or a boy soon?"

"No, I don't think so. I wasn't planning to ask. Somehow it seems part of the mystery of it all to wait and see."

Once they'd finished their drinks and said goodbye Rose headed back to the flat. As she walked along Queen's Road under her umbrella she found herself smiling. Sally was going to be a very enthusiastic stepgranny. Maybe not having had her own children made her more excited about the baby.

When she'd returned to Bristol a month ago Rose had been extremely nervous about making the announcement of her pregnancy to her dad and Sally. She was expected for Sunday lunch and caught the eleven o'clock bus to Bath. Her dad had been sitting reading *The Sunday Times*, waiting in his car, by the bus station. He whizzed her back to the house where Sally emerged from the kitchen. They hadn't seen Rose since early December so she was very conscious of her increased girth. It seemed to be successfully concealed under the floaty top that she'd chosen to wear, as there were no comments while they greeted her and settled together in the lounge, preparing to exchange belated Christmas presents. Then drinks were offered.

"You know, what I'd really like is a cup of tea," Rose had said.

"But I've been saving this bottle of Prosecco especially for today." Her dad had sounded put out, bottle poised.

So then she'd felt she'd better just go for it and get the announcement over with, having previously planned to wait until after presents. She'd blurted out her news, including dates, and was met with an initial stunned silence.

"And what about the father?" her dad had finally asked, his words soft and clipped as if he was bottling in a flood of other words with great difficulty.

"He's not really on the scene." Rose had explained that they'd broken up and that she hadn't told Mark about the pregnancy yet.

"Jesus Christ, point him out and I'll tell him," Angus had exploded.

"Angus." Sally put a restraining hand on his arm. He shrugged it off, irritated. Meanwhile Rose had been digging in her handbag. She found the photograph of her ultrasound scan and handed it to her father.

"This is your grandchild," she said.

This tactic had seemed to deflate her dad's anger. He'd studied the photograph in silence and Sally had quickly taken over with questions and enthusiastic comments.

"I will tell Mark, Dad," Rose had promised. "I just needed some time to get over him and to think about what I wanted to do. But I'm acting with him in the play so it'll be pretty obvious soon."

"Rose, it's not what I'd have planned for you, but you know we'll support you in any way we can." Angus had eventually handed the photograph over for Sally to look at and Rose had smiled, tearfully.

"Thanks, Dad. I'm getting all emotional now. It's partly hormones, but mainly relief that everything's out in the open."

"OK. I'll go and make that cup of tea you asked for," her dad had relented.

Since then Dad and Sally had been great, Rose thought as she walked up the driveway to her flat. She glanced at her watch wondering if she might manage to fit in a 'power nap'. She'd always loved to lie on in bed in the mornings if she had nothing planned, but prior to pregnancy hadn't tended to sleep during the day. Now she seemed to be able to drop off at any time, and now might be a good opportunity as her rehearsal tonight would probably be a long and intense one. She rootled in her pocket for her keys, already looking forward to snuggling in under her downie.

⁕

Simon, the director, called for a rest break at nine o'clock that evening. The cast fell out to eat their snacks and sandwiches and gulp down drinks from cans, bottles and flasks. They congregated loosely into two groups: one contained Rose and the other Mark. Becky hung on the fringes of Mark's entourage. Rose found this polarisation awkward and tried to ignore it. It was none of her doing. Somehow, when word got out about her pregnancy, people took sides. In contrast, she was much more at ease with Mark now. They exchanged greetings when they met and were working well together in rehearsals with no obvious awkwardness.

In the end she'd decided on writing a letter to tell him. It had taken her several attempts to compose and she'd sent it to his flat by post with a first class stamp.

Dear Mark,

You'll be surprised to receive a letter from me but I have something important to tell you. In fact I came to tell you this on that day when I found you with Becky.

I am having a baby and you are the father. I don't expect you to do anything about this, or to be involved with the baby. However, I think it's your right to know about it and my parents agree. After their initial shock they are both being very supportive.

I'll be starting to show soon, so I thought it was best to tell you now so that you'll be prepared when people start to notice and ask questions. The baby is due in July and I'm planning to take a year out from uni but hopefully might be able to complete my course the next year. I need to find out more about this but am too busy with the play right now, so I'll investigate after.

I'll talk to you if you want to know more,
Rose.

Two days later there was a ring of the flat doorbell. Joanna answered and then called to Rose.

"Rose, it's Mark. Do you want to see him?"

Claire, Trish and Joanna now knew about the pregnancy too. They'd all seemed overawed at first and Claire had been very surprised that none of them had suspected a thing before Christmas. After their initial shock, they now had a tendency to be protective of her. Rose had found it amusing at first when they tried to wrap her in cotton wool, but she soon started to get irritated and rebel.

Joanna let Mark in and led him through to the kitchen. Rose made tea in two mugs and then produced the photograph of their baby on the scan to show to Mark.

"I don't know what to say. You must think I'm a complete shit." Mark had been unusually quiet after studying the photograph.

"Well, I know it's a shock for you. I've had a lot of time to get used to the idea. I just thought you should know."

"And are you OK?"

"Yeah. I'm better now, over the morning sickness. Look, can we just stay in touch? Be friendly but not best mates or anything?"

"That would be good. I'd like that."

Since then things had been civilised between them, although Mark had never mentioned the baby again.

"OK, people, break time's finished." Simon called the actors to attention. "I want to run through Act One again before we finish tonight. A few points before we begin. Pete, you need to concentrate more on your accent, it's all over the place, man. Angie, you were late on your first entry. Mark, I think you need to run over your dialogue, you're still a bit hesitant and your character is meant to be forceful at this stage in the play. Everyone will need to be more aware of their stage positions, but we can work more on that once we're in the theatre on Monday. Otherwise it's coming on. And can I just remind you all to see the costume girls at some point tomorrow for a last fitting. Let's get going."

"Yeah, Rose, your costume might need letting out," Becky muttered, but was easily heard by everyone in the silence after Simon's instructions.

"It's a voluminous sort of dress so I'm sure it'll be fine. To your places." The director quashed any further discussion.

Rose tried to ignore Becky's cattiness, after all they weren't in any kind of competition. It wasn't Rose's fault if Mark's attention had moved on from Becky.

Marion

Marion went around her house on a final check. All the windows were closed, the bins empty and three lamps were set up on timer switches. She consulted the clock on the mantelpiece; the taxi should be here in five minutes. Her suitcase was sitting by the front door. She flipped through the documents in her carry-on bag to check that everything was there: all of her tickets, confirmations for her hotel reservations, passport, Euros and a few Swiss francs. She decided to sit down to wait and perched on a chair with a view of the street. She'd finished up at work last Friday, been on holiday for nearly five days now, but still seemed to be rushing about to get ready at the last minute. She loved the carefree feeling of being away from work and had definitely needed a break after her recent stresses, but she wouldn't relax properly until she was sitting in the taxi. Once her trip began she would try hard to shrug off her worries about Betty and get into real holiday mode.

This was easier to plan than it was to put into practice, and once she was settled on the plane and it had reached cruising altitude Marion found herself ruminating again. No one had questioned her decision to move Betty to the nursing home directly from hospital. The unexplained wandering from the house (no reason had been gleaned from Betty) with its resulting worry and upset was understood to be reason enough. If she was honest with herself Marion was unsure whether she would have made a different decision if the relationship with Robert was still undiscovered. Luckily Hilltop was able to accommodate Betty straight from hospital and it was also fortunate that Betty was content at Hilltop. She'd settled in remarkably well. Sometimes she asked when she was going home, but that seemed to refer to a childhood home with her parents. She seemed to enjoy the company of the other residents and was very happy that there was a piano and regular music sessions. Marion wasn't quite so sure what the other ladies in the lounge made of Betty's Prima Donna-like performances. She'd always been a keen participant and a willing soloist but now she had become quite uninhibited. The staff thought that her loud renditions were largely appreciated by the other residents. However, her cutting remarks about some of the ladies' dress sense and tips on how to improve their looks hadn't been so well received.

"Would you like something to eat or drink, madam?" The flight steward was making his rounds.

"A gin and tonic, please."

Marion fished her purse out to pay; there were no complimentary drinks on easyJet. She planned to catch the Airport Flyer bus into the city and then take a taxi to her hotel. She would have dinner on arrival and Rose was going to come to meet her after tonight's dress rehearsal. Apparently her character didn't appear in the final act so she might even manage to join Marion for dessert. It depended on how strict the director was tonight. Marion was pleased that Rose sounded happy again this term. The preparations for the play had kept her very busy and it seemed to be going well. Rose didn't seem too concerned about catching up with her coursework, counting on putting in a lot of effort over reading week and the Easter break.

The seatbelt sign came on and there was an announcement that they were preparing to land. Marion folded up her tabletop and looked out of the window at the illuminated city below.

⸺◦∞∞◦⸺

Marion picked up her coffee cup to take a first sip when a message signal pinged from her phone. It was a text from Rose.

'Leaving now. With U in 20. R x.'

She returned to browsing through a local information booklet that she'd picked up in the lobby. She knew that Rose would be busy and was therefore unlikely to be available to accompany her around the city, so she was planning some activities for the next two days. As it was so near, she thought she'd walk across the suspension bridge and there was the old observatory on the Downs just past the bridge which might be interesting. She was reading about tours on the *SS Great Britain* when she felt a tap on her shoulder.

"Rose, hello." She stood up to hug Rose in greeting and was aware of her bump pressed between them. "Whoops, you've definitely got bigger. How did the rehearsal go?"

"Pretty well. It's so much more atmospheric now that we're in the theatre. I think it's going to be good."

"That's great. Have a seat, and would you like something to eat or drink? I checked, and they'll do sandwiches, or get you a dessert?"

"A cold drink and sandwiches would be great. I need a loo stop, so I'll ask on the way. Do you want anything?"

"A glass of the Pinot Grigio. Just get them to put it all on my room, number 30."

"OK, back in a minute."

Marion studied Rose as she crossed the lounge. Her walk was bouncy and confident and she'd left her hair loose; it hung in a smooth, glossy sheet to her shoulder blades. She seemed to be very upbeat, the play must be going well. But also, she must be feeling healthy and be much happier. Marion's assessment was borne out when Rose returned and plumped down into the chair beside her.

"That's better. I think I know where all the local loos are these days. I've ordered the roast beef sandwiches. I see you're studying the local attractions. What're you planning?"

"Well, I've got a few ideas. I was pretty sure you'd be busy, so I've found some things to amuse myself."

"Yeah. I've got a tutorial tomorrow morning, but I could meet you for lunch and part of the afternoon. Obviously I'm in the theatre all evening but you could come to have a drink with us after the show if you'd like to."

"OK. Any idea what the weather's to be like? I thought I'd walk across the bridge and up onto the Downs."

"I'll check." Rose consulted her phone. "Looks OK tomorrow, maybe a bit of rain by the evening."

The sandwiches and drinks arrived and Rose took a large glug of Appletiser and attacked her food hungrily.

"I see you're in the blooming stage now," Marion teased.

"Yeah, I feel pretty good. I told you I had my check-up last week and it was all fine, didn't I?"

"Yes, that's good."

"Hey, maybe we could go and start looking at some baby stuff tomorrow. Sally bought me the cutest baby blanket but I've not looked at anything like that yet."

"Sure, if you'd like to." Marion sipped her wine, secretly pleased to be asked. "So Dad and Sally have been OK about the baby?"

"Well, I thought initially that Dad was going to explode, but he calmed down. And Sally's just so excited. Mum, you realise you'll see Mark at the play?"

"Yes, he's got one of the leading roles, hasn't he?"

"Yeah, John Proctor. I just thought I'd say – we don't mix socially but we're friendlier again."

"And what's his opinion about the baby?"

"We haven't mentioned it again. I imagine he's still thinking about it."

"Mmm."

"Mum, don't be all judgemental. I had ages thinking about it and getting used to the idea before I spoke to you. And it's kind of more immediate for me cos it's my body. It'll be harder for him to feel involved."

"Although, acting with you, he must notice your figure changing."

"Yeah. So how's Gran doing?" Rose decided to change the subject.

"She's settled in really well at Hilltop. I think she likes the company. Remember you thought maybe she was lonely before?"

"Uh-huh. Is that why you decided not to try her back at home?"

"I don't know exactly. It was all a bit of a shock and so worrying when she wandered off. And we still don't know why she did it. But I realise now, once you came back here she was still on her own in the house for a long time on the three days I work." Marion had decided against telling Rose anything about her gran and Robert.

"So do you think this is permanent?"

"Yes, I think on balance that she's just as happy if not even more so at Hilltop. And it's so close I can pop in every day, so overall it gives me more freedom. Also, once they stopped coming, I recognised that I was relieved not to have the carers trooping in and out of the house every day."

"What does Auntie Peggy think?"

"She's fine with it. She thought I was taking on too much having Gran at the house anyway. And Uncle Douglas is happy about it too."

"So will you sell Gran's house now?"

"Yes. I'll have to get that organised once I get back from my holiday. I'd already started doing some sorting out and cleaning and Douglas cleared out the attic before he left."

"I suppose you need the money from the house to pay for the nursing home."

"Well, not immediately. But given that Gran's physical health has been good, we could be looking at years of care."

"I wasn't too keen on the idea of the home, but if you think it's working out then I think you should stick with it."

Marion proceeded to entertain Rose with descriptions of her gran's performances at the music sessions.

"Maybe that's who you take after with the acting."

"Could be. Talking of acting, I'd better go home now and catch up on my sleep so that I'm fit for the opening night. So let's firm up on where we're going to meet tomorrow. I'll be out of my class at twelve. Have you got a map in that wee booklet?"

Marion unfolded a map of central Bristol at the back of her guide and they agreed to meet by the Wills Building tower on Queen's Road at ten past twelve. Then Marion walked with Rose through the lobby of the hotel to the front door. Mum and daughter embraced.

"Bye Mum."

Rose waved from the street as she set off on her walk home. Marion waved back, then once Rose had gone from view she turned her gaze to the floodlit suspension bridge. She breathed a sigh of relief, thankful that her daughter was coping so well.

Marion found her seat and looked around the theatre before sitting down. It was small with a very basic set-up; its simplicity reminded her of some of the Edinburgh Fringe venues that she'd been to. She counted the rows of bench seats and guessed that it could hold an audience of about fifty. So, it shouldn't be too difficult to achieve a full house. The review of last night's performance in today's *Bristol Post* had been very good; it might have encouraged any remaining tickets to be scooped up. She opened her programme and tried to match the actors that she'd met last night with Rose in the adjoining tavern to the characters that they were playing. It had been fun to be included in the post-show drinks. Everyone had been in high spirits and very supportive of each other. And because Rose also worked here, the bar and theatre staff all knew her and had been caught up in the excitement too. Although she'd probably been the oldest person in the gathering by far no one had made her feel out of place. She hoped that this would also apply this evening when she was due to go out with Rose and her three flatmates who would be at the play tonight. The plan was to go for pizza together.

The theatre lights began to dim and Marion felt her guts flip in anticipation as she turned her attention to the stage. Her nervousness around Rose's performances had receded greatly over the years, but there was still some remaining angst.

By the interval Marion felt exhausted. She was wrapped up in the intense atmosphere and growing hysteria on the stage. She couldn't help feeling awed by her daughter's portrayal of Abigail's cunning and manipulative character. She could also see why Rose had been attracted to Mark. He was very handsome and exuded confidence from the stage. She could imagine that, if he chose to, he could use that magnetism to attract many young women.

That kind of male charm reminded her of Angus as a young man. Maybe he still had it, but she hadn't seen him in years. She was glad that she'd be gone, in France, when Angus came to see the play tomorrow. She didn't want to meet him. Even after all these years and many hours of therapy she knew that she was still angry with Angus because of what she had always felt was his betrayal of her. She hadn't forgiven him. She managed to keep those feelings well buried most of the time and had been able to be civil to Angus on the phone making arrangements for Rose over the years. It was important to Marion that Rose shouldn't be caught up in any bad feelings.

But the anger had bubbled up to the surface again since learning about her mum and Robert. Marion still believed that Angus had wounded her when she was at her lowest and most vulnerable. The postnatal depression had not been her fault. It was a recognised clinical condition and she was just unfortunate to have been severely affected. That Angus had deserted her because of this, when he'd actively encouraged the planned pregnancy, seemed particularly cruel. Of course, later she found out that he'd been with other women before this occasion. She sometimes wondered if he still had affairs on the side, and if Sally knew about it and put up with them. Or maybe Sally, being a different character from Marion, was enough for Angus. Well, she'd never know and it was none of her business now either. She'd really like to be able to bury this rage towards Angus again. Maybe she should go back to see her psychologist. But the idea of returning to therapy seemed to represent failure.

The repetitive, intrusive thoughts about Betty, Robert and Angus were beginning to wear her out, though, and she wasn't sleeping very well. So maybe she had to be sensible and accept that she needed some help again.

She decided to see how she felt after the skiing week and to consider more therapy if the Betty and Angus thoughts weren't subsiding. She was due to meet Jenny at Gatwick Airport tomorrow, catching the train to take her there first thing in the morning. A week of exercise, fresh air and Jenny's good company might help to put things back into proportion.

As she reached this conclusion the lights dimmed again for the end of the interval and she quickly became immersed in Act Three.

Nyaga

Nyaga narrowly missed a collision with the postman; he was coming up the stairs of her building as she clattered down on her way to work.

"Hello Miss Sejewe. I've got an airmail letter for you. Do you want to take it with you or will I put it through your letterbox?"

"I'll take it, thanks," Nyaga replied and shoved the letter into her bag, hurrying on her way.

She was working a late shift and at her teatime break she went to her bag to retrieve the watermelon that she'd diced and packed into a Tupperware box, intending to eat the fruit with her sandwich. She discovered the letter nestling there and took it along with her to read. She slit the envelope open with her knife making a wrinkled, jagged edge. As she eased the contents out a photograph fell onto the coffee table face up.

"Oh, is that your girl?" Sonia was also having tea and the fallen photo caught her attention.

"Yes, she's just started school."

"Oh, doesn't she look smart?"

163

They both surveyed the picture of Lesedi who had a wide grin and neatly braided hair. She was wearing a yellow school polo shirt with a badge sewn on the pocket and held a pencil case featuring a motif of giraffes. Nyaga picked the photograph up and stroked the image of her daughter's face gently with her right index finger. Sonia noticed tears beginning to well in her colleague's eyes.

"You must miss her."

"Yes, I do. But I've promised myself that I'll be home to see her before the end of this year," Nyaga said, blinking back her tears.

"Well, I'll leave you to read your letter in peace. I'll go and remind everyone that we've got an entertainer coming in tonight. Get them to start gathering in the lounge."

"Oh yes. Is it the magician? He was good last time. I'll come and do the six o'clock drugs, get that out of the way before he comes."

"Read your letter first."

The letter was from Nyaga's mum and quite short. The main purpose had been to send the school photo. However, she did give news of one of Nyaga's friends, Tumi. She was pregnant with her second child, but unfortunately her antenatal blood tests had shown that she was HIV positive. She was now receiving anti-retroviral treatment. Nyaga's mum thought that she'd want to know.

Nyaga sighed; poor Tumi.

And it could so easily have been me that was infected, she thought.

At least now in Botswana there was excellent treatment for HIV and therefore a good chance that Tumi's baby would escape placental transmission. She'd known Tumi for years, they'd been at school together, and Tumi's son was just a few months younger than Lesedi. Nyaga could remember their last outing together, just before she came to Scotland. They'd decided to treat themselves to the Sunday buffet lunch at the Gaborone Sun Hotel. There was always a fantastic spread of food and the added bonus that lunch guests could stay and use the swimming pool after they'd eaten. The main problem for Nyaga and Tumi had been to interest Lesedi and Tsholo in eating some lunch. The children would have been quite happy to skip the food and go straight to the pool. That afternoon they'd both splashed around for hours, wearing water wings to keep them afloat. Nyaga hoped that Tsholo was well; maybe Tumi caught the virus after he was born. She'd try to email her friend on her next day off. But now she'd better get on with the drug round. She carefully stowed the letter and photograph back in her bag.

Nyaga's next day off was on Tuesday and she planned to visit Betty at Hilltop. She'd promised that she'd pop in while Marion was on holiday. She decided to visit the library first to use the internet. That way she could check exactly where the care home was situated and research the best bus to take. She also intended to email a message to Tumi and one to her mum to thank her for the photo of Lesedi. After discovering the local library, which was almost on her doorstep, she was a regular visitor both for borrowing books and to use the internet. She had a note of the opening hours and arrived sharp at ten o'clock, just as the librarian was unlocking the doors. Often it was busy and she knew she might have to reserve a computer for later in the morning. But she was lucky and there was a free slot straightaway. She logged on to her email account and found lots of mail sitting in her inbox, including messages from Tumi and Rose.

Tumi supplied more information about her health. She was HIV positive, but didn't have full-blown AIDS. However, to give the safest outcome for the new baby she'd been started on treatment. That was also a good thing for her own outlook too, giving her a better prognosis. 'If I hadn't been pregnant I'd never have known yet that I have the virus, because I didn't feel ill so I wouldn't have gone for a test. So my baby has helped me. I only hope I'll be around to look after him for a long time.' Nyaga knew that Tumi had been in a relationship with a new man, not Tsholo's father. But she didn't know if they were still together or if he was healthy. If she'd been at home she'd have known all of this through regular contact with Tumi. But she didn't feel that she could ask these questions in a letter if Tumi wasn't volunteering the information. However, she had no qualms about asking after Tsholo who, like Lesedi, would have just started school. She fired off a supportive response.

Rose's letter was full of the theatre and the play, which had gone very well and got good reviews. She also mentioned Marion's visit and that they'd gone to look at baby things together. Nyaga replied that she was planning to start knitting some little clothes for the baby, but would stick to white wool since Rose didn't know the sex of her baby. She also mentioned that she was going to visit Betty later today.

Next Nyaga logged on to the website for Hilltop Care Home and also to the one for Lothian Buses. Her most straightforward route was to walk along to Broomhouse Road and catch a number twenty-one bus. Then she should get off at St John's Road and walk along from there to Clermiston Road. Hilltop was just off that road. When she connected back to the care home website to double-check the address she noticed a bar marked 'jobs' at the top. She clicked on it and it gave her a dropdown menu. Out of curiosity she entered her staff grade and a few other details. It seemed to be a big coincidence, there was a position listed at Betty's home – Hilltop Care Home, Hawthorn Care Group, Corstorphine, Edinburgh. Maybe she'd ask more about it when she was there. Some of the other staff at Dellview had been grumbling recently because they reckoned that other care providers were paying better than theirs. She hadn't felt strongly enough about it to go actively looking for another position, but if she could get a rise in pay that would be good. She noted down all the details for her journey and logged out from the computer. Her hour was up in two or three minutes anyway.

Nyaga went home to change before setting out to visit Betty. She remembered that Betty was interested in clothes so chose a bright turquoise jumper and put in the large hoop earrings that had grabbed Betty's attention at Christmas. Despite the bright sunshine the wind was coming from the east bringing a definite chill to the air. She donned a hat, scarf and gloves and her thick jacket, although she'd noticed on her earlier outing that some of the local population were braving the day without coats.

The instructions for her journey worked out easily and she was soon climbing the steep hill up Clermiston Road. She remembered that Marion's house was on a hill but it hadn't seemed so extreme in the car. Halfway up, with the sun warming her back, she began to feel the prickle of perspiration at her hairline and had to stop to remove her hat and scarf. Three months ago she'd never have imagined that she'd ever feel too hot in the Scottish climate. And now she was able to tackle this hill without being out of breath. Those vitamin injections had made her into a new woman.

When she arrived at Hilltop she was very impressed by the façade of the old mansion house. Everything about it looked neat and well cared for. The windows and gable boards were freshly painted and there were tubs containing snowdrops and crocuses in flower by the front door. She rang the bell and the door was opened by a member of staff. Marion must have told the carers that Nyaga planned to visit as her name was familiar to them.

"Betty's just finishing her morning coffee in the lounge. I'll take you through to see her."

They entered a large sunny room. Light poured in through two bay windows and tall patio doors that led out into the garden. The windows were framed by floral curtains; blue and yellow blossoms cascaded over a cream background. These colours were reproduced elsewhere in the room. The carpet was cornflower blue, armchairs and cushions were various shades of blue, yellow and gold and the walls were cream. The chairs were arranged in clusters facing the windows and the fireplace.

At first Nyaga didn't recognise Betty, as her hair which had been dyed black when they met before had been allowed to grow out while she was in hospital. She'd arrived at Hilltop with a bedraggled piebald mop. Their hairdresser had fashioned a short pixie cut to eradicate the final dyed ends and so Betty's hair was now pure white. Nyaga thought that she bore a definite resemblance to the actress Judi Dench. She'd seen her portrayal of M in the recent James Bond films.

"Hello Betty. How are you?"

Of course Nyaga didn't expect Betty to remember her so she wasn't surprised or offended by the vague half-smile that she gave in greeting.

"I'm quite well, thank you. That jumper is a lovely colour on you. Is it angora?" Betty's hand came over to stroke Nyaga's arm, testing out the fabric of her sleeve.

"Yes, I think it has some angora in it."

"It's lovely and soft. Do those earrings not hurt you? They look very heavy."

Nyaga reassured Betty once again that they didn't weigh very much.

"I wondered if you'd like to come out with me for a walk today," she suggested.

"That's very kind of you, but would you know where to go? I'm not from here myself, you know, and my mother told me not to go out on my own in case I get lost."

"That's quite right, you shouldn't go out on your own. But I'll make sure you get back safely."

"Well, that should be alright then. I'd like to go."

Betty was quick to rise up from her seat and walk across the lounge. However, when she came to the door into the hall she hovered looking into the corridor uncertainly.

"We'll just need to collect your coat and shoes first. Can you show me the way to your room?" Nyaga was following after Betty.

"It's along this way... somewhere," she said, gesturing imprecisely, obviously hoping that Nyaga would know the way.

"Let's ask the nurse," Nyaga suggested. "We'll need to let her know that you're going out anyway."

Once she'd helped Betty to find her room and don suitable outdoor clothes they set off together. Betty was keen to wear a pair of high-heeled patent leather court shoes with red velvet bows on the backs. Tactfully Nyaga managed to persuade her that they didn't really match her good camel coat and to try a comfortable pair of brown walking shoes instead. Betty held on to Nyaga's arm for support as they walked down the gravelled drive, the top of her head only reaching up to Nyaga's shoulder. She glanced up at her companion in a shy, admiring way.

"Would you like to stay for your tea? We can ask my mother if you're allowed."

"That would be lovely," Nyaga replied, refraining from correcting Betty's orientation. They walked along some of the neighbouring streets, admiring the spring flowers in the gardens and looking out over the sprawl of the city and the Pentland Hills to the south. Nyaga wasn't sure if they passed Marion's house as she'd only visited once and it had been dark. Betty didn't comment, as everything seemed entirely unfamiliar to her.

When they returned to Hilltop Nyaga discovered a loose button on Betty's coat. She went to the laundry to see if she could borrow a sewing kit. Then she sat in the lounge beside Betty and sewed on the button, fixing it firmly. Betty snoozed in her chair, tired after her walk. She certainly revived quickly when lunch was announced and was pleased that her visitor was staying to eat.

"You eat up now," she encouraged Nyaga while attacking her own food with gusto. Her appetite had been fully restored on recovering from her recent illness. Nyaga enjoyed the meal. The portions were small but there were three courses and all of the food was fresh and tasty. After lunch she said goodbye to Betty and promised to visit again soon.

Before leaving Hilltop she knocked on the office door. Aileen, the manager, was in, and after introducing herself and explaining that she was a friend of the family visiting Betty, Nyaga mentioned that she was aware of a staff vacancy and might be interested in applying for the post. Aileen asked her a few questions about her qualifications and experience.

"I think you could suit us very well. We've been short-staffed for quite some time."

Nyaga asked what she might expect to be paid and was told an amount that was substantially more than her present salary.

"I would definitely like to apply," she said.

"OK. I'll give you these forms to fill out and you'll need two references. If you bring them back to me, or post them, I can take things on to the next stage."

She pulled open a drawer and produced some papers from between cardboard dividers. Nyaga noticed that the office seemed to be neat and well organised.

"Thank you. I'll try to get them back to you soon."

The women shook hands as they said goodbye and Aileen accompanied Nyaga to the front door. As she retraced her steps to catch her bus Nyaga was feeling very positive. It would be great if she could earn a better salary and she liked the ambience of Hilltop; it would be OK working there. She'd given up on the idea of living permanently in Scotland and having Lesedi come here too, but extra money to take home would be very helpful. She'd originally thought that coming to Scotland would give them both a better life, and maybe she was also trying to escape from the AIDS crisis in Botswana. But she hadn't counted on the deep feelings that she had for her own country and its culture. She didn't expect to be so homesick and to miss her family and friends so intensely. Ironically she'd begun to like Scotland much better since she'd decided to leave. She'd become more accustomed to the climate and some of the strange-seeming customs. And she'd made some good friends.

Marion

"So, how was the skiing holiday? You look well." Susan greeted Marion as she arrived in the staffroom on her first morning back at work. They were obviously the last two to make it up for their coffee break as the room was otherwise empty and a crowd of upside-down mugs was dripping on the draining board by the sink.

"It was great, thanks, lots of snow. And it was good to see Rose too, her play was fantastic."

"Well, you've arrived back here to the usual mayhem. And we still have that referrals review to complete by the end of the month."

"Yeah, it doesn't seem to matter how much we try to keep up over the year, we always seem to be scrabbling around at the last moment."

"It's so annoying that we can't just be paid for doing a good job clinically for our patients. But we have to rely on all of this information-gathering to make ends meet. I nearly punched Hari and Judy last week," Susan continued. "They presented me with an enormous list of patients' records to wade through and then expected me to have completed everything by the next day."

Marion grimaced in sympathy. Hari did get carried away sometimes.

"I take it you said you weren't quite ready," she said.

"I did, in no uncertain terms. Some of this stuff is just nonsense."

"Well, most of it probably makes sense, and it could help to make access to secondary care more even across the board for our patients, maybe even cut down waiting times. But I agree that the amount of extra work that it creates can be daunting. I'm sure we all just have to use our common sense and fit it in when we've got time."

"But then we might not meet the deadline and we've got Hari breathing down our necks."

"I think it's good that someone in the practice is enthusiastic, though. Otherwise we'd never make any of the targets. You know, he gets upset that you're so antagonistic towards him."

"Humph. Well, I'm sure he'll be pleased to hear this news: I went to a BMA meeting about pensions last night. I'm thinking of retiring early."

"Was the meeting helpful?" Marion refrained from making a comment about it not being very early to think of retiring in case she gave offence, but she knew that Susan had celebrated her fifty-eighth birthday just before Christmas.

"It all seems quite complicated. I think I'll try to make an appointment with their financial adviser to explain it on a personal level and get Bill to come along with me."

"We'd obviously miss you, but if you can do it, why not? How about Bill? Would he work on?"

Susan's husband was an anaesthetist.

"Well, he's always planned to work until he's sixty-five. But he might change his mind if I'm lazing about with lots of free time."

"Well, keep me posted, Susan. It sounds exciting."

"Yes, it is exciting. Now, I suppose we'd better get around to looking at how many visits they've left for us."

The women consulted the list for that day's house visit requests and shared out the remaining four according to their knowledge of the patients.

Twenty minutes later Marion parked her car in front of a semi-detached two-storey house. It was situated in an area that had originally been built as council housing. Over the years most of the tenants had been able to buy their houses at a very reasonable price under a government scheme introduced by Margaret Thatcher in the 1980s. It meant that the neighbourhood was now smarter, but Marion knew that the legislation had also led to a shortage of houses available for needy families, with some of her patients living in very cramped conditions and having to wait years to be allocated accommodation. She was about to visit Mr Thomson who'd been discharged after a lengthy hospital stay following a severe stroke. She'd had a lot of communication from the hospital unit about his homecoming. They'd really recommended long-term institutional care to deal with his complex nursing requirements. But his wife and daughter were adamant that they wanted him back home and that they would cope with looking after him. So he now had carers in attendance four times a day and the district nurses also called daily. Inside the house the area previously used as a dining room had been converted into a mini hospital ward with a proper hospital bed, a hoist and a reclining chair provided courtesy of the occupational therapist. Mrs Thomson showed Marion into this room.

"I had the carpet taken out and this laminate flooring laid to make things easier and more hygienic," she explained, seeming very satisfied with all of the arrangements.

"Hello Mr Thomson. How are you?"

Marion approached the bed and grasped her patient's good hand. He was lying askew in the bed and one side of his face was so badly puckered up that it appeared to be caved in. He wasn't wearing any false teeth which caused the chasm of his mouth to be accentuated and there was a trickle of drool running down his chin. But he looked at her with bright, intelligent eyes and squeezed her hand in greeting.

"Oh, he's very pleased to be home, aren't you, Jimmy? We have a code, Doctor. One squeeze means 'yes' and he gives two for 'no'. He can do the same with blinks, can't you, Jimmy?"

Mr Thomson's good eye blinked once.

"That's very helpful that you've got a way to communicate," Marion commented. "Well, I know it's early days but is there anything you're worried about or want me to look at?"

"I think we'll need you to provide us with more medicines soon. We only got a week's supply when Jim came home. There's a letter here about it all."

Mrs Thomson produced a document from the sideboard and handed it to Marion. Looking at it Marion could see that there were a few changes when compared to the list she had of his drugs prior to admission.

"Are you using the same pharmacy as before?"

Mrs Thomson nodded.

"I'll get all of this changed in Mr Thomson's electronic notes back at the practice and send everything he needs along to the pharmacy. You'll be able to collect from them later in the week."

"That's good, Doctor."

Marion opened her medical bag.

"Now, I'll just check your blood pressure, Mr Thomson."

And after she'd finished, "All fine."

"What about his diabetic control, Doctor?"

"The district nurses will do the checks for that and also look after his catheter. They're coming in every day and they'll let me know if there's a problem with either."

Marion packed up her bag and said goodbye to her patient. As she made her way out of the house she paused on the doorstep where she felt she wouldn't be overheard.

175

"You're very brave to take this on, Mrs Thomson."

"It's what I wanted to do. I hated him being in that hospital."

"Well, you have to be careful not to overdo things. I don't want you to get worn out or ill."

"Thank you, Doctor, but the carers and nurses seem very helpful, and my daughter can come to sit with Jim if I need to get out to the shops or anything like that."

"Do you have any other friends or family nearby?"

"Oh yes. We've lived in this house all of our married life, so we know a lot of people locally."

"Well, I want you to accept help if people offer it, don't try to do everything yourself."

"Yes, Doctor. It's good to know that you're looking out for me as well as Jim."

Marion waved back at Mrs Thomson who stood on her doorstep to watch the car drive away. *What a huge burden for an elderly woman to take on*, she thought. And the outlook for this kind of dense stroke was hard to predict. Mr Thomson could survive like this for ten weeks or ten years, or anything in between. Marion hoped that they were all going to manage the situation without too much stress. Her next visit was to Dellview Nursing Home so she turned left at the end of the street, heading in that direction. When she arrived, she was greeted by Nyaga at the front door.

"Hello. I hope you had a nice holiday."

"Yes I did, thank you. I'll tell you all about it later. It's Bob Young that you'd like me to see today?"

Nyaga explained why she was worried about Bob. He'd been complaining of abdominal pains, seeming very distressed by them, and he'd also vomited a few times this morning.

"When did it all begin?" Marion asked as they walked along the corridor together to Bob's room.

"Yesterday, he didn't feel like eating any of his evening meal and then the pain seemed to build up overnight."

When Marion saw Bob and examined him she was very concerned.

"I'm going to give you an injection for the pain and arrange for you to go to hospital for assessment," she told him.

She administered an intra-muscular injection of morphine and then went to the office to use the telephone. She arranged an ambulance and an emergency surgical opinion.

"I think he may have an intestinal obstruction," she explained.

Once she'd organised all of that she was free to chat to Nyaga briefly about her holiday. They'd left one of the care staff with Bob to keep him company until the ambulance arrived.

"I had an email from Rose telling me about the play," Nyaga told her.

"Yes, it was amazing and hard to believe that it was my daughter up there on the stage. She played the role so well, really got into the part. Her character was scheming and manipulative, not at all pleasant."

"And is she well in herself?"

"She's so well, Nyaga. She's definitely in the blooming stage of the pregnancy and she seems quite calm and serene about everything, long may it continue."

"I saw Betty last week. She seemed well too."

"Yes, I popped in yesterday and she was in good form."

Marion kept her true feelings well hidden. When she'd visited Hilltop yesterday it was the first time that Betty hadn't seemed to know who Marion was. Sometimes in the past she hadn't been able to make the right connection about their exact relationship, but she'd always seemed to recognise that Marion was a significant figure in her life. Yesterday her greeting had been polite but vague, with no glimmer of recognition. Maybe it was to be expected after an absence of twelve days, but Marion had been upset.

Nyaga checked that no one was approaching the office from the corridor then said to Marion, "I hope you don't mind. I wanted to ask you a favour. There's a job going at Betty's nursing home and it would be better pay than here. If I applied would you be willing to give me a reference?"

"Of course I would, it'd be no problem at all."

"Thank you. Now I'd better phone Bob's relatives to let them know he's going to hospital."

"Yep and I'd better get back to the surgery and write up everything from my visits. Good luck with the application."

Once she was back in the car Marion wondered why she hadn't confided in Nyaga. She'd had a chance to share an upset. She knew from past experience that bottling feelings up was bad for her and would lead to sleepless nights and stress. She hadn't managed to raise the subject of Betty and Robert's relationship with Jenny while they were in France either, and there had been plenty of opportunity. The insomnia had started already. She sighed.

It looks like I'll have to go back to Rosemary, she thought. *If I'm paying someone to listen to me, then I suppose I'll spill the beans.*

"Now, Marion, I want you to think back into your childhood. What are the good things that you remember about your mother?"

Marion's psychologist, Rosemary, wore glasses with large, thick lenses that magnified her eyes. Marion thought that there was a resemblance to the intense gaze of an owl. Maybe she also blinked less frequently than was usual too. Her scrutiny and searching questions usually got to the heart of a problem.

"Mum was good fun, she laughed a lot. She made me great costumes for dressing up and Halloween. And she wasn't too fussy about the house being shipshape and tidy. My friends liked to come around to play, and then to hang out when we were older. I suppose she was more relaxed than their mums were."

"Any bad memories?"

"She was often busy, between her job at the shop and evening choir rehearsals. If I had a problem I'd probably ask my dad, he seemed to have more time for us."

"How about as a granny to Rose?"

"She's always loved Rose and had a close relationship with her. In the early baby days I couldn't have managed without her. As you know I was depressed and even though Mum was still working when Rose was born she took time off to come and help me. And she'd take Rose away for half days to give me space. She'd retired by the time Angus left and she and Dad helped out a lot, especially at weekends when I used to have to be on call for the practice and later with school holidays. Rose spent some holiday time with her dad but a lot of it with my parents."

"It sounds as if she was a good mum. Did she ever do anything to hurt you in any way?"

Marion shook her head.

"So why are you so angry with her?"

"Because she cheated on my dad."

"Was your dad unhappy?"

"No, he adored her and he was always delighted to see her. His face would light up when she came into a room, even latterly when he was ill."

"Do you think he knew about the affair?"

"I can't believe that he did."

"And your aunt told you that your mum would never have left your dad."

"Yes. She has an idea that maybe seeing Robert on the side actually protected the marriage because it stopped Mum from being restless."

"What do you think?"

"I don't know. It's possible. Auntie Peggy's pretty shrewd and she obviously knows my mum really well."

"It sounds from what you've told me, Marion, that your mum didn't hurt your dad. He was happy. Does he need you to be angry with her on his behalf?"

"But she was unfaithful."

"Yes."

"It's like Angus and it's made me angry with him all over again. So maybe that's why I'm angry with Mum too."

"Yes, I think that's certainly happened. However, remember that Angus was never discrete. You certainly knew about his extramarital affairs. And, Marion, I don't think you've ever really let go of your anger towards Angus. I think you've suppressed it and buried it but the anger has still been there. Why can't you let it go?"

"He hurt me. I'd really prefer not to have any strong feelings left for him, good or bad, because I know they still tie me to him. But I can't seem to forgive him."

"I think that this may be where you need to direct your energy. Instead of being angry with your mum and with Angus, focus on cutting the tie with him. You say you want to do that, so maybe it would be a relief. Imagine taking a pair of very sharp shears and hacking through the rope that binds you to him. Close your eyes for a few minutes and think about it."

Marion closed her eyes. The consulting room was part of a converted stone house set in mature gardens. The window was open and she could hear birdsong from the chestnut tree outside and occasional passing traffic. She tried to concentrate on the picture that Rosemary had given her. The rope in her mind seemed to have the features of an umbilical cord – twisted, grey and knobbly. Would it bleed if she cut into it? Perhaps despite her protest to the contrary, she kept hold of her anger because it connected her to Angus. Did she really want to let go completely?

When she opened her eyes, she mentioned this thought to Rosemary.

"Yes, Marion. After fifteen years do you want to let go? I want you to consider this and come back to see me next week."

Rose

Rose was desperate to get to the loo. When she arrived back at the front door she let herself in and dived into the toilet immediately, glad that it was unoccupied. It was a relief to sit and let go. Recently she seemed to have to plan every outing around places that she knew had toilets. This morning she'd enjoyed a relaxed wander around the farmers' market, taking in the colourful stalls and varied aromas, glad that the semester was finished. Claire had asked her to pick up a cake for their tea party this afternoon and she'd been swithering in front of a selection of baking when suddenly the urge had struck her. She'd quickly chosen any cake and hobbled back home as quickly as she could. Thankfully her pelvic floor exercises must be doing their job and she'd made it on time.

Today was the last time that all four girls would be together. Exams were over and everyone was packing up and preparing to leave. Joanna and Trish were about to set out on a backpacking holiday in the Far East, taking in Thailand, Vietnam and Cambodia, and Claire had a job lined up in a coffee shop near her home in London. Rose was looking forward to going home to Edinburgh, but if she allowed herself to think further forward to her impending labour she was filled with trepidation. The idea of caring for a tiny baby was also quite scary.

There was a tap on the door.

"Are you still in there?" It was Joanna's voice.

"Oh yes, sorry to be hogging the loo. I'll be out in a sec."

Rose dried herself off, washed her hands and rearranged her clothes. She'd eventually had to give in to her expanding girth and start wearing maternity clothes. Today it was a wafty, lacy top over an enormous T-shirt and expandable denim shorts. She picked up the shopping bag that she'd abandoned by the door and emerged into the hall to find Joanna waiting for her.

"Did you get the cake?"

"Yes, it's a lemon drizzle I think."

"Great, give it here and I'll take it into the kitchen. Why don't you go through to the lounge and take the weight off?"

"It's OK, I'm not that tired."

"Well, I'm sure you could do with a rest anyway."

All of the girls tended to be protective of Rose but today Joanna seemed particularly solicitous as she herded Rose towards the lounge. Rose was about to comment on this but as she opened the lounge door a cacophony of voices cried out, "Surprise!"

The room was filled with Rose's girlfriends and classmates all giggling and waving at her. While she'd been out someone had been busy hanging up bunches of pastel balloons tied with trailing ribbons and pinning up pictures of cute babies. There was a pile of gift-wrapped parcels on the coffee table.

"Come and sit down." Claire invited her further into the room.

As she came in one of the girls dropped a shiny sash over her head. It was emblazoned with the words 'Mum to Be'.

"Wow. Well, this certainly is a surprise. I had no idea."

"No. It was quite hard work getting you out of the way this morning to let everyone gather," Claire admitted.

Rose remembered that she had been gently but firmly shepherded out to the market earlier with the instructions about the cake. But she'd never suspected that anything bigger than their afternoon tea party for four was planned.

"Welcome to your baby shower, sit down, there's a space next to me," Corinne, a fellow student from the English faculty, invited.

"We've all got a drink. What can I get for you?" Claire asked.

"Apple juice would be nice, thanks.". Rose gave in to the pampering and sat on the sofa, allowing Claire to fetch a drink for her.

"So, how did your meeting with Prof. Jones go yesterday?" Corinne enquired.

Rose had met up with her course director to finalise the arrangements for her year out.

"It was fine. As long as I've got good enough average marks this year they're happy to hold my place open. My grade was on track from my class work and I think the exams went alright, so I should be OK."

"Won't it be funny coming back in a different class? We'll all have moved on."

"Well, I think that by then my life will have changed so much in so many other ways that it won't matter to me too much, no offence."

"Sure, I can't really imagine."

"Rose is planning to stay in Bath with her dad and stepmum and travel in for classes," Claire stepped in to explain as she delivered a glass of chilled apple juice to Rose.

"Yeah. My stepmum works intensive shifts but has a lot of time off in between, so she says she's happy to help out with some of the childcare, and I can apply for a place at the university nursery for days when I know I'll have a regular class."

"You're going to have to be sooo organised."

Rose was beginning to bristle at Corinne's comments which came across to her as either incredibly naïve or slightly catty. She was saved from making a reply as Joanna appeared with a tray full of baking and a pile of plates and offered the selection to Rose.

"Have some cake, need to keep your strength up."

"Then you can open the pressies. I want to see what's in all of those parcels," Claire added.

Rose chose a slice of the lemon cake and Claire began to ferry some of the wrapped parcels from the coffee table and pile them up beside Rose's feet. Soon there was a scatter of ripped paper on the floor and many comments of, 'Ooh' and 'Isn't that cute' and 'Sooo adorable' as Rose unwrapped and displayed the gifts. There were clothes: seven mini vests with poppers underneath and the days of the week embroidered across the chest, a white velour sleep suit with rabbit ears on the hood, a pair of rainbow-striped soft corduroy bootees and a red quilted jacket. Some packages revealed toys: a tiny cream teddy bear wearing a tartan bowtie, a mobile of butterflies to hang above a cot, a family of rubber ducks for the bath and some first picture books. Then there were baby care items: soft white towels, bibs, a sippy beaker and cutlery with Peter Rabbit motifs, and a papoose-style baby-carrying sling.

"Thank you all very much." Rose was warmed by the girls' generosity. "I had thought that my packing was done, but I'm sure I can find space to squeeze all of this in."

"When do you set off?" Ruth, a friend from the theatre, asked.

"I'm catching the train on Monday morning. I've got quite a lot of luggage to move so I'll take a taxi to the station. And my dad's coming across tomorrow to take some of my stuff to Bath, things I'll need when I come back."

"I hope you're going to keep in touch," Emma chipped in.

"Well, I expect I'm going to be pretty busy, so don't expect individual messages, but I'll try to keep my Facebook page up to date."

"And you've got to put lots of pictures of the baby up for us to see," Julia called over.

"I'll do my best."

"So do you have some names chosen yet?" Emma asked.

"Nothing definite," Rose admitted. A general discussion of names began, starting out with some fairly sensible and suitable suggestions and then gradually moving on to jokey and ridiculous ideas which caused general hilarity to break out.

―❧―

"Right, that's the lot then." Angus deposited the last of Rose's boxes into his car and pulled the hatchback down firmly.

"Thanks, Dad."

"Not a problem. And you will take a taxi to the station tomorrow? And get help once you're there. I don't want you trying to lift a lot of luggage."

"One advantage about being this shape is that everyone suddenly leaps to help me and fusses over me. I'm sure it'll be easy to get help."

"You'd think the least that boy could do would be to see you onto the train." Angus found it hard to believe that Mark was just leaving Rose to get on with things. "You said you were seeing him yesterday."

"Yes."

Rose thought back to their awkward encounter. They'd agreed to meet at Caffe Clifton, one of their old haunts, at five o'clock. Rose had gone along there after the baby shower broke up. She hadn't seen Mark since the play in February. They were on different courses and without the focus of Drama Soc didn't mix in similar circles. Also, they'd both had a lot of catching up to do with their coursework after the run of the play. Obviously Rose's figure had expanded a lot in the past three months. She could see Mark absorbing the change as she walked towards him across the café. They attempted a clumsy embrace around her bump. Their polite conversation stuck to facts about their work, exams and moving on from Bristol. No feelings were mentioned, emotions were kept well wrapped up.

"He's going home until graduation and then he'll be touring in the States over the summer. He's got a conditional acceptance for a postgrad theatre course at Columbia, New York. So he's not going to be around for the baby, Dad. There's no point in wishing for it."

"And what about his parents?"

"I've no idea. I don't know if he told them or not. Dad, I don't want to make a big thing of it with him. Please let it go."

Angus smiled and shook his head.

"You know you've got me wrapped around your pinkie, so I'll do what you say. Anyway, look after yourself and keep in touch. Sally and I will come up to visit once the baby arrives. We've got some holidays in July, so we'll maybe do a wee tour up north and take in the grandchild along with the other sights."

"OK, Dad, and thanks for saying I can live with you next year."

"You could always have lived with us at any time, Rose. Our place is your home as much as Corstorphine is. Sally and I think so anyway."

Father and daughter hugged and then Rose waved until her dad's car turned the corner out from her street. She felt at a loose end now, but there was cleaning to be done in the flat if the others would allow her to help. They needed to have it spotless in order to get their rent deposits refunded. She could tackle the cooker or the kitchen cupboards, that wouldn't require too much bending. She walked slowly up the drive. She'd miss the freedom of being in Bristol and living with people of her own age. However, she appreciated the fact that both of her parents had rallied to support her. And she was probably going to need their help for some time to come.

Marion

This weekend Marion's aim was to clear out the remaining belongings from Betty's house in Joppa. The 'For Sale' sign was due to go up next week and the estate agent had recommended that there be no clutter left behind when viewing commenced. She planned to leave the furniture in place, but to empty all of the cupboards and drawers and clear the surfaces and shelves. She'd previously made good progress with the upstairs bedrooms, the kitchen and the dining room, and most of the belongings from the downstairs bedroom had been moved when Betty had come to stay in Corstorphine. However, there were still a lot of clothes hanging in various cupboards throughout the house and all of the boxes that Douglas had brought down from the loft were stacked up in the lounge unopened. She decided to tackle those first.

She'd donned old clothes as she knew that the boxes were dusty. She armed herself with a duster, a brush and dustpan, scissors and a roll of plastic bin bags, and steeled herself to tackle the first box. She brushed a layer of gritty powder from the top and slipped the scissor blades under the adhesive tape. As the box flap was freed it caused an explosion of dust to rise, resulting in a sneezing fit for Marion. After blowing her nose into a tissue, Marion lifted the flap fully to meet the intense blue stare of a Sindy doll. Sindy was wearing a bright yellow jumpsuit with matching shoes and was lying on a thick mattress made from dozens of customised outfits. Marion remembered how she'd saved her pocket money, or money given as presents for her birthday or at Christmas, and then gone to the toy shop to choose another set of clothes for the doll. In addition to this Betty had fashioned amazing creations from material left over from her dressmaking. So Sindy had everything she could ever need, from bridal wear to baby doll pyjamas, smart business suits to swimsuits. Paul also had a sizable wardrobe but it wasn't as extensive as Sindy's. The couple had a resurrection when Rose came of an age to play with them. But they'd been consigned to the attic for eight or more years now. Marion's fingers lingered over the smoothness of an emerald satin cocktail dress with black beading around the neckline, one of Betty's designs. She'd forgotten the care that her mum had taken over the tiny outfits. She put everything back into the box. Should she give it all away to charity or keep hold of it for Rose's baby? She supposed it might depend on whether the baby was a girl. While she didn't want to stereotype children, she couldn't imagine that a future grandson would be very interested in the dolls and their clothes. She decided to hang onto the dolls in the meantime and placed the box in the hall to be taken back to Corstorphine. She had a capacious attic where it could easily be stored for a while.

In box number two she discovered musical scores. Some of the music was bound in hardback, but the majority had yellowing floppy covers. She flicked through the scores. Most of the music was for choral arrangements or songs for soprano voice, but there were also some pieces for solo piano. She decided to take all of it to the paper recycling and placed the box on the other side of the hall from the one containing the dolls. She sighed. This was very time-consuming. She'd hardly started out and it was already nearly lunchtime. She'd make herself look at two more boxes before she allowed herself a break to eat her sandwiches.

The next two boxes both contained photographs of all descriptions. Some were studio portraits, loose and in frames. The older ones were in black and white but there was a collection of coloured school photographs featuring Douglas and herself and also some of Rose. She uncovered old albums containing small greyish pictures held in place by triangular papers at the corners. She recognised some of the people: her grandparents, Auntie Peggy and Betty as children and young adults, and then her dad as a young man. But other photos of both people and places were a mystery to her. She'd better take everything here home with her; it would take time to create some kind of order from the jumble. Maybe Auntie Peggy could help to identify some of the subjects and perhaps she'd like to have a selection of the photos. Marion put both of the boxes into the hall and then collected her bag which contained her sandwiches. She decided to go out into the back garden to enjoy the sunshine while she ate her picnic. She settled herself on the wooden bench that had been a present to her dad from his colleagues when he retired. She'd arranged for a gardener to continue to cut the grass and tidy the hedges and flower beds until the house was sold, and on looking around she was pleased to note that everything looked neat and well cared for. As she munched on a cheese and pickle sandwich she became aware of a face looking at her from over the hedge. She waved and called out, "Hello Rita. How are you?"

"Oh, I'm fine, dear. I heard some noises from the house and I thought it was your car out front. How's Betty these days?"

"She's settled in well at Hilltop, but she's definitely getting more confused."

"That's a shame, dear. It's a pity that it's so far away or I would have come to visit but it would take me over an hour each way on the bus and it's up that steep hill."

"Don't worry, Rita, it's nice of you to think of it, but she probably wouldn't know who you are anymore."

"Oh dear, I hadn't thought of that. So, is the house going to be sold now?"

"Yes, hopefully. It's going on the market next week that's why I'm trying to clear the decks a bit, but it's hard work."

"Aye, it's not easy to tidy away the belongings from a lifetime."

"I've got a friend coming to give me a hand tomorrow, so maybe I'll do better then."

"Well, why don't you both come in at lunchtime and I'll make some sandwiches and coffee?"

"That would be very nice. I've promised to take her out for dinner tomorrow night as a payback for her help, but lunch would be good."

"Right. I'll let you enjoy your break but I'll see you again tomorrow. Just come in by the back door when you're ready."

"OK, thank you. See you tomorrow."

Marion felt cheered by the encounter with Rita and was glad that she'd have Jenny's company tomorrow. Rosemary had warned her that she shouldn't tackle too much on her own. And she didn't just mean the house clearance. She'd recognised Marion's tendency to keep worries and strong emotions bottled up inside. This was something that Marion had been doing for years now, one of her ways of surviving after Angus left. But the habit caused her to have sleepless nights and headaches; it wasn't good for Marion. If she wanted to move on she had to begin trusting in other people again and Rosemary had recommended that Marion try to share some of these issues with her close friends. She'd set her a goal of one disclosure before their next session. Marion was hoping that tomorrow she might be able to open up in some way to Jenny. As she was mulling this over, there was a loud whirring by her left ear and a robin fluttered past, then landed to stand on the path only two feet beyond her left shoe. It cocked its head to one side and regarded her with lively black eyes.

"Hello. Are you missing the supply of crumbs and seeds from my mum?" she asked it, breaking off a corner of cheese and dropping it onto the path in front of her. The bird hopped twice and pecked up the food. Marion wondered how its tiny legs managed to support it, they looked so fragile. It gave her another appraising glance.

"I'll give you some crumbs once I've finished," she told it, and it hopped onto the grass and over towards the flower bed as if it understood her.

I'm getting as daft as my mum, talking to the birds, she thought.

But once she'd finished eating she was careful to shake out the crumbs from her sandwich bag and brush down her lap, leaving a feast for the robin. She paused on the doorstep before she returned into the house and on looking back could see that the bird was already busily pecking at the paving stones around the bench.

On Sunday morning Marion set out to drive to Joppa again but this time her route took her via Ravelston Dykes where Jenny lived. She'd called Jenny as she left Corstorphine and her friend was standing waiting by her garden gate.

"Hello. How's it going?" Jenny enquired as she settled herself into the passenger seat.

"Pretty well," Marion replied and reported on her progress from the previous day. She'd made better inroads into sorting the boxes in the afternoon – finding china and ornaments that could be taken to a charity shop and old faded curtains and bedspreads that joined the music scores and an additional three boxes of old books for recycling.

"I left at four and drove via the British Heart Foundation shop in Portobello and then the dump at Seafield. I was quite efficient really."

"OK, so what's in store for me today?"

"Well, I thought I'd ask you to sort through the clothes that are still there. Work out what can go to charity and what's to be binned. Check through the pockets and for any jewellery. There are a few handbags too and lots of shoes. I'll carry on with the boxes."

"OK. Does Betty have all the clothes that she needs at Hilltop?"

"Yes, definitely. Probably more than she needs. She had masses of outfits and rarely threw anything out in case it would come back into fashion, or could be adapted in some way. Wait until you see the cupboards."

"Fine, I'm sure I'll cope. So, how's it going with your new lodger?"

Jenny was referring to the fact that Marion had recently invited Nyaga to come and stay with her. After she'd accepted the new job at Hilltop, Nyaga had mentioned to Marion that she might move flat to help cut down on travelling time. Marion found the words were out of her mouth without planning or forethought – "Why don't you come and stay with me? I've got a spare room now that Mum has moved out."

And so three weeks ago Nyaga had come to live with Marion.

"Actually, it's working out very well. I hadn't admitted it to myself before, but I don't really like living on my own. I'd been missing Mum and Rose. Nyaga and I are both busy, so some days we don't see each other at all. But so far we've been eating together a couple of times a week if we know we'll both be home. We agree that whoever is going to be back first does the cooking. It's lovely to be welcomed by a home-cooked meal after a harassing day. And a new experience for me."

"Mmm, it would be a novel experience for me too. I'm glad it's suiting you both. And you'll have Rose home soon. How will she feel about Nyaga moving in?"

"In fact she's travelling up tomorrow. She seems to really like Nyaga and was quite excited about her coming to live with us."

"And how's she been keeping?"

"She seems to be absolutely fine, no pregnancy complications and she's done well in her coursework. She doesn't have her exam results back yet, but she thinks they went OK."

Then, mindful of Rosemary's task, she ventured, "I'm amazed at how cheerful she is too, managing to stay positive and take things in her stride, but I can't help worrying that it'll all crumble after she's had the baby. What if she gets postnatal depression like we did?"

Marion hated to remember those terrible dark days. Although she was a much-wanted baby, when Rose was born Marion felt constantly anxious and worried that she wasn't up to the task of caring for her. Because her nervousness concentrated around the baby, at the time she couldn't feel that she loved her new daughter unreservedly. That gave her a huge burden of guilt. She was a bad mother and nothing that she did felt good enough. As a consequence of the illness Marion couldn't work out how anything she did would change the situation, and therefore she gradually became totally passive. She wanted to do nothing and to disappear. It became a huge effort to get out of bed, and once she was up she often couldn't manage to wash, or dress in her day clothes. She stopped eating, and lost a lot of weight as she was still trying to breastfeed Rose. It took months of medication and therapy to feel well again. Throughout that time she relied heavily on help from Angus, her parents, the health visitor, her psychologist Rosemary and the other women that she met at the support group, Jenny in particular. Now Jenny's voice interrupted her reverie, responding to her question.

"Well, I think Rose might have a slightly higher risk because of your history, but she's a different character, Marion. And anyway, if you're aware of the risk and looking out for any signs, she'd get prompt treatment. You know, I wasn't nearly as bad after Mhairi as I'd been with Callum, and I think it was mainly down to Martin looking out for the symptoms and then my GP starting me on treatment immediately."

"Yes, I'm sure you're right."

Marion felt that Jenny's comment made sense.

"It should certainly be lively enough in your house once the baby arrives on the scene. Then you won't be lonely. You might be trying to escape for some peace and quiet."

"Maybe. Who knows? Here we are now."

Marion parked in front of her mum's house.

"I forgot to mention that Mum's next-door neighbour Rita has invited us in for sandwiches and coffee at lunchtime."

"I hope that's not the meal out that you promised me."

"Oh no, of course not. Rita was just being nice and looking for some company. I booked us a table at Blonde for six thirty. That'll be your reward."

"Yummy. Well, let's get cracking." And Jenny opened the car door.

"Now Rose is home. That must be lovely." Rosemary opened their discussion at Marion's weekly therapy session.

"Yes, she seems really well and she came laden with gifts from her friends at uni; they'd held a surprise baby shower for her. Between those presents and Nyaga's knitting she's got a start on things for the baby, but we'll need to go shopping soon for some of the other stuff she needs – a cot, a car seat and a pram of some sort."

"And how did you get on with your task for the week?"

Marion reported on clearing out Betty's house and her chat with Jenny.

"So you shared your worry about Rose with your friend, that was good. How did you feel having done that?"

Marion was subjected to Rosemary's intense scrutiny.

"Well, it did help, because Jenny's had the experience of postnatal depression so her view has validity for me. And she knows Rose so well too."

"And do you think you'd be able to consult her again? For instance, could you confide in Jenny if you began to suspect that Rose was beginning to display symptoms of depression after the baby comes?"

"Oh yes, definitely."

"It seems that Jenny's a good support for you."

"Yes, we've been close since our kids were small. Her help on Sunday made much lighter work of the house clearance too."

"Yes, I think it makes it easier if you have a companion for that kind of task, I'm glad you asked her for assistance. How are things with your mum?"

"She's just the same physically, but her dementia seems to be progressing. She really doesn't know who I am now, and she's stopped trying to hide it. Before when she was having difficulty placing me she'd try to make some kind of social connection, ask if she'd met me at the church or something like that. Now she just looks at me blankly."

"Difficult for you," Rosemary sympathised.

"Yes."

"And are you feeling warmer towards her again?"

"Well, it's hard to get over the feelings because the woman I'm visiting isn't the same character as the one who was unfaithful to my dad, and there's no way I can talk to her about it. I probably just have to let it go. In a way it lets me off the hook a bit."

"In what way?"

"Well, I think I gave myself a hard time about my marriage failing because I was measuring it against my parents' perfect example. But now I know that wasn't the case, maybe I don't need to be so perfect either."

"An interesting observation. And your current thoughts about Angus?"

"Oh, I don't know, not so different I don't think. I still think that we might have had a chance to fix things between us if he'd waited around until my depression was fully treated. But I don't really know that. Maybe we were always unsuited and would have broken up eventually anyway. I'm probably going to have to see him soon. Once Rose has the baby he's bound to visit and I don't suppose I'll be able to avoid him totally."

"Maybe that will be a positive thing. When you actually see him, your emotions could be different from what you expect. When did you last see him?"

"Oh, about eight years ago, and only very briefly when I dropped Rose off at his house."

"That's a long time. You've probably held onto an outdated picture of him in your mind and then elaborated on it over the years. I'm sure he'll have changed. Perhaps he won't spark the same feelings as before."

Marion hoped that this would be the case.

<hr />

Marion heard a tentative knock at her door. She was munching on a tuna and sweetcorn sandwich, so had to chew quickly and swallow before calling, "Come in."

Laura, the current medical student attached to the practice, put her head around the edge of the door. She was fair and slight and spoke with a strong Northern Irish accent.

"Dr Wallace, you said you'd be OK to meet up after lunch?"

"Yes, sure. Come on in, I'm running a bit behind, still writing up my visits. Can you give me a few seconds to finish this? Then I'm all yours."

Laura settled herself into the chair that was placed beside the desk for patients and began to flick through some papers she had brought with her while Marion resumed tapping on the computer keyboard and chewing her lunch. A few minutes later she minimised the screen, wiped her hands on a tissue and swung her swivel seat to face her visitor.

"So, tell me how you got on."

The practice accommodated third year medical students for a month at a time, giving them an introduction to general practice. During their attachment they had to complete a small project. There was a list of suggested topics, or the student could follow a theme that interested them. Laura had chosen to look at problems encountered by families with a relative suffering from a chronic health condition. Hari, who mentored the students, had asked Marion if she could think of any patients who would be happy to talk to Laura and she'd suggested Mr Dickson, whose wife remained in Liberton Hospital, and Mrs Thomson who was still nursing her husband in their dining room.

"Well, both of the relatives were very happy to see me and have a chat. Mr Dickson was delightful, really courteous, an old-fashioned gentleman. The focus of his day is the visit to see his wife, although he does take one day off; apparently a cousin visits on a Wednesday. His son drives him there on a Sunday but on the other five days it's a complicated journey with two buses and a substantial walk. I did it myself when I went to see Mrs Dickson; it must be very tiring for a man of his age and he goes in all weathers too."

"Did he complain about it?"

"No, not one bit. He said he has lots of time and he wants to spend as much of it as he can with his wife while she's still with him."

"And how was Mrs Dickson? I haven't seen her since her second stroke."

"She seemed quite contented and smiled a lot; she's not able to talk. Though the whole time I was there she clung onto my hand really tight; I almost had to prise myself free when I went to leave. So maybe there's a bit of anxiety underneath."

"And what did you make of the Thomsons?"

"Mrs Thomson was exhausting, just full of nervous energy and babbling non-stop. She wanted me to know how well she was coping and how wonderfully everything was going."

"Did you think she was well in herself?"

"She looked very thin and worn out."

"And Mr Thomson?"

"He was pretty dozy, he opened his eyes once or twice, but I'm not sure if he knew I was there or who I was."

"So, what were your conclusions?"

"Well, when you first described the different situations, I thought that the patient being at home must surely be the best outcome. After visiting it looked as though both of the invalids were well looked after, and that both of the spouses were worn out, Mrs Thomson probably more so. So now I'm not so sure."

"Of course the ability to cope depends on each person's character but I worry about how long Mrs Thomson can keep this up for. There's no way of predicting Mr Thomson's life span, he's been back home for about three months now. She's doing a marvellous job, but at a cost to her own health. However, she wasn't at all happy when he was in hospital and we have to support her as well as we can. Do you have some other families to see?"

"Yes, I'm going to see the Gourleys tomorrow. They have a teenage boy with cerebral palsy, and also the Smiths. Mrs Smith has MS. I think that probably four cases will be enough to write up and compare."

"Good. I'm sure Hari will keep you right."

"Thanks for suggesting the cases and for checking that they'd be happy to see me."

"No trouble. What are you up to this afternoon?"

"I'm sitting in with Dr Choudhury for his surgery, so I'd better be getting along."

Marion smiled at the young woman as she left. She pondered over the 'home's best' argument. It seemed to her that often there were no ideal options and so you just had to choose whichever solution appeared to be the least bad.

Nyaga

K6, *yfwd, K2tog, K4; rep from * to end.

Nyaga began to knit another row of the lacy white cardigan intended for Rose's baby. Nyaga was convinced that the baby would be a girl but if Rose knew, she wasn't giving it away. So she was sticking to white wool, although this pattern had a row of eyelets underneath the yoke where a pink or blue ribbon could be threaded later, once the mystery was revealed.

When she'd finished the row, Nyaga looked at her watch. She should make a round to check on the residents in another five minutes. She enjoyed the night shifts at Hilltop. The atmosphere was hushed and there was an aura of warmth and security. Occasionally a resident would wander and she'd lead them back to bed, or if they were wakeful she'd make them a cup of tea or hot chocolate and chat to them for a while. There were a lot of toilet calls but there was another staff member with her, so between them they could easily cope.

She got up now and began her round. She knocked gently on each door and then entered quietly. In most rooms there was only the sound of snoring or deep breathing. Nan was awake but didn't need to use the toilet or want anything to drink, so Nyaga tucked the downie snugly around and tiptoed out into the hall. When she returned to the office Tracey, the other helper, was there.

"All OK?" she asked.

"Yes, all quiet. Nan is awake, but didn't want anything."

"I'll pop in on her again in a wee while."

Nyaga picked up her knitting again.

"When's your friend's baby due?"

"In about three weeks."

"Did you ask the boss yet about chumming her?"

"Yes. She was very good about it and said that if necessary she'd come in and cover for me herself."

"Wow, you must be Miss Popular."

"Mmm."

Nyaga had been surprised but pleased when Rose had approached her last week to ask if she'd be her companion during labour.

"My midwife suggested I ask a friend or relative since I don't have a partner," Rose explained.

"But won't you want your mum?" Nyaga had asked.

"Well, you know, Mum's been great. But I just feel she might be too closely involved with me to be a good help. I'd worry the whole time that I was doing it all wrong, or that she was going to take over from the midwife and tell them what to do."

"I'm sure she wouldn't do that."

"Maybe not, but I might be needier, revert to being like a wee girl if she was there. I think I'd be able to be more relaxed with you."

"Well, I'm honoured and I'm happy to say yes on two conditions. One, that I can get away from my work. It might not be easy at short notice, but I'll ask my manager. And two, you make sure it's OK with Marion."

"Cool, I'll speak to my mum. And I hope you won't regret saying yes, I'll probably be a nightmare. I'm beginning to get really scared about it all."

"Every woman is nervous." Nyaga had tried to be reassuring. "I'm sure you'll do just fine."

Nyaga's life had changed completely since the beginning of the year, and only for the better. She loved her new job. Dellview had been fine, but Hilltop was much smaller and also homelier. She liked the old house with its quirky rooms and elegant furnishing. The garden was wonderful and she felt that it was so beneficial for the residents to be able to walk there and to sit out in the sun on a good day, improving their mobility and getting a dose of vitamin D. She was always encouraging them to make the most of the facility.

When Marion had asked her to come and stay she'd had mixed feelings. A huge part of her had wanted to agree immediately. Who wouldn't want to live in such a lovely environment? But she'd also had some reservations. What was Marion's motive? Was she really just being friendly or did she think that Nyaga was some sort of a charity case? Her pride bristled; she'd insist on paying her way if she agreed to the arrangement.

"The room is empty now that Mum's at Hilltop and to be honest I could do with the company," Marion had admitted.

"What would you want for the rent?" Nyaga had asked.

"I don't need any rent, but a contribution for groceries would be good. Take some time to think about it and let me know."

Nyaga had slept on the offer and when she woke up in her flat the next morning she knew immediately that she should accept the invitation. After all she could also benefit from some regular companionship. Her life had been improved by better health, some friends, the library and a new job but this flat was still dreary and soul-sapping. She calculated a monthly amount that was less than her current rent but more than what she usually allowed for provisions. When she'd phoned Marion to agree to the arrangement and had named her suggested payment there had been no quibble from her new landlady.

"That would be fine. When do you want to move in?"

So now she had nicer lodgings and a better job. She was also earning more and paying less for subsistence. She felt very fortunate and was squirrelling away the extra money, saving for her return to Botswana.

Being so far away from home was still tough, and last week especially so as it had been Lesedi's birthday. Nyaga had planned her strategy well ahead and had thought that she'd be able to cope OK. She arranged a shopping trip with Rose in plenty of time to post her gifts to Lesedi. Rose was very helpful, suggesting that they begin with a visit to the toy department at Jenners. Nyaga hadn't ventured into the department store before. The building was ornate and had looked too imposing to Nyaga. She'd been intimidated, but had also reckoned that everything inside would be well beyond her budget anyway. Rose led her through the perfumed haze of the cosmetics section into the central hall. She described how special it looked at Christmas time when a huge decorated tree filled the space, stretching up to the highest gallery. The stairway down to the basement was quite grand, with wide carpeted steps and carved wooden bannisters, and it felt to Nyaga that she was entering a magical world, there were so many amazing toys on display. She could imagine how wonderful it must seem to a child's eyes and wished that Lesedi could be there with them. It took a long time to choose something that they thought would appeal to Lesedi without it being too heavy to post. Eventually they'd settled on a girly Lego hair salon set and a cuddly Highland cow soft toy. Their next stop was Marks and Spencer to look at clothes. They chose a navy, sailor-style mini-dress with matching short stripy leggings for everyday wear and an elegant ivory party dress embellished with a scattering of beads and sequins. Of course in both shops a few baby toys and clothes proved to be irresistible and also found their way into their shopping bags. And there were several stops for Rose to visit toilets and a much-needed reviving café break.

On the day of Lesedi's birthday Nyaga had arranged to work an early shift so that she was at home by late afternoon to speak with Lesedi on Skype. Lesedi was very excited, bouncing and fidgeting while chatting to her mum. She remembered her manners, though, and politely thanked Nyaga, saying how much she'd loved the presents that her mum had sent. Nyaga gazed at Lesedi, proudly wearing her party dress, and listened to her chatter about her party. She mentioned names of classmates from school and told her mum all about Pass-the-Parcel and another game that had involved chasing balloons. Her inability to put faces to the names of Lesedi's new friends and not being a part of the events had made Nyaga feel rotten that day. After the call was over she'd retreated to her room and shed bitter tears. In her interaction with Lesedi she'd felt more like a benefactor aunt, not the girl's mother.

Since then Nyaga had made a more definite plan for going home. Sure, she'd thought about it before and had mentioned to a few people that she'd like to be back home by Christmas, but now she had dates in mind. She wanted to be in Gaborone at the beginning of December in time for the end of school. That way she could attend any end-of-term concerts and sports events. Then she could spend the long summer holiday re-forming her bond with Lesedi. They might even take a trip somewhere; she should have enough money saved to be able to afford that. And once school began again in January she'd look for a job. It felt good to have made these decisions; she now had a firm target to aim for.

While Nyaga had been musing and knitting the day was quickly lightening and loud chirping and twittering from the birds in the garden could be heard through the open window. Used to living near the tropics where days were always much the same length, Nyaga found the change in the amount of daylight to be a strange phenomenon. The light from the early dawns not only roused the birds but also seemed to waken a few of the residents. She would expect to hear some of them stirring soon. Betty was often one of the early risers. Until recently she was still able to dress herself and would often appear wearing one of her colourful costume combinations looking for a cup of tea. However, on this spell of night shifts Nyaga had noticed a change. On the past two mornings Betty had emerged from her room still wearing her nightie, and with bare feet. Both times Nyaga had gently escorted her back to her room and helped her into a dressing gown and slippers before making her a cup of tea. Betty was also less chatty and there were definitely fewer of those sharp disinhibited remarks that had previously caused offence to some of the other residents. Nyaga was familiar with this diminishing of ability and fading of personality that Alzheimer's caused, as it had happened to other residents that she'd cared for. She also knew, from Marion, that the lady of the pithy comments was yet another manifestation of the disease. Betty might have thought such things before her illness, but she'd have been much too polite and tactful to voice them out loud.

At seven o'clock Nyaga began to make another review of her residents. Some were still peacefully asleep, some liked breakfast to be brought to their room and others preferred to eat in the dining room. She reached Betty's door, a little surprised that Betty hadn't surfaced yet. She knocked and opened the door, calling, "Good morning, sleepy head."

At once she stiffened, alert. Her instinct told her that something was wrong. She became aware of the sound and pattern of Betty's breathing as she crossed the room to the bed. The breaths were rough and fast, but changing pace even as Nyaga approached. Gradually slowing, then an eerie silence as Betty's respiration stopped. Nyaga counted. After fifteen seconds the fast breathing began again.

Nyaga pulled back Betty's downie and tried to rouse her, although she knew from the pattern of breathing that she was unlikely to respond. She called loudly, shook Betty by the shoulder, pinched her earlobe and rubbed hard on her sternum. Nothing.

Nyaga left the room and hurried to the office.

"Something wrong?" Tracey asked noticing Nyaga's expression and reading the urgency in her pace.

"Yes, it's Betty. I think she must have had a huge stroke. I'm going to call Marion and the GP."

"She was OK when I last looked in."

"How long ago was that?"

"At six."

"Did you go right into the room?" Nyaga asked, while dialling Marion's number.

"No, I just looked from the door, she seemed fine, peaceful."

The phone was ringing and then Marion picked up, sounding sleepy. It was a Wednesday, her day off, so she wouldn't have set her alarm early today.

"Hi Marion. It's Nyaga, I'm sorry to wake you, but you need to come to Hilltop. I think Betty's had a big stroke. I just discovered that she's not right. She's got Cheyne-Stokes resps and she's unresponsive. I'll call the GP right now."

Marion

The room was dimly lit. Soft light filtered through closed curtains which fluttered gently in a draught from the window which had been left ajar. A candle guttered faintly, releasing a vanilla scent. The slow movement of the Mozart clarinet concerto was playing at low volume as Marion kept vigil by Betty's bed. She held Betty's hand and spoke quietly from time to time as subjects came into her head. There was a possibility that Betty was cognisant and would know that someone was there keeping her company. The cyclical pattern of her periodic breathing still held centre stage in the room. At each halt Marion found that she also held her own breath, waiting to see if Betty's respiration would resume. She'd been sitting for two hours now and there were signs that Betty was weakening. Her breaths were shallower, the hand that Marion clasped was colder and the fingertips had a blueish tinge.

Betty's GP had arrived at Hilltop shortly after Marion, and after he'd made his assessment both had agreed that moving Betty would not be of any benefit to her. Something catastrophic had occurred in her brain, a bleed or an infarct, and it was obvious that it would be fatal. Their main aim now should be to keep Betty comfortable.

Nyaga had offered to stay on after her shift had finished, but Marion had asked her to go back to the house in order to tell Rose what had happened. Marion wasn't sure if Rose would have heard the phone or her own departure. In this late stage of pregnancy her nights were often restless, leaving her dozy when everyone else was waking up. The chances were that she was oblivious to the current crisis. It would be better for Rose to hear the news in person from Nyaga than to receive a phone call or text message. Marion also asked Nyaga if she or Rose could alert Peggy to Betty's condition in case she wanted to come and see her.

"I'm not sure what I should do about Douglas, though," she spoke out loud to Betty. "They're seven hours behind us just now, which makes it two thirty in the morning there."

Even if he wanted to come, he's not going to get here before Mum dies, she thought, but didn't say aloud.

"I think we'd be better to let him sleep and phone first thing in the morning before he leaves for work. Maybe about two o'clock our time."

She paused for one of Betty's apnoeic phases, twenty seconds. The chugging, fast breathing resumed; that was a long one.

"I'm sure he'll come over," she resumed her soliloquy. "And thinking of that, I realise that I've 'forgotten' to tell him about Rose. Now, what would Rosemary make of that particular lapse? Maybe I'm not as comfortable with having a young, unmarried, pregnant daughter as I'd like some people to think. Well, I have to admit that, although I'm proud of the way that she's coping, it's not what I'd ever have wished for her. And I'm so used to thinking of Douglas as being unapproachable and judgemental. We're getting on better now since his last visit, after you went wandering and I learned about your secret past. But old habits die hard."

Another pause. Twelve seconds. She studied Betty's face as she talked to her. Her skin was remarkably well preserved and free of wrinkles for her age. Apart from gardening, she hadn't spent much time out of doors in the sun and had always worn a hat to shade her face. Both eyes were closed, but Marion knew that their bright blue colour had faded in recent years to a more subdued greyish shade. The pixie haircut had been squashed up on one side where she'd been sleeping on it, making a fuzzy ridge on the left side of her head. She was currently lying on her back – the care staff had been altering her position every two hours – and her nose stood out sharp and angular above her gaping mouth, a black hole from which the rasping, hypnotic breathing emerged.

"Maybe they'll all come. It's a long time since we saw Mandy and the kids. I don't think I've seen them since before Dad died. You made a trip out to visit shortly after that, didn't you? But that was nearly six years ago now. Kids change a lot in that sort of time. I'm sure you've got some recent photos somewhere. I'll have a look."

Marion relinquished Betty's hand and stood up, rummaging to find Betty's photograph album. She discovered it on the top shelf of the wardrobe and brought it back over to the bed just as Betty commenced another surge of rapid breathing.

"Here they are, that's what I was looking for. I think these were taken about four months ago. Gregor must be seventeen now, and he's definitely got the Wallace colouring, looks just like Douglas and me. Caitlin is completely different, more like Mandy with that dark blonde hair. Douglas mentioned recently that she's keen on gymnastics and had won a regional competition. It would be nice to see them. Hello?"

There was a soft tap on the door and Aileen put her head into the room.

"How are you doing? Would you like a break or a cup of tea?"

"Tea would be lovely."

"OK, I'll bring you a cup. Also, there's a message from Rose. She'll be along soon."

∞

Rose arrived an hour later. Her bump, now tense and very round, preceded her into the room. The bottle-green T-shirt dress that she was wearing, although designed for maternity wear, seemed clingier than some of her other outfits and accentuated her condition. She didn't look her best. Her long dark hair had been scraped back hastily into a ponytail. Red, puffy eyes showed signs of recent crying and her face was marked by multiple dark pigmented splodges, the chloasma of pregnancy. She did manage to produce a watery smile for Marion.

"Hi Mum. How is she?"

"Rose, come on in and sit here." Marion vacated her position.

"Nyaga explained to me about the breathing."

"Yes, it sounds bad to us, but Gran won't be distressed by it. She's very comfortable. We're not sure if she knows that we're here, but I've been talking to her and holding her hand to keep her company."

"Should I say something to her?" Rose sounded unsure.

"That would be a great idea. I could do with a loo break and while I'm out I'll find another chair and join you shortly."

As she left the room she saw Rose pick up Betty's hand.

"It's Rose, Gran. I'd have been here sooner to see you, but Nyaga had trouble waking me up. The baby was turning somersaults all night so I didn't get properly to sleep until about six o'clock and then..." The rest was muffled as Marion gently closed the door. She stretched and walked along the corridor to the toilet.

Next she went to look for Aileen. The office was empty and she found her in the lounge where she was assisting one of the residents with filling out a form.

"Rose is spelling me for a bit. I don't think it'll be much longer."

"OK, Marion. Just let me know if you need anything. I'll get someone to bring you a jug of water."

"Is there another chair we can use?"

"Sure, you can take one from the dining room."

When she returned carrying the chair Rose seemed to have adopted an American accent.

"… done your duty…"

She stopped mid-sentence as she noticed Marion's arrival.

"Oh, I was demonstrating to Gran how I had to talk for the play, since she couldn't come to see it," she explained, seeming embarrassed.

"She'd have been very proud to see you perform in a real theatre. Remember how much she enjoyed coming to your school productions?"

"Yes, but she always gave an honest opinion too. No getting away with the odd duff note when Gran was in the audience. Mum, how old is Gran now?"

"She's seventy-six."

"That's not so very old, is it? My other gran was eighty last year. We had a big party for her. She's still pretty fit, does country dancing every week."

Rose hardly ever mentioned the other side of her family and so Marion sometimes forgot that Rose was also a member of the MacMillan clan. Was her reticence tactful? Or had it just been easier for Rose to compartmentalise her relationship with each parent? Angus was the youngest of four brothers, so there was quite a crowd when the whole family congregated. She wondered how the MacMillan grandparents had reacted to Rose's pregnancy.

"So Gran was twenty-five when you were born? That's not much older than I'll be."

"No, I suppose it isn't."

"You were thirty-one, though."

"Yes. I wanted to get established in my career before taking a maternity break. I wouldn't have been entitled to paid maternity cover if I'd gone off too soon after joining the partnership."

There was a lapse in their conversation which allowed Betty's breathing to become their focus again. In the silence of an apnoeic phase Marion noticed that the CD must have finished.

"Why don't you sing something? Gran would like that," she suggested to Rose.

"What sort of thing?"

"How about some of the Scottish songs you learned at school?"

Rose thought for a while then began softly,
"Bheir me o, horo van o,
Bheir me o, horo van ee.
Bheir me o, oro o ho,
Sad am I without thee."

Her voice was sweet and true and it gained a little in volume as she sang through the verses. Marion closed her eyes and allowed herself to sink back into her chair, relaxing. She hoped that Betty was able to hear the song, it was one of her favourites.

Peggy joined them at eleven fifteen, moving to Marion's place at the bedside. Ten minutes later Nyaga reappeared.

"Do you mind if I sit with you?" she asked. "I tried to sleep, but it wouldn't come. I wanted to be with my friends."

"Of course you're welcome," Marion reassured her. "You've met Peggy before, haven't you?"

"Yes. She's been a regular visitor," Nyaga replied. She crossed the room to embrace Peggy. "I'll find another chair."

When she returned she also brought a tray with sandwiches and mugs of tea.

"Don't forget to eat. You didn't have any breakfast, Marion, and Rose didn't manage much either."

"It's good we've got you to look after us." Rose smiled up at Nyaga as she selected a sandwich.

"Her breathing is fainter than it was," Nyaga commented quietly.

"Yes, she's getting weaker," Marion agreed in a whisper.

The women talked to Betty and conversed among themselves, always mindful of steering away from talk of illness or death in case Betty was listening. From time to time Rose gave them another song from her Scottish repertoire and Nyaga introduced a couple of Botswanan folk melodies in her deeper contralto voice.

At ten to two Betty's breathing failed to resume after the pause. The women waited, counting the seconds in case they were mistaken. But there was silence in the room.

Rose

Rose's feet were aching. She'd had to force them into a pair of smart shoes despite end-of-pregnancy puffiness, and now she'd been standing at the funeral reception being polite for what seemed like hours. She tried to concentrate on what the lady beside her was saying.

"Your grandma was so talented and chic. She could make everyone look their best with her advice on styles and colours and sometimes a little alteration. We all missed her so much when she retired."

"Well, I remember she was good at fancy dress outfits too, for Halloween," Rose contributed.

"Yes, I'm sure she would be, and such a shame that she got that Alzheimer's, cruel for someone who was so sharp."

"Yes, it certainly changed her. Excuse me, do you mind if I find a seat? All of this standing is a strain on my back."

"Of course. Yes, dear, you have to look after yourself in your condition. When is the happy day?"

"In about two weeks." Rose gave the woman a little wave as

she headed for one of the chairs at the end of the room. Her back was bothering her today. It had been sore ever since she'd woken up, and the standing around seemed to be aggravating it.

"Whew," she sighed as she sat down; she felt about a hundred years old.

"Hi, you OK?" It was Caitlin, her young cousin, now morphed into Cate. Rose had forgotten that her Canadian cousins would be growing up on the other side of the Atlantic. Cate was now a very feminine, confident teenager, not the tomboy nine-year-old she remembered from their last meeting.

"I'm a bit whacked. Sore feet, sore back. A seat will help."

"Do you want me to fetch you a drink or some of those little snacks?"

"Yes, go on. Get me a selection and a glass of water. You don't mind?" Rose didn't want to sound too bossy.

"No, glad to help out." Cate threaded her way through the groups of people to the buffet table at the other end of the room.

Rose gazed out of the large bay window next to her; it overlooked a series of gardens behind the smart New Town hotel. The sun was shining and lots of rose bushes were in bloom in the flower beds below. She and Marion had chosen a large bouquet of scented roses as their floral tribute for Betty. Gran had always liked the perfumed varieties and had grown them in her garden. She'd miss her gran. Even if her personality had changed, there was still a 'granness' that remained at her core. Everyone was saying how the stroke was a blessing, taking Gran away suddenly instead of the long, slow decline and possible indignity of progressive dementia. Maybe it was selfish, but Rose wished that Gran had hung around longer.

"Here we are." Cate in her role as waitress proffered a plate with a selection of canapés and a glass of iced water. She sat down next to Rose.

"Is it kicking much?" she asked.

"Not so much today. Maybe after I eat something it'll wake up, food often has that effect. I'll let you feel if it starts up."

Cate smiled.

"I guess it must feel real strange."

Cate seemed to be fascinated by her pregnancy and had bombarded Rose with questions when the families first met up yesterday. Mandy had quickly called her off.

Probably doesn't think that I'm a good example, Rose had thought.

The Canadians were staying just down the hill from Marion's house at the Holiday Inn by the zoo. Marion had considered having everyone squash up to make room for them at the house and then quickly decided that it wasn't practical. And they couldn't stay at Joppa as Betty's house had been sold. The speed of the sale had surprised everyone. Marion had arranged for a house-clearing firm to tidy out the remaining furniture as the buyers wanted a quick entry at the beginning of July.

"I'm missing the last week of school to be here," Cate said, swinging her legs to and fro under her chair.

"Do you mind?"

"No, not much. I'd have been real mad if I'd been away for the gymnastics training squad, but that's not until the end of July."

"Yeah, Mum said you're a good gymnast."

"I want to try to get into the regional team. Then maybe I'll get a chance to try for the national. But that's way off."

"I'd like to see you."

"Well, a lot of what I do needs apparatus, but I could show you my floor routine sometime if we can find a suitable space."

"I'd like that. What else will you do in the summer holidays?"

"We're going to Vancouver Island with Mom and Dad. We go there most summers, to a cottage that my mom's sister owns. It might be the last year that Greg comes with us. But Mom says I can bring a friend along to keep me company next year if he goes off on vacation with his own friends. That's a kinda tradition after leaving high school."

"Yeah, I did the same. We went to a Greek island. Whoops, looks like we're getting company."

An elderly man was approaching. He had a full head of floppy silver hair and was dressed conservatively enough in a mid-grey suit, apart from his flamboyantly large red paisley bow tie. Marion had encouraged people to wear colour, and not black, for Betty's funeral, as her mum had so loved wearing bright clothes herself. This gentleman was obviously following that request.

"I hope you young ladies won't object if I join you, but I need to have a rest," he announced. "Robert Gilchrist."

He proffered his right hand to each of the girls and shook with a firm grip, then sat down in a neighbouring chair.

"I'm Rose and this is Caitlin, we're Betty's granddaughters," Rose explained.

"Ah yes. Well, your grandmother was the star in my choir, a wonderful voice and a talented musician."

Despite his glowing comments about Betty, Rose thought that he sounded pompous.

"Then you'll be pleased to know that Gran retained her love of music even once her memory began to fail," Rose told him. "Listening to music always gave her pleasure." She was trying to give back her own experience of her gran in response to all of the little snippets that people at the funeral were telling her.

Suddenly she had an awful sensation. She felt that she'd wet herself. God, she hadn't done that before! She'd better get to the loo, quickly.

"Could you excuse me? I need to make a dash."

She hauled herself up from her seat and lumbered as quickly as she could go across the reception room. She was making for the entrance hall where she'd clocked the sign for the ladies' toilets when they'd arrived. She couldn't walk very fast, her ankles and feet felt so stiff and her sore back wasn't easing up at all. Once in the toilet she quickly entered a stall. When she lowered her underwear, her pants were quite damp and before she could sit down a great flood of fluid poured from her, running down her legs and splashing onto the tiled floor.

I don't think that's pee, she thought.

She heard someone else enter the toilet.

"Rose? What a weird man. What was with the bow tie? Once you left I didn't know what to say to him, made an excuse that I needed to check up on you to get away from him."

When there was no immediate reply, "Rose, are you OK?"

"Cate can you get Nyaga or my mum? I think my waters have gone."

She heard the outer toilet door slam, as she lowered herself onto the toilet. The liquor was still coming, although more of a trickle now compared with the initial gush. Then the pain in her back intensified and gripped her like a band, encompassing her whole lower abdomen and causing her to double over with its strength. She heard the door opening then Nyaga's voice.

"Rose, can you open the door?"

Rose was trying to do the breathing that she'd been taught at her antenatal class.

"Just… a… minute," she gasped.

The pain subsided and she managed to stand to unlock the cubicle, then sank back onto the toilet as more fluid leaked from her. Nyaga took the situation in at a glance – the large puddle on the floor and the white-faced, gasping girl. She stepped into the cubicle and squatted down in front of Rose, embracing her.

"Oh, Nyaga, look at the mess," Rose wailed.

"It's OK, Rose, don't worry about that. You've gone into labour. That liquor's clear, no meconium, so that's a good sign that the baby's healthy. I'm going to call a taxi to take us to the hospital and I'll ask someone to go home and collect your things to bring them on later. Cate will stay here with you until I come back."

Rose only now noticed Cate, mouth gaping, half hidden behind Nyaga.

"Cate, just stand here and hold her hand and rub her back. Have you got a watch?"

Cate nodded.

"Good. If another contraction comes tell me how many minutes since this last one. OK?"

Cate nodded again and Nyaga left them.

"Well, at least all this gloop is on the toilet floor, not on their good carpet." Cate found her voice, trying to cheer Rose up.

"It looks like you're going to meet the baby in person before you head back home," Rose said, aiming to match her cousin's upbeat comment.

The drive in the taxi was the most uncomfortable journey of Rose's life. Every bump sent a piercing jolt up into her womb. The contractions were coming every four minutes and Nyaga was trying to help her to breathe through them and relax. This was against Rose's instinct, which was to clench up tight, resisting the pain. Nyaga had managed to whisk Rose out of the hotel quickly without drawing the attention of people at the funeral party, although obviously she'd alerted Marion to what was occurring. Marion had felt torn; it would be hard to dash out of her mother's funeral gathering but maybe Rose needed her. Nyaga had reassured Marion that she had everything organised and that she'd keep in touch. It took thirty minutes to reach the maternity unit and Rose felt a huge sense of relief that now experts would be on hand to take control.

From the taxi Rose was transferred into a wheelchair and pushed along the corridor to the assessment suite. A midwife welcomed her and helped her out of her clothes and into a hospital gown, then up onto a trolley. They stopped as required for contractions.

"You're doing really well, Rose, already five centimetres dilated," she reported after her examination. "We'll take you along to Labour Ward and consider what's best to help with the pain."

"Wow, five centimetres already! You realise now that the back pain today has been the start of labour," Nyaga said.

Rose burst into tears.

"It's been a horrible day," she sobbed. "I miss my gran and I so wanted her to meet the baby. She was still clued up enough to be interested in it. She liked to feel it kicking. Lots of the other ladies did too."

Nyaga hugged her close.

"Most of the women are mums and grandmas, some of them are great-grandmas, so pregnancy is familiar to them. You're right, they do take an interest and you could still visit with the baby to see those other ladies. They'd like that."

Rose nodded, bracing herself as another contraction began to build up.

"Aaaah," she screamed. "I wish they'd hurry up with that fucking pain relief."

Twenty minutes later Rose was coping much better. The injection that she'd been given was beginning to take effect, lessening the intensity of the pain. She was still aware of the contractions but was now able to concentrate on her breathing, and between pains she could relax and chat to Nyaga and the midwife. The contractions were spaced about three minutes apart and the monitoring of the baby's heartbeat indicated that the baby appeared to be coping fine. There followed a spell of about two hours when the process seemed to be falling into a routine. Then Rose sensed that something was changing. She felt more restless again and wriggled to try and get comfortable.

"You feel like pushing, don't you?" The midwife had been observing Rose's behaviour. "Let's examine you and see if it's time."

This was the beginning of a new phase. Nyaga and the midwife supported Rose's feet when she felt a contraction coming on, she lowered her chin onto her chest and pushed as hard as she could into her bottom.

"Great, you're doing really well. Try not to waste any energy making a noise, just put it all into the pushing," the midwife instructed.

Eventually Rose felt that she might split in two, the pressure was so enormous. But at the end of that push there was a shout. "That's the head! Just one more push should do it, Rose."

Then before she could take it in there were cries of, "It's a girl!"

She got a glimpse of the baby as it was held up for her to see. It was still attached by its umbilical cord.

"We're just going to lay her down here on your tummy to cut her cord. Then we'll dry her off and wrap her up. You'll be able to hold her in a jiffy."

Then a warm bundle was placed in her arms. Rose was smiling and crying simultaneously, she was so relieved that the baby was here. The baby girl had a slick of dark hair, still held tight to her head by white, waxy vernix. Her face was pink and her eyes were open and looked dark grey in colour. They didn't seem to be quite in focus which gave the newborn a rather dazed expression. As Rose gazed, her attention fixed intently on her new daughter's face, the baby poked out her minute pink tongue.

"Oh, so you're going to be a cheeky girl, are you? Sticking your tongue out at your mum when you've only just arrived," Rose teased.

The tiny girl squirmed sufficiently to enable a hand and arm to emerge from her swaddling blanket.

"Nyaga, look how perfect her fingers are, and her tiny nails."

Rose felt that she could look at the miniature features forever. She was vaguely aware of the midwife still pulling on the other end of the cord between her legs – must be waiting for the placenta.

"So do you have a name for this wee girl?" the midwife now enquired.

"Yes. I'm calling her Beth, after my gran."

Standing under the hot shower spray was incredibly refreshing. Rose's legs felt a bit wobbly and she didn't want to think about her nether regions, she was sure they were bruised and swollen to about twice their normal size, but the hot water and shampoo were heavenly. A midwife hovered nearby in case she felt weak or faint. She escorted a revived Rose back to the postnatal ward with a promise to return in a few minutes with tea and toast.

When Rose entered the four-bedded ward she found that Marion had arrived. Her mum was sitting in an armchair cradling Beth and talking to her. Beth, now bathed and wearing a pristine white Terry-cotton babygrow suit seemed to be listening, her eyes were wide open and she was looking in the direction of Marion's face.

"Rose, there you are. I'm so proud of you. Look at this wee darling."

Marion rose from the chair and Rose fell into her embrace with Beth sandwiched between them.

"I hope you like her name," Rose said.

"Beth MacMillan. Yes, I think it suits you," Marion addressed her granddaughter again.

"Where did Nyaga go?" Rose asked looking around as she settled herself on the bed, leaning back on a stack of propped-up pillows.

"She went to the loo and to find a cold drink. I think she was being tactful and leaving me on my own for a while getting to know Beth."

"She was just such a fantastic help today. I don't know how I'd have managed without her."

"How're you feeling?"

"A bit battered and bruised and absolutely famished. The midwife said she'd bring me some toast, I hope it arrives soon. How did the end of the gathering go? Did anyone miss me?"

"A few people did ask after you. It went fine, I thought, as these things go. Did you speak to your dad yet?"

"Yes. He's gutted that he's working all this week. He arranged his holidays to start on Saturday, thinking that was still a week before the baby would arrive. So he and Sally will come up at the weekend. I'm to send him some photos. Maybe you could give Beth back to me and take a few. I'll give you my phone, it should be in this drawer."

She leaned over and produced the phone from her bedside cabinet, making sure that it was set to camera mode. Then Marion transferred baby Beth back to Rose in exchange for the mobile. Marion then proceeded to take a series of photographs which later would be saved for posterity. Those important first photographs of baby Beth, cradled by her smiling and delighted mum.

Marion

Marion needed two hands to open her front door. She put her work case down on the step, inserted her key into the Yale lock and turned it with her right hand, using her left for the lower handle. As soon as the door opened a chink she could hear the baby wailing. She sighed, picked up her bag and closed the door.

"Hi Rose, I'm home," she called.

The lounge door was ajar and the crying noises increased in volume as Rose appeared in the doorway snuggling a baby papoose to her front. Marion kissed the top of Beth's head, the only part of her which was visible. The baby's hair was dark – no redheaded genes had been passed on – and damp with the exertion of her crying.

"How was your day?" Marion asked.

"Not too bad. She just started crying at about five o'clock. She's a wee bit better in the sling and if I walk around. I made a start on cooking our dinner, but then I had to feed her and change her nappy. Nyaga's on an evening shift, so it's just the two of us."

"OK. I'll head into the kitchen and get the meal on the go. I can spell you for a bit after dinner if you like."

"Thanks, Mum."

Marion shed her shoes and jacket and washed her hands at the kitchen sink. A board with a selection of thinly sliced vegetables was on the table and a pack of salmon fillets sat by the hob. It looked like a salmon stir-fry was on the menu. Marion heated the grill and fetched the wok from the cupboard. Then she located some teriyaki sauce and noodles in the store cupboard and began to cook.

She'd forgotten how demanding a small baby could be. Beth had been a model baby until three weeks ago; then she began to cry all evening every evening. She was good at feeding, her weight gain was satisfactory and she was well otherwise, so it seemed to be a classic case of infantile colic. It was amazing how wearing the crying could become, though, especially at the end of a busy day at the surgery. No one was at their best by that time of day anyway and they all just longed for some peace and quiet. At least there were three adults living in the house so the whole burden didn't need to fall on Rose. Most nights the baby settled around midnight or shortly after. She woke up again once in the night to feed, and once sated seemed happy to go straight back to sleep.

Marion was relieved that Rose was coping so well. Once she'd been reassured that the crying didn't mean that Beth was ill, she seemed able to take it in her stride. Sometimes she got tired and tearful, but Marion had been watchful and had seen no signs of depression or a sustained low mood emerging.

All of the ingredients seemed to be cooked. Marion gave the vegetables and noodles another thorough stir then ladled the mixture onto two plates and slid a salmon fillet on top of each.

"OK, Rose, food's up," she called as she took the plates to the kitchen table. Rose appeared and filled two water glasses before sitting down.

"This smells great. I'm starving, though what's new? It seems to be a permanent state with breastfeeding." She began to eat, careful not to drop any of her hot food onto the top of Beth's head.

"Were you at the baby clinic today?" Marion asked.

"Oh yes, it was Beth's six-week check. There was a different health visitor there, covering for holidays I think. She was really nice. I told her about the colic and said that the gripe water and Infacol drops didn't seem to have made any difference at all. She thinks Beth's weight gain is good and she suggested maybe I try cutting out dairy products from my diet. Something about foreign proteins in the breast milk. What do you think?"

"I don't know how much evidence there is for that theory, but I've heard it can sometimes help. I suppose there'd be no harm in trying."

"I don't really drink milk, but I do like my cheese and yoghurt."

"And ice cream."

"Mmm, yes."

Marion and Rose both laughed. As Rose had already stated, she was constantly hungry while breastfeeding Beth. One of her 'life savers' was Ben and Jerry's Chunky Monkey ice cream. She had been known to eat a tub overnight while up feeding the baby. Despite this she'd already regained her pre-pregnancy weight and figure. The extra calories must all be going Beth's way.

"I'm sure I'd still find plenty of things I can eat and it would be worth it if Beth could be more settled."

Just at that Beth began to fuss again, whimpers rising in a crescendo to full-on bawling.

"Might she be hungry again?" Marion asked.

"No, I just fed her half an hour before you came in."

"Well, I'll take her out in the pram if you do the dishes. I'll have my coffee when I get back. I love the long summer evenings, so I might as well make the most of the light while it lasts."

Marion scooped her granddaughter out from the papoose and jiggled her on her hip. She tucked her into the pram under a soft blanket then returned for her jacket and shoes.

"See you in a bit."

"Bye Mum. I've decided, I'll definitely start that diet tomorrow."

The next day Marion had an appointment with her lawyer. The office was on the site of the former Edinburgh Royal Infirmary. It was ultra-modern with glass walls from floor to ceiling, soft pile royal blue carpets and pale wood and steel furniture. The views out over the remaining old stone hospital buildings to the Meadows and the south side of the city were amazing. Marion thought it would be distracting to actually work here. She'd spend far too much time window-gazing. Carolyn, the lawyer, returned to the room from the copying machine. Marion knew her well by now. She'd dealt with her father's estate and then set up a power of attorney for Betty as her capacity decreased. More recently she'd helped with the sale of Betty's house and now there was another estate to be settled.

"As I said, it was fortuitous that the house sale was all signed and sealed before Betty died. Otherwise it could have been postponed for some time while awaiting probate. Since that did all go through, everything should be quite straightforward. I still have a few investment valuations to confirm, then we can calculate and settle any inheritance tax. The will leaves the remainder to you and your brother fifty-fifty, as you know." Carolyn put some documents on the table in front of Marion.

"Yes, I've been thinking and I wanted to ask you about putting my share of the estate into some kind of a trust fund for Rose and Beth."

"OK, what do you envisage?"

"Well, I'd like it to be for their education. Rose still has a year of her degree to complete and may want to move on to a postgraduate qualification. She's going to find things hard enough, I don't want her to have a lot of student loans to pay off."

"Yes, I see." Carolyn was scribbling on a pad of paper as Marion spoke.

"Mum and Dad both thought that education was very important, so I think they'd be happy that their money is used for this. I wouldn't want to oversee the fund, though. Rose should have someone to contact when she needs money. And it should only be for studying or for Beth's school, or uniform, equipment she needs, or school trips. That kind of thing."

"That should be possible to arrange. I'll need to consult with a colleague, but I'm sure that we could oversee the money on your behalf."

"And if there's any left over it can go to Beth once she's twenty-five."

"Do you want all of your share from the estate to be in this trust?"

"I'd like to keep a small amount aside to give to charity. I thought St Columba's Hospice in my dad's name and Playlist for Life in my mum's name."

"I've not heard of that one?" Carolyn enquired.

"It's a music charity for dementia sufferers; they help to create a personal collection of music that's meaningful from different times in a person's life. It's been found to be enriching. Mum was very musical and I know that she still got huge enjoyment from listening to music despite her memory loss."

"Yes. OK, Marion, I'll get something drafted up about the trust fund and send it along for you to look at. We can't put any definite figures in until the estate is settled, but that shouldn't take too long."

"That's fine, there's no rush. Rose is having a year out just now, but I'd like this all to be in place before she goes back to uni next year."

"No problem. I think that's us for today then."

"Thanks." Marion collected her belongings and shook Carolyn's hand before leaving the room for the journey back down to the ground in the glass-sided lift.

In the afternoon Marion had another appointment, this time with Rosemary, her psychologist. It was her first visit since Betty's death and Beth's arrival. Rosemary came into the waiting room to find her.

"Well, Marion, such a lot has happened since your last visit. I was sorry to hear about your mum. Come and have a seat and let me know where you'd like to start."

Marion settled herself in a winged armchair.

"Since you mentioned Mum we might as well begin there. I've been feeling pretty mixed up since she died. Part of me misses her, although I've really been missing her for a while now anyway. The lady I've been visiting and looking after wasn't the same character as my mum at all. Part of me feels a huge sense of relief that the burden of responsibility for Mum has been removed. But then I feel awful and so guilty for thinking such a thing. And another part of me is still angry with her and I know we can never sort that out."

"Marion, I think you tend to be too self-critical. You and I both know that it's not unusual to feel relieved when someone dies, especially when they've had a lingering illness. It's been hard to be a witness to that decline."

"Yes, but on the whole Mum was quite happy and contented. Especially once she moved into Hilltop. We realised that she'd probably been lonely at home and perhaps got a bit anxious when she was left by herself."

"Well, it's good that you were able to provide that secure environment for her. I think you'll eventually realise that there's no need for you to feel guilty. You cared well for your mum and did your best by her. Do you think you can let go of the anger?"

230

"I hope so, with time. I talked to my brother about it when he was over for the funeral and that helped. You know that man, Robert Gilchrist, turned up at her funeral? Douglas and I were horrified."

"It seems that one good thing to emerge from this is a better relationship with your brother. That's definitely something to be grateful for, and something that you can take forward."

"Yes, you're right. Maybe I should concentrate on things in the future instead of worrying so much about the past. Beth is going to help me with that."

"Of course. How is your daughter coping with the baby?"

Marion was able to tell Rosemary all about the colic and the new diet starting today.

"And you'd been worried that Rose might be affected by postnatal depression like yourself."

"Yes, I was worried. I thought she might be a higher risk because of me and the stress of being a single mum. But she's been fine. Just the normal ups and downs that go with being tired out."

"That must be a relief for you, and of course she has you and your friend to give her help and support."

"Yes, and I coped OK with seeing my ex. You were right."

It was interesting that Rosemary's prediction about meeting Angus again had been accurate. The man who came to visit Rose and Beth bore no resemblance to the Angus of her memory and imagination. He'd changed physically, obviously: greying hair, bushier eyebrows and thicker round the middle. Despite these signs of ageing, she had to admit that in her eyes he was still a handsome man. The biggest change she found was in his character. He'd lost that predatory aura that used to make him seem edgy and slightly dangerous. These were the traits that had originally made him attractive and exciting to Marion and had probably also helped him to become a successful surgeon. When she'd lost her own self-confidence, his sharp edges had bruised her and his razor wit had cut her to the core. Now he'd definitely mellowed. He came across as approachable and calm. Marion thought that his patients must love him and feel very safe in his care; and while she still wouldn't choose to socialise with him, their interactions had been easy and harmless.

"And Sally, his wife, seems so nice too. Rose has always liked her and she was obviously besotted with Beth. I think that meeting Sally and seeing Angus again has reassured me that things will be OK for Rose when she goes down to stay with them in Bath next year."

"From what you're telling me I think that you're well on the way to an improvement in your mental well-being. How are you sleeping now? And the headaches?"

Marion was able to report fewer headaches and, apart from sometimes waking through the night when Beth cried, both the quality and quantity of her sleep had improved. Rosemary soon wound up their session and they agreed to meet again in four weeks' time for what would hopefully be a final appointment.

"That view is so like the one in Gran's painting, Mum," Rose declared as she gazed from the castle gardens out across the Irish Sea to Ailsa Craig.

"Yes, it's quite dramatic, isn't it? Whoops, careful of the pram on this bit of path, it's pretty uneven." Marion helped out by lifting the front wheels of the pram over a skewed flagstone.

"Hey, Marion, isn't that where all of your curling stones come from?" Auntie Peggy who was walking behind with Nyaga pointed out to the island.

"Supposedly," Marion agreed.

The four women were exploring the gardens at Glenapp Castle Hotel after putting away a sumptuous afternoon tea. Today would have been Betty's birthday, so Marion, Peggy and

Rose had decided that it would be an appropriate point in time to scatter her ashes. Deciding on a site for the scattering had been more difficult.

"Gran was really a towny kind of person, wasn't she?" Rose had commented. "Her favourite places were department stores but you can't really scatter ashes in Jenners or John Lewis."

"She liked the Botanic Gardens, but I don't think that would do." Marion had been doubtful.

"What about Portobello beach?" Rose had asked. "She used to live so nearby."

"Yes, but I still think it's a bit too urban for ashes," Marion said.

"You know she chose the seashore near Girvan for Peter's ashes. Maybe we could take her there too," Auntie Peggy had suggested.

"Isn't that where they went for their honeymoon?" Rose asked.

"Yes, it obviously still meant a lot to her if she chose it for Peter," Peggy had said, looking directly at Marion.

"Yes, that's a valid point. Let's do that," she'd agreed thoughtfully.

"And I think we should treat ourselves to a slap-up afternoon tea while we're there. That was one of Betty's favourite treats, she would definitely approve of that," Peggy had added.

Although Nyaga wasn't officially family the women included her in their planned trip.

"After all, she looked after Gran and she was there with us when she died." Rose spoke for them all.

So today they had gone to a quiet beach at Lendalfoot and scattered Betty's ashes at the tide's edge. Then they retreated to the luxury of the five-star hotel for their afternoon tea.

"And Beth has been a perfect baby all day," Rose declared as they began to make their way back towards the hotel car park.

"Yes, I'd like to give that health visitor a medal," Marion announced. It was like a miracle. Two days after Rose had stopped eating dairy products Beth was transformed from a miserable squalling infant into a contented, smiling cherub.

"Mum, can you hold the pram for a minute?" Rose asked. "I've just got a wee errand to complete."

Marion watched her as she walked over to a flower bed filled with roses. She took what looked like a handkerchief from her pocket and waved it gently over the flowers. A soft dust of ash fell gently to the ground.

"Thanks," she said as she reclaimed the pram. "It was just a tiny bit of her. I saved it for here because I thought she'd appreciate the surroundings."

Marion gazed around, taking in the warm stone of the magnificent baronial-style turreted house, the mature trees and topiary, well-kept lawns and flower beds, then the wilder forest leading towards the sea.

She smiled and nodded her agreement and then added, "Roses were her favourite."

Nyaga

"Good morning, Helen. Just checking if you want to come through to the lounge for the music this morning." Nyaga stood in the doorway of the elderly resident's room.

"Will the wee one be there?"

"Yes, I think so." She smiled as Helen began to lever herself out from her armchair, then offered an arm while placing a Zimmer frame in front of the old lady's slippered feet. "Let's go then, but take your time, there's no rush."

Nyaga had noticed that, after all of her friends returned to their universities for the new term, Rose often seemed to be at a loose end. So, she'd suggested that the Hilltop residents would enjoy some piano playing and singing. Rose had agreed to come for a short spell twice a week and her sessions were a huge success. But, much as the residents liked the music, the star attraction was baby Beth who accompanied Rose on these visits. She was four months old now and happily sat in her pushchair bestowing smiles on the assembled group. The residents vied with one another to gain her attention, waving, clapping, making little clucking noises and calling to her. After the music was finished Rose was very patient and took the baby out of the pram to visit everyone closer up.

Just as she'd seated Helen safely, the doorbell rang and Nyaga went to admit the stars of the show.

"Hi there. You've got a crowded house, as usual," she greeted Rose. She held the door wide open as Rose manoeuvred the pushchair in from the porch.

Nyaga was standing at the back of the room as Rose played and sang. The residents joined in with some of the choruses and Nyaga realised that she'd now been to two of the places made famous in Scottish songs. A month ago, she'd taken a week of holiday and gone travelling around Scotland with her friend Amelia. They'd hired a car and, advised by Marion, had booked overnight stays in B&B accommodation. This made their trip less expensive and also gave them a chance to meet and talk to local people. Rose had helped plan their route. First, they drove to Inverness and visited Loch Ness and Urquhart Castle. It was very atmospheric, but no sign of Nessie. Then they went west to Kyle of Lochalsh and across to Skye. They spent two nights on Skye before driving south via Oban, Inveraray and Loch Lomond. So now she could join in with 'The Bonnie, Bonnie Banks of Loch Lomond' and 'Over the Sea to Skye' with some kind of authority, even though she'd crossed to the island by the bridge. She was pleased that she'd managed to see a little of Scotland before leaving the country. Her visit to Glenapp to scatter Betty's ashes had only been her second time away from Edinburgh and it had spurred her on to plan the sightseeing trip. She'd really enjoyed the whole experience; the views across the sea to the scattered islands off the coast of Argyll had been her favourite thing, especially in the colours of the setting sun. She'd also forgotten how much she liked driving. At home she shared a beaten-up old Toyota Auris with her mum, but she hadn't driven for over a year now. It had been so liberating to get behind the steering wheel again and set off on an independent course. Coming from Botswana she was quite at home with driving on the left, so Amelia had been happy to leave the driving to her and it was also cheaper to insure for only one driver anyway.

Once the music session was finished and Beth had made her round of honour she waved to Rose and Beth from the front door.

"See you later," she called as she returned to organise the medicine round before lunch.

That evening the three women were sitting round the kitchen table and tucking into a spaghetti carbonara prepared by Rose. Beth was sitting in her bouncy seat waving her arms wildly which had the combined effect of jiggling her seat up and down and creating a rhythmic rattling noise from the toy that she was holding.

"Well, I've done it," Nyaga announced. "I handed in my notice to Aileen before I left today."

"How long do you have to work now, then?" Rose asked.

"It's a four-week notice period, but I haven't taken all of my holiday entitlement, so just over three weeks."

"You must be so excited to be going home." Rose gave Nyaga's arm a squeeze.

"Yes, I am. But I've got mixed feelings about leaving Hilltop. I've loved working there and I know it might be hard for them to find a replacement for me. They were short-staffed before I came along and although she tried to look positive I think Aileen was quite upset at my announcement."

"Well, Nyaga, you have to do what's best for you and Lesedi. It's not your responsibility to keep the nursing home staffed." Marion tried to reassure her.

"I know but I don't like to think of my friends on the staff struggling to cope, or of the residents not having someone they like and trust to help them."

"Well, I promise that Beth and I will keep up our music sessions until we move down to Bath. Will that help?" Rose asked.

"Thank you, Rose, it will. And I wonder could I borrow a laptop this evening to look into booking my flight?"

"Sure. You can have mine," Rose offered.

One of the many great things about living with Marion was the easy access to the internet. The house had broadband and both Marion and Rose had laptops that they let her use. It was so much easier to be in touch with everyone at home.

After dinner Nyaga collected the laptop from Rose and settled down in her bedroom to look at potential travel dates and compare flight costs. The cheapest flights went via the Middle East and seemed to take a very long time. Eventually she settled on a route via Frankfurt and Namibia which wasn't too expensive and didn't involve long stopover periods hanging around in airports. She was just about to email her mum with the details when there was a tap on her door.

"Can I come in?" It was Rose's voice.

"Of course." The door opened and Rose slipped in.

"Phew, I've just managed to get Beth down to sleep. She was so wound up tonight and wanted to keep playing after her bath."

"Trying to keep your attention and putting off going to sleep, it's a great game for children. It'll only get worse with Beth. I remember Lesedi would be all tucked up and I'd be about to kiss her and leave and she'd suddenly ask 'Mummy, do you want to know what I did with Nkuku today?' or 'Mummy, do you want to know what I'll be when I'm grown up?' Things like that to hook me in, just as I was about to say goodnight."

"It'll be so great for you to be with her again."

"Yes. I've booked my flight now. I was just going to let my mum know."

"Well, I've got a favour to ask you. I feel that Beth and I should go down to my dad's at Christmas because he's really not seen much of us at all. But I hate to think of Mum left here on her own over the holiday period. She does well at hiding things, but I know she's been struggling with Gran being ill and she's seemed much quieter than usual since Gran died. Anyway, I wondered if you might think of asking her to come over to visit you in Botswana for Christmas?"

"Rose, what a brilliant idea. I agree that Marion needs something different to take her out of herself and a big trip could be just the thing. Also, I'd love to have her to visit so that I can repay some of the hospitality that she's given to me. It's a wonderful plan."

"OK, well, I'm pleased that it's fine with you. I'll mention about visiting Dad within the next couple of days, so any time after that you could ask her."

"I will. And sometime you must come to visit me too. When Beth is bigger."

"Thanks, Nyaga. I'm not sure how we'll be for money but I'd love to come."

"Once you're with me it will be inexpensive and a baby is free to fly under two years old."

"Wow, you're serious. Well, I'll keep it in mind. We'll definitely be staying in touch with each other, so you can keep nagging me. I'll leave you in peace to finish with your emails now. Thanks again, Nyaga."

Rose left the room and Nyaga began to write to her mother about her return home and of a plan to have her friend visit for Christmas.

Marion

Marion surveyed the piles of clothes laid out on her bed and tried to think if she'd forgotten anything. Because the clothing was lightweight summer wear she still had the potential to fit more into her suitcase. However, she knew that she could do some washing while she was away, so it seemed silly to carry extra. No, that was probably it. Anyway, a bit of space might be handy to accommodate any purchases for coming home. She set off downstairs to the hall cupboard in search of plastic bags to hold her shoes and toiletries. The house was eerily quiet. Yesterday she'd taken Rose and Beth to the airport. They were off to spend Christmas with Angus and Sally. When Rose had first mentioned this plan Marion had to admit that her heart sank. She'd had to work hard not to let Rose see that she was upset.

"Mum, I know you won't be offended. Because we live with you just now I think it's fairer to go to Dad for Christmas. He hasn't seen that much of Beth. And then next year when we're living in Bath we'll come here for Christmas, I promise."

Marion had smiled and said that yes, of course it was fine. She admired Rose's tact and forethought, but it was an effort to keep up an adult façade and not to feel like an abandoned puppy. Also, she knew that she wouldn't have to be alone; she'd always be welcome to spend the holiday with Auntie Peggy or with Jenny and her family. Then a couple of days later Nyaga had extended an invitation for Marion to come to Botswana and spend Christmas with her. Were Rose and Nyaga in cahoots? Anyway, it was an amazing idea and here she was getting packed, almost ready to go. She collected a bunch of bags and trotted back upstairs. She began to wrap her sandals up and place them in the base of her suitcase and soon everything was transferred from the bed into the case.

Then Marion went through to her study to sort out the documents that she needed to take with her. She collected her passport from her safe-box and then sat down at the computer. First she printed off her boarding passes. She'd chosen a different route from the one that Nyaga took, and the journey seemed quite straightforward. A flight down to London, then overnight to Johannesburg. Because she was sticking with British Airways she wouldn't need to change terminal at Heathrow; that was good. The overnight flight was eleven hours long, which sounded a bit grim. But she was hopeful that she'd sleep for some of it, and because the journey was mainly on a north-south axis there would be no jet lag. The connecting flight next morning to Gaborone was only an hour long and Nyaga would be there at the airport to meet her.

Next she printed off the confirmation for the accommodation that she'd booked at Mokolodi. The game reserve was very close to Gaborone and she was taking Nyaga and Lesedi there to stay in one of the lodges for two nights as a treat. She hoped that they'd get a chance to see some animals together. Then she collected the information and tickets for her trip to the Okavango. She was slightly nervous about the idea of going off on her own, but she wanted to see the delta and Nyaga had said that these trips weren't suitable for a child. So she'd booked what appeared to be a very well-organised safari lasting for six days. She'd be part of a small group, so hopefully she should find some convivial company. The last papers that she printed were for a trip to Sun City after New Year. She and Nyaga were going to drive down there with Lesedi and stay for four nights to enjoy the facilities of the upmarket resort. She checked that she had her driving licence and travel insurance documents, and then stowed everything in chronological order into an A4-sized plastic wallet.

The phone rang.

"Hello?"

It was Auntie Peggy calling to wish her a happy holiday. Marion told her that she was nearly organised, packing almost finished.

"I've ordered a taxi for half past one."

"It sounds like a grand adventure. And did Rose get away alright yesterday with the wee one?"

"Yes. She called last night after Beth had settled down to sleep. Apparently Sally had a nursery all beautifully decorated and prepared."

"That was nice, but I suppose she's going to be living there next year."

"Yes. Well, I'd better go and get the house sorted out. I don't want to come home to mouldy bins or a festering fridge. We'll see you the last Saturday in January."

Marion and Rose had agreed to have a family lunch and exchange presents after Marion's return, a postponed sort-of Christmas, to which Auntie Peggy was invited.

"Yes. Have a great time, see you then. Bye bye."

Marion stowed the wallet of documents together with her foreign currency into her hand luggage and then went to the kitchen to fill a small watering can. She went around the rooms in her house methodically, watering the house plants, collecting rubbish from the waste-paper bins and checking that the windows were all closed and securely latched. She poured a generous amount of water into the holder for the Christmas tree. She planned to decrease the house temperature on the thermostat, so she hoped that it would hang on to its needles. Last night she'd rigged up automatic timers to some of her lamps, and to the Christmas tree fairy lights, so that the house would have some lights on when it was empty. Rose and Beth would be back between Christmas and New Year but it was best to make the house look occupied.

In addition to Rose's call last night Marion had also heard from Douglas.

"Hi sis," she'd heard when she picked up the phone. Since Betty's death communication between the siblings was more regular and less complicated. Douglas had been calling to wish her *bon voyage* for her African holiday. He'd also suggested that Marion, Rose and Beth come and visit Canada next summer.

"You have to say yes or Cate will be seriously disappointed. You could come to the cottage with us, that would be a very relaxing holiday and easy with a baby. Anyway, think about it and see what Rose says."

Marion thought that Rose would be keen to see her cousins again but she couldn't make presumptions. She had to remember that there was the whole MacMillan clan who might like to see Rose and Beth too.

"I can say yes from me," she told Douglas. "But I can't speak for Rose. She's down seeing Angus right now, so Cate will have to wait for her reply. I expect that it's Rose and Beth that she really wants to hear from rather than me."

"Don't do yourself down, Marion. She's very fond of her Scottish auntie."

Marion laughed now, thinking about his reply. She'd never told him about her psychotherapy sessions, but it was the kind of comment that Rosemary might have made. She'd stopped going for therapy several months ago. As the weeks passed, her anger with Betty had gradually receded and, without the focus of Betty in person, the confusion of mixed loyalties seemed to settle.

As she completed her circulation of the house Marion was struck again by the silence. She peeped into the back bedroom. There had been so much change here recently. Originally the spare room, it had become Betty's room, but only for two short months. Then Nyaga stayed in it for seven months. Since she'd gone Marion and Rose had rearranged the room again, this time as a nursery for Beth. Until now she'd shared with Rose, but the plan was to move her into her own space when they returned home from Bath. From what Rose had said on the phone it seemed that she already had her own room down there. So, if she became used to sleeping on her own while she was away on holiday it should be a smooth transition to this room on their return. Marion's eye was caught by a stuffed toy lying on the armchair – Minnie Mouse. She went over and picked it up. Rose had been very upset by the toy, a Christmas present for Beth from Mark. It did seem a bit strange; it was the first acknowledgement or communication of any sort that they'd had from him since Beth was born. Rose had registered Mark as Beth's father on her birth certificate, but Beth was to be named MacMillan, her mother's name. A few weeks after her birth Rose had sent a message and a photograph to Mark but received nothing in response until Minnie Mouse. Rose's theory was that it was a sentimental holiday gesture, probably bought under the influence of alcohol. But Marion wasn't so sure, maybe Mark was more interested than Rose thought. She couldn't imagine how any of them would react if he did decide he wanted to be more involved with his daughter. Oh well, no use worrying about something that might not happen. Ironically Beth loved the toy on first sight, beaming and chatting to it, so Rose didn't feel she could discard it, much as she might like to. However, it didn't seem to have accompanied them to Bath. Marion replaced Minnie onto the chair and left the room.

She'd only been on her own in the house for a day, and she had lots to do, but already she felt that she was rattling around in all of the unoccupied space. She'd got used to having lots of company. She was going to have to think about that once Rose and Beth moved to Bath next year. She was considering the idea of getting a dog. She liked dogs and enjoyed the outdoors, so it might be a possibility. She knew that there were dog-walking services that she could employ for her long days at work, and also an organisation called BorrowMyDoggy which was more informal, matching up dog lovers with owners. She could also think about taking in a lodger for company – maybe a student or someone visiting from abroad. When Nyaga came to stay it had seemed to widen Marion's horizons. And now it was doing that literally; she was about to fly off to Botswana.

She checked her watch. One hour until the taxi was due to arrive. She decided to have a cup of coffee and some toast with honey before getting changed and closing her bags. She put the kettle on to boil and popped a heel of bread into the toaster. Once her snack was ready she sat down at the kitchen table and decided to try giving Jenny a call.

"Hi Jenny, can you talk? I'm just about to go."

"Sure. Are you all packed? Tickets, passport and money?"

"Yeah."

"Did Beth cope OK with the flight yesterday?"

"Yes. Rose said she was fine, slept most of the way."

"That was good. And how did that final curling match in your competition go last night?"

"Oh, we got beaten. So no trophy this time around. But I did have an interesting encounter."

"Tell me more."

"Well, after the match when we were having a drink this chap came up to me and said 'Marion?' I didn't recognise him. He was about our age and had that little fringe of hair, close cut, that some guys have, greyish. Anyway, he said, 'You don't recognise me, do you? It's Ken Blakey.'"

"And did that mean something?"

"Yeah. He was a guy from my year at uni. I remember going for coffee with him a few times before Angus was on the scene. Anyway, he's moved down from Inverness and I might meet up with him after I get back from Botswana."

"Wow. Well, keep me informed. Have a great time, Marion, I'd better get back to work. I see my boss approaching. Bye."

Marion replayed her meeting with Ken yesterday. She'd had trouble matching her memories of a boy with long, dark, curly hair with the figure of the man in front of her. She'd known back then that Ken had a soft spot for her and would have liked to go out with her. But at the time his shy, gentle character was no match for the charisma of Angus. She knew through the grapevine that he'd specialised in psychiatry and had moved up north somewhere. Yesterday he told her that his wife had died three years ago after a battle with breast cancer. His children were away from home at university and he'd been struggling along in a big empty-feeling house in Inverness on his own. Then an opening had come up at the Cullen Centre in Edinburgh, so he'd decided to apply. He'd been in Edinburgh for six months now and had joined a curling club at the beginning of the season.

"So, what are you up to these days? And how's Angus?" he'd asked.

After she'd filled him in about her current circumstances she'd also agreed to contact him in January. He'd seemed very keen to see her again, and they'd exchanged phone numbers. Well, she could meet him. There was no harm in that. He'd always been a nice chap, a good listener. No doubt that would make him good at his job too. Better keep quiet about the psychotherapy sessions for a while, though.

She drained her coffee cup and then washed her dishes. Only twenty minutes until the taxi. Once upstairs she undressed and stepped into her travelling clothes: a trouser suit in royal blue cotton jersey over a blue and gold-coloured T-shirt. She'd found a pair of summery moccasins in pale golden leather to match. She fastened on a gold chain necklace and a bracelet, then brushed her hair quickly. She decided against make-up. Why bother on a long flight? She put the cosmetics bag into her suitcase and then zipped it up, securing the locks and tying it around with a colourful red band to make it easier to identify.

Her phone rang twice, then stopped. The taxi. She manhandled the suitcase downstairs, returning for her inflight bag. When she opened the front door, a black cab was parked level with her gate. She set the burglar alarm, closed the door, locked the mortice and set off down the path.